WICKED ANGEL

A DARK MAFIA ARRANGED MARRIAGE AGE GAP ROMANCE

SINISTER ARRANGEMENT
BOOK ONE

LUCY SMOKE

A.J. MACEY

For the readers who use trigger warnings as shopping lists.

This one's for you.

TRIGGER WARNING

This book contains very dark content that may be triggering for some readers.

Some of these themes include, but are not limited to, graphic violence, explicit sexual situations, masochism, sadism, degradation, humiliation, sexual bondage, pussy fisting, dubious consent, sexual violence, murder, loss, and other themes that are common in dark romance.

All of the events and people contained within this book are works of fiction. Any similarities to persons living or dead are purely coincidence.

If you do not enjoy these themes listed above, or have specific triggers that are harmful to your mental health, please do not read.

This book is recommended for 18+ due to sexual content and adult situations. ***Please read responsibly.***

CONTENTS

PROLOGUE
ANGEL

11 years old ...

Black cloaked bodies moved in sync as they surrounded my father, my sister, and me—leading the three of us from the limo we'd just stepped out of towards the hill where several more figures dressed in black waited. Dry, slightly cool air slapped me in the face. I turned to look up at the clouds hovering overhead, threatening this already dreary day with more rain. At the sight of more men in black stationed around the cemetery, my insides rolled. Nervous, I reached out for Dad's hand, pausing when he pulled away.

"Remember the rules, Angel," Dad said.

As if to prove that she was better, Jackie leaned around his back and scowled at me. "You know better," she snapped before falling back into place. I bit my lip so hard I swore I could taste blood. She was right, though; I did know better. I'd just hoped that under these circumstances we could be a little different … we could be *normal*. Apparently not. Even at Mom's funeral, we weren't allowed to show affection.

There were so many rules. Where we could eat —never anywhere Dad hadn't yet approved. What we could wear. Where we could shop—only the best brands and only from certain stores that would allow extra security while we were inside. Who was allowed to pick us up or drop us off at school— never anyone we hadn't been expressly introduced to before. Who was allowed *in* the same school— certain family's children were never allowed within a certain distance of us. I never understood any of it until this moment.

All those secrets. All those times when I couldn't understand why we had so much security detail and so many people living in the mansion. It all became clear here. We weren't a normal family, and we never had been. We were different, and the things my father did … they weren't good. He had enemies and as his blood, so did we.

My flat, black Mary Janes slid through the dirt of the ice-cold ground. Everything was numb. My eyes were sore and raw from the amount of tears I'd cried. They felt swollen, and whenever I reached up to touch them, it only hurt more. I felt all cried out. I was so drained of tears I wondered if I'd ever be able to cry again. The dark, itchy dress I wore was a stark contrast to my fair skin. My shoes were quickly getting dirty from the light rain misting our faces as we trudged through the cemetery. Mom was being buried today—in the mud and rain and cold wintry air. I could hear the dull thud of raindrops when one of my father's men opened an umbrella and held it over our heads as we finished making our way up the hill. It only made the sadness I carried weigh heavier, and I felt as though my heart had cracked a little more with each passing moment.

My footsteps slowed as I saw the dozen or so wide-chested men crammed into suits, looking like overstuffed penguins standing around the casket. Dad didn't look back as he moved forward, and the men that came today reached for him, offering their hands in condolences. I guess the funeral of a beloved mob wife was a pretty big deal. I looked around for somewhere to tuck myself away so I wasn't in the way but could remain close to Dad and his bodyguards.

"What are you doing?" My sister's sharp voice startled me, disrupting the quiet in my head. Jacquelina scowled at me as she hovered nearby. Her thin lips tightened with the sharp look, making her face appear even more bird-like than it already did with her slightly larger-than-average nose and the widow's peak at the top of her forehead. She looked more like our dad with her dark hair and olive skin, but me—I looked like our mom. Softer, rounder, and shorter.

At nearly seventeen, Jackie was almost six years older than me, and other than our similarly shaped eyes—though hers are brown to my hazel—the reality of being related to her seemed near impossible. There were few other similarities, both physically and personality-wise. I had emotions, but she … well, even at her own Mom's funeral, her makeup was completely untouched, no tears or mascara smeared down her cheeks. It was as if it was just a normal day.

Whereas I'd typically duck my head and apologize for the unseen insult. Today, I was different. I was tired and angry and sad. I found a chair in the first row and sat on the edge before looking up at her expectantly waiting face. "Sitting," I snapped back.

Jackie's eyes widened at my tone. She stepped back and folded her arms across her chest. "Touchy much?"

I bit my lip again but didn't reply. Instead, I turned my gaze to the casket. Closed, of course. Why wouldn't it be? There's nobody inside. From what I'd overheard from Dad's men, Mom's body had been so badly beaten, it was hardly recognizable. No eleven-year-old should have to hear that, but I had only myself to blame. I'd been eavesdropping near Dad's office, and when I wasn't in their direct line of sight, Dad's men weren't all that great at tempering their words.

Swallowing the lump that formed, I tried not to flinch when people moved around and between Jackie and me. My heart felt like it was hammering at a million miles a minute. Sweat collected in my palms even as I tried to squish my fingers into them to stop it. Jackie's stare continued to bore into me for several moments until she seemed to get bored and finally gave up. I was thankful when she flipped her hair off her shoulder and headed across the space toward our dad. That was just who Jackie was, and it wasn't like we'd ever been particularly close.

Closing my eyes and resting back against the seat, I sucked in a breath and then slowly released it as I thought about the fact that despite the big mouths of my father's bodyguards, Jackie was the one who'd told me the truth about how Mom had died.

I'd been crying in my room several days ago when she'd popped inside and leaned against the jamb, watching me with cool, unbothered eyes. It always freaked me out when she did that. Sometimes, Jackie would just show up somewhere, and instead of saying anything at all, she would stare at you. Watch you. Then she'd ask strange questions like, "Does it hurt when you cry?" or "Why do you feel bad about lying?"

And the day we'd been told about our mother's death was the same.

"Do you know what killed Mom?" she'd asked.

I sniffled hard. "Car wreck? Th-they said it was an accident." I swiped angrily at the wet streaks on my face. Did she really have to question me today, of all days?

Jackie nodded and sighed, but she didn't look exactly comforting. I used to think it was just the way her face naturally fell, but at that moment, I realized it was because she truly didn't seem to care about me. There was no reaction to my tears, no attempt at consoling. Her lips were twisted in more of a downward, irritated scowl. "Ah, so that's what he told you."

My hand slowed, pausing against one cheek as I processed her words. "Told me?" I repeated. "What do you mean 'told me?'"

"It's just because you're still pretty young," she replied without actually answering my question. "Young enough to be kept in the dark…" She trailed off, turning to leave.

Confusion swirled within me. What did she mean? I jolted forward.

"Wait!" I called, grabbing hold of her arm to keep her from leaving. "What do you mean 'kept in the dark?'" Dad wouldn't lie to me, I thought. Sometimes he was mean and he yelled, but he loved me—us—and Mom. He wouldn't lie about how she died, but Jackie sounded so sure. I had to hope this was just one of her mean tricks.

Jackie angled back to look at me, her expression devoid of any pity or guilt. I hated that too. I knew Mom always said that Jackie was special and she needed help understanding emotions more, but it was just too hard and she was just too freaking mean sometimes. I swore she did it on purpose.

"Mom didn't die in a car crash," she said as she turned back to face me. She tilted her head to the side. "Dad pissed someone off and they went after her."

My jaw dropped. "What?" She couldn't be right. I shook my head. That didn't make any sense. Why would—before I can finish my thought, however, Jackie's talking again.

With an eye roll and a huff, she took her arm from my hand and folded it along with her other one across her chest.

"Ugh, grow up, Angel," she snapped. "We aren't a normal family. Dad's a criminal. We are criminals, *and criminals don't get happily ever after's. We won't get into heaven, no matter how many times you get told you're daddy's little angel. Dad's a powerful man, and he has enemies, enemies that got too close and Mom paid the price. There was nothing accidental about her death."*

My head started to throb. "I don't understand—why are you telling me this?"

"Because I'm tired of everyone in this house protecting you from the truth like the little princess," she growled at me. "It's annoying. The sooner you realize the truth, the better. Mom's gone now, so that means I'm the next lady of the house. What I say goes."

I ignored her last statement. Whatever she wanted to be —in charge, in control, or whatever—I was not going to even acknowledge it. "You have to be wrong," *I insisted.*

"I'm not," she sneered. "It's because of who he is. Who we are—the Price Family. Syndicate. Read the papers, or better yet—why don't you just ask Dad?"

"I will," I snapped, pushing past her and into the hall.

IMAGINE MY SURPRISE WHEN IT ALL TURNED OUT TO be true. The illusion of a normal life, of a normal family with loving parents, came crashing down the day my Mom died—its destruction illustrated by my own sister. It all made sense, then. The rules. The reasons. Dad was a criminal; not just any criminal, though. He was powerful, and that meant that Mom had died because of something he did.

Even if he felt regret, even if he felt sadness, the truth was now in front of my face in a cold casket with a bunch of men in black gathered around. I pinched down my fingers against the outside of my thigh, trying to feel something because everything was quickly growing numb all over again, when a deep voice startled me.

"You shouldn't do that." I jumped at the sound of a man and a moment later, the chair next to me creaked under fresh weight. I looked up and up and up some more into a pair of startling blue eyes.

"W-what?"

The man was tall with a straight back, a proud nose, and a sharp jawline. His hair was a sandy blonde, swept away from his face and his eyes were the deepest shade of blue I'd ever seen in my life. I was so mesmerized by them that it was only when he blinked at me that I realized I was staring. He nodded down to my thigh, where my fingers were still lightly rubbing against the sore spot. "Once you start, you won't be able to stop," he advised.

I pulled my hand away immediately and faced forward as heat rocketed up my cheeks. "I don't know what you're talking about," I lied.

The corner of the stranger's mouth tipped upward, and somehow I found that to be even more intimidating than he was before. However, even with that intimidating air, something told me he wasn't an enemy. My attention continued to follow him out of the corners of my eyes.

"Then let me just offer my condolences." He

gestured to the casket and I saw the black gun strapped to his chest beneath his suit coat. The sight of it made my insides coil.

I could feel the scowl form on my face. "I don't want your stupid condolences," I snapped. "Go talk to my Dad or something. Leave me alone." I folded my arms across my chest, but beneath one, I turned my hand and sunk my fingernails into the underside of my bicep.

The man didn't get up immediately though. Instead, he turned fully in his seat and looked down at me. "You're angry, kid," he said. "I get that, but anger isn't going to bring her back."

"Nothing will bring her back," I pointed out. "So what else can I do but be angry?" Why the hell hadn't he left yet?

The man's eyes roved over my face, but I turned away, forcing my own eyes down to the ground so I wouldn't meet his. "It's a rough world." His voice remained clear and even. I still didn't look up. "If you're Raffaello's daughter, then there will be more where this came from. My advice—"

"I didn't ask for it!" I finally looked up and immediately regretted it.

His eyes weren't on me at all. In fact, they were somewhere behind me. It wasn't that, though, that freaked me out—it was the cold look in them. The icy fire grew as he glared at someone, but when I moved to look back, he stopped me with a hand on my shoulder. "Don't," he warned quietly.

"W-what?" Looking up at him, I spotted a tiny

little sliver of a scar coming out of the neckline of his dress shirt, slightly curved. For some reason, I focused on that scar. Curious and also a little afraid. How many more did he have? Where did he get them?

"Take my advice, kid," he said. "Don't let one loss kill you. Life is all about fight and vengeance."

"Vengeance?" I repeated the word with a little hint of confusion. What did he mean by that? Once again, I tried to turn to look over my shoulder and see what it was he was glaring at, but he stopped me.

"Yes," he replied, this time grabbing hold of my chin and turning my face forward forcefully. A loud car honked in the distance, making me jump as the man's eyes returned to mine. "Everyone's lost someone. The best way to move on is to make sure that whoever took them from you pays."

"But … I'm too young," I said.

His lips twitched again and his head bobbed up and down in agreement. "Yes." His voice rumbled deeper. "But I'm not."

Before I could ask what he meant, someone behind me shouted and his arms closed around me, dragging me into his chest and then down onto the cold ground as a gun went off and a bullet whizzed over our heads. More shouting. Screaming. A woman yelling. My dad … my dad yelling and cursing. Then the man holding me disappeared. Another gunshot rang in my ears, so loud and so close that I had to cover them with my own hands as tears streamed down my cheeks.

Firm hands lifted me up and the man's face reappeared in front of me. "Hold on, kid." I didn't know why he was asking me to hold on, but for some reason, I didn't question it. I latched on, wrapping my arms around his shoulders as he started running. I was too big to be carried by an adult, but he acted as if it was nothing, with one hand under my legs and the other around my back.

The weight of the man pressed into my much smaller body and with it, the fresh scent of soap and spicy cologne. My nose wrinkled. It was too much, too strong, and too close. As he shifted, something from his chest touched me and I froze. I knew it for what it was, the outline was too distinctive for me not to recognize it; it was the same gun I'd seen before. Now, though, the weight of such a weapon didn't scare me. It made me feel safe, just like the arms around me.

Pulling away, I looked into the man's face and asked for the one thing I thought I didn't want anymore. I asked for the truth. "Did you kill them?" I asked. "Did you kill the person who murdered my mom?"

The man's steps slowed to a stop and when I took a look around, I realized we were back in the cemetery parking lot and there were loads of other men in black suits carrying guns. "Not yet," he said. "But I will."

Somehow, that one promise was the best condolence I could've ever asked for.

1

GAVEN

7 years later …

Expensive sports cars were a luxury I didn't usually allow myself to enjoy. Though I could readily afford anything and everything that I wanted, the Aston Martin purring beneath me was far too ostentatious for my line of work. It commanded attention something I only used as a method of distraction. It wasn't necessary, however, to remain inconspicuous when my business was to be conducted face-to-face. So, for the moment, I enjoyed the feeling of the rumbling engine as the speedometer reached a hundred miles per hour and then ticked past that.

I tightened my fingers around the taut leather of the steering wheel and wove the speeding vehicle in and around all obstacles in my path. Packed city streets gave way to trees and green landscapes, all blurring past the windows as I pushed the little car faster.

It wasn't long until I rolled up to a country estate that could rival a military compound in size. The two men standing vigilant in front of the tall iron fence turned to meet my gaze through the windshield of the car. Smirking at them, I waited as another guard leaned out.

"Name?" he barked, eyeing me with suspicion and distaste.

"Gaven," I drawled, lowering my sunglasses to look the man over, "Belmonte."

There was an obvious brutality already settled into the guard's youthful face. A long scar marred the side of his cheek, from his chin to the corner of his eyebrow. It wasn't surprising. Any man in this business who was lucky to make it past thirty likely felt much older than that.

At the thought of getting older in this career, I started to wonder if retiring was in the cards for me. It had nothing to do with the money; I had more than enough, that was for sure. But I was depraved enough to enjoy the work that I did— thrived on it—so I doubted I'd be stopping any time soon. Not unless something more interesting came along.

The guard blinked at my name and quickly leaned back into the guardhouse, his fingers flying over the keyboard of his computer. "I apologize, I didn't recognize you. Welcome, Mr. Belmonte," he said after a moment.

"I'll let it slide this time," I said calmly. "Though, I suggest you amend your tone in the future."

THE BUZZING SOUND OF THE GATE OPENING DREW MY attention. "Of course, sir," the guard replied quickly. "Mr. Price is awaiting your arrival at the mansion."

"Thank you."

The security guard gave me a quick once over, his lips thinning before he nodded respectfully. Leaving the window down, I slid my sunglasses back on and pressed gently on the gas, letting the car roll forward, past the gates. The only noise that filled the interior of the vehicle as I drove farther up the drive was the soft breeze mixing with the rumble of the engine.

It only took a few minutes to reach the top of the courtyard circle drive, and I threw the car into park before climbing out. The face of the mansion was elegant. Each nuance of the extravagant stone was lavish and the lawn was groomed to immaculate perfection. Anyone looking on from the outside would assume a wealthy family resided here, and they wouldn't have been wrong. A wealthy family did live here—one of the wealthiest in the United States but also one of the deadliest.

The ornate wood and glass doors opened as I approached. Two more guards walked out to hold them open for me. Noting their presence but ignoring their stone-cold expressions, I stepped into the entryway toward the older man waiting within.

I'd been here a time or two in the past, but Raff had obviously done some renovations since my last visit. It was wider now, showcasing an impressive circular staircase leading to the second floor. My steps echoed off the shiny marble flooring that had once been a rich hardwood the last time I'd been a guest at the Price estate—almost seven years ago now.

My eyes focused on the pepper-haired man standing next to a large painting hung between the walls of two doorways, one leading to a guest lounge of sorts and the other farther into the mansion. Raffaello Price was just as I'd seen him the year before at an intimate business gathering in Sicily. It was rare for a man such as myself—a born American, non-Italian—to be invited to such gatherings, and I had the feeling that it was thanks to him.

Raffaello Price was sturdily built with a dark-colored suit clothing his fit frame. I took him in, noting the calculating gaze that trailed over the art, the shrouded almond-shaped eyes hinting at his Italian and Welsh descent. Despite the wrinkles that now creased the corners of his eyes and the white sprinkled through his hair, he seemed to exude the cold confidence he always had.

"Gaven," he greeted warmly. I smiled as he turned toward me, offering me a firm handshake. "It's been a while, my boy." Amusing as it was for the man to call me "boy," despite my many years of service, I didn't comment. Hell, I'd been working for the man for nearly a decade or more at this point, having started as a cleaner for one of the families he allied himself with at barely twenty. It was because of him, however, that I'd managed to move up and become something more. More dangerous. More deadly. And far more prosperous than any cleaner. His voice was rough, like a smoker after thirty years of enjoying his favorite Marlboro several times a day.

"It has," I agreed. "It's good to see you, old man."

While my statement was true, and our banter was genuine, Raff was still the head of the Price Family. Deadly and well-connected with friends in lots of high and low places and whatever it was that brought me here today, I knew what was to come if I ended up on the wrong end of Raff's scope. While I gave him my attention, most of my focus was on the several armed guards that remained within Raff's line of sight.

He chuckled as he dropped my hand and gestured for me to step through the door that led to the main part of the house. "Thank you for coming, my friend. We have much to discuss."

"Do we?" I inquired. "Is there a job you have lined up for me? I must say, if you wanted me to kill someone, you could've just gotten to me through the usual means."

"No." He strode forward, forcing me to follow. "This isn't about a contract, though I hear your business is doing quite well these days. Heard about the Perelli girl. Didn't know you and Jason didn't get along."

I shrugged. "He was an offensive man," I replied blandly. Business was business, and regardless of my personal views of Jason Perelli and how he ran his business, his daughter's contract had been too good to pass up. Plus, unlike Raffaello or the majority of other mob families, I didn't find a woman in power to be as shocking. Times were changing, after all. The very fact that America Perelli had managed to get ahold of me and offer a contract to take out her father had proven that she had what it took to be a Queen in a criminal world ruled by men.

"Yes," Raff agreed. "He was quite brash and rude, even to his betters." Only a man like him would be so arrogant to see himself as above an equally dangerous family. "Regardless, very intriguing, that girl. Never would have thought she had it in her."

"You met her then?" I asked.

Raff nodded. "Only once. She was a mousy, quiet thing though. I thought she would have befriended my daughters if Jason hadn't kept her away from his world. Perelli should have had a son, we could've joined houses. Or if I had one…"

"Unfortunately, America's already married," I replied. "But you're right, she is an interesting woman."

"Indeed."

When he didn't elaborate, I pressed forward. "Are you going to tell me exactly why you've called me here for this meeting? Seeing as how it's not for a contract." I withdrew the notice I'd received two days prior. He paused and smiled as I handed it to him. "Because last I checked, saying 'an offer you can't refuse' tends to get a man killed."

He laughed, the sound loud and barking. It was odd and rough to hear, especially coming from a man who so seldomly found such amusement. "Only if you're stupid," he said with a shake of his head, "and you, Gaven, are the furthest thing from it." His age-spotted hand waved in my general direction before he started walking again. Raffaello Price was an odd combination of genuine man and conniving fucker. He was one of the few mafia men I'd ever seen actually form a family unit and truly love his wife and children. It was something for those lower in ranks to achieve, but not a Kingpin. To be King was to be lonely. And as the loneliest bastard around, I couldn't help but admit—even if just to myself—that I'd fucking love to be King. "Besides, tradition and the classics have a certain ... elegance to them, wouldn't you agree?" Raffaello continued.

"Like having an entire hall of gaudy paintings of Price Heirs?" I countered with a smirk, glancing around at the art spanning back generation after generation. Raff's laugh was once again choppy, but he didn't disagree when we reached the door to our destination.

"Ah, yes, our ancestry," Raff said as he looked up at the walls and slowed his pace. "Sometimes, I look at these walls and think to myself, who else but the Prezzos would immigrate to America and change their name only to form an empire of blood and money."

I considered his expression for a moment before looking at the paintings myself. A tall, bulbous man with a thick mustache that was popular back in the 1920s stared back at me from one. "And?" I asked my old friend. "What do you derive from that?" I returned my attention to the man standing next to me.

"I think they wanted to remind our family and those who came after them that Prezzo or not … the Price is what we should always be looking for. After all, we did sell our souls to the devil for a damn good one, didn't we?" Raff winked as he said that last part, but before I could respond, he turned and kept walking.

"The Price Syndicate is actually something I'd like to discuss with you." The office we entered was as ornate and gaudy as the rest of the mansion. It smelled of paper, wood polish, and the slightest scent of tobacco. Raff strode around the massive desk before sitting in his office chair. When I made no move further into the space, he gestured to the leather chairs facing him. "Please have a seat." My fingers brushed over the front of my suit jacket, undoing the single button as I moved to oblige him.

"I'm going to cut right to the chase, Gaven," Raff started bluntly once we were alone and out of the guards' sight. "I'm getting older, and Dahlia is gone." He paused for a moment, a dark look crossing his face. One I remembered well as I'd seen that very same look when he'd called me seven years ago and ordered me to find and bring him his wife's murderer. It took only a moment for it to clear, and once it did, he was back to the smiling, albeit sharp-eyed, Raff that I knew well enough.

Had he ever gone legit in his business, he might have made a fine politician. Very few knew *just* how dark parts of him that lurked beneath the surface were, having chosen to keep it hidden beneath layer after layer of mask and façade. The only reason I'd ever been privy to such details of the man's life had been because of my assistance in finding his wife's killer and the enemy that had taken her from him. If I were honest with myself, though, it wasn't just the request from my old friend, but also from that of the young girl I'd met at the funeral. Her big eyes had looked up at me, and through her own innocence, she'd asked me to do something no child should ever even think of … and she'd done so without any hint of regret.

"I have no sons to pass the Price business to when I inevitably pass," he continued. "You and I have worked together on many occasions over the years. I respect the code you follow when carrying out your contracts and how you conduct yourself. You should know that I've always cared for you as if you were my own."

I nodded. "Yes, if I recall, you were one of my very first clients as a hitman."

He grinned. "And you performed it beautifully,"

Raff replied. "I'm quite proud of the man you've become."

"Even though you stole me away from your competitors?" I chuckled as I asked the question. The truth was that even allies in our world were competitors. I might have gotten my start cleaning up kills and progressed into the direct act of killing, but Raffaello Price had given me the first shot it took to showcase my darker talents. Even afterward, it wasn't until the death of his wife that I'd truly begun to shine as a man who could make the impossible … possible. I'd found the enemy responsible for his late wife's murder and I'd sent his heart back to the family before slaughtering the lot of them—from the head to the heirs.

"It has been a lucrative relationship for the both of us," Raffaello said, pulling me back to the present.

"It has," I agreed. "I've always respected you and the way you do business." The circles and banter, while piquing my curiosity, were also wearing on me. None of it explained what I was doing here now. "Did you call me here to placate my ego, old man, or is there a point to this meeting?"

"Did you know that I was not always a Price?" he asked by way of answer. I frowned, confused by the strangeness of the question. I shook my head and he continued, "Dahlia wasn't an heir to another family, and though we'd hoped for one for the Price Syndicate, it didn't happen. I contemplated remarrying after she was gone, but…" He trailed off as if recalling some long-ago memory. He doesn't need to say it. The love he had felt for his wife had been obvious to everyone in the underworld. It was why she'd made the perfect target, the perfect weakness. Even though I felt for him, he'd been stupid to get so attached. A sigh accompanied the rhythmic tensing of his jaw, the brief wistfulness in his gaze hardening at whatever he was seeing in his mind.

"Raff." I leaned back against the chair as my frown deepened. "All this talk of marriage and heirs. Please explain what this has to do with—" It hit me, causing me to cut off my own words even as I spoke them. "You want me to marry into your family and take over the place of heir." It's not a question but a statement, and a damned shocking one at that.

A smile stretched his wide face. "Like, I said, you're far from stupid, Gaven," Raff replied with a nod. "Yes." He straightened in his wingback chair and folded his hands over the surface of his oak desk. "I intend to offer you just that."

"What about your current lieutenants? I'm sure they'd be pretty pissed to find out the organization is being handed over to a stranger," I countered, relaxing back into the cushions of the chair. "I don't exactly want—or need—any more enemies gunning for me."

"They're devoted to the Price Syndicate," he replied with a dismissive wave of his hand. "Their families have been a part of our organization for generations, so they're well versed in how the head of the family is passed down when no heir has been born."

"Mhmm," I murmured skeptically, "and what makes you think *I* want to be the next head of the Price Family?"

"I'm sure I don't have to tell you that men in your line of work, or rather, *our* line of work tend to find themselves in an early grave, Gaven. You've surpassed the typical lifespan of a contract killer— no doubt because of your skillset. The question is: do you want to continue to live your solitary life- style? Worried that at any given point you could be next on the chopping block?" There was a pregnant pause before he finished the open-ended question- ing. "Or do you want power?"

That was an easy question to answer. I wanted fucking *power*. In this business, however, revealing your cards too soon was dangerous. So, I schooled my face as I dragged a hand down my jaw. Wearing a mask was a means of survival, even among friends. I stared back at my old friend and considered his question a bit more carefully before answering. The fact was, I enjoyed my work, but I couldn't deny that he was right. The life of a hitman was short-lived in comparison to the average person, and I wanted a change.

Taking on a Syndicate was a once in a lifetime opportunity. I was rich from all of my contracts, but the Price Family ... they were the kind of wealth that shot first and didn't question whether they'd be able to buy their way out. It wasn't a safer life, but I would be insane not to realize the benefits of accepting it.

"What if I decline your offer?" Raff's eyes narrowed on me. He knew what I was truly asking. He wouldn't have asked me here, brought me in, and practically slapped adoption papers in front of me despite my age if it weren't for the sheer fact that he knows I'm not going to say no. However, if I did… well, he wouldn't want it to get out that he was looking for an heir to marry one of his daughters. There was no gain without loss, and I was anxious to know the specific details of this position. As he said, there was always a price.

"I don't think we need to go into those specifics, Gaven, you're smart enough to know what the potential downsides are." Raff's rough chuckle filled the room as he gestured to my expression. "And regardless of your expression, I know you. You're as ambitious as they come."

"So astute," I muttered with a shake of my head, earning another laugh from Raff.

"There's only one thing you would need to do." He reached into the top drawer of his desk. When he pulled two pictures and laid them out for me to see, I stood and leaned over to scan them. "My daughters—Jacquelina and Evangeline," he said, pointing to the corresponding portrait with each name. "You would only need to choose one."

A wife, I mused, *is not something I ever thought I'd have.* A wife such as the one that Raff, himself, had was one that I wouldn't tolerate. These girls, whichever one ended up being the pawn, needed to understand that if we were to wed—things would be vastly different from their parents. If I was to become the head of a family, I refused to have a weakness. Even if it meant strapping one of them with a lifetime shackled to me in misery.

The first, labeled in clear black letters at the top —Jacquelina—was darker in both complexion and hair. She clearly resembled her father. It was as if I was looking into a strange, warped image of the man in front of me. Still, though, she was feminine in her own way, with a slender figure and hooded eyes. She was the older of the two, with a mature face and expression, but there was an iciness to her smile that gave me pause.

She would likely make for a powerful ally, but a wife? Dangerous. It was a well-known fact that keeping your friends close was a good tactic, but keeping your enemies closer would keep you alive. This woman would not be easily malleable. She was far too much of a risk. I knew the kind of look she exhibited. I'd seen it countless times in prostitutes, escorts, and other mafia women. There was nothing but a serpent slithering around underneath her skin. One wrong move and she'd unhinge her jaw and attempt to swallow me whole—and it wouldn't do to kill my own wife. I may not want to love her, but I would respect the hell out of the protection part of our vows as any man who laid claim to a woman should. Too bad, really. I recognized a bit of myself in Jacquelina. She had the expression of someone who understood pride and greed. Someone who was more than willing to use herself to get what she wanted.

I turned my interest to the second image, pushing Jacquelina's away as I pulled it closer to me and examined the photograph: Raff's youngest daughter, Evangeline. The murky memory of a young girl with soft, dirty blonde hair, several shades lighter than her sister's, and big eyes resurfaces. I lifted the photograph and brought it closer. Even as I do so, though, I could practically feel Raff's interest. If I had to guess, I would bet he's banking on me being more interested in Evangeline.

In the image, she was older than she was the last time I met her at her mother's funeral. In this picture, she was far more to my taste. While some sick fucks craved young girls, that never was and never would be my preference. The Evangeline in this photograph no longer resembled a child. Instead, she had the look of a young woman. Soft, rounded cheeks and pink, parted lips. Her eyes glittered even in the still image.

Unlike her elder sister, Evangeline had no such calculating look in her eyes. Instead, they were wide and round ovals of purity, albeit a little mischievous. The slight quirk in the corner of her lip, as if she were holding back a smirk, makes me want to know what's happening in her mind. Big, luminous, hazel eyes that begged a man to take her under his protection, under his command. She was far too innocent for a man such as myself. Still, I would have her.

If Raff bet on his youngest, then he would be right. Evangeline would be the perfect bride. Young. Innocent. Easy to please and ship off. I'd ply her with treats and gifts and then keep her tucked away. She would be simple to use or, even better, to *control*. In fact, the longer I stare at her picture, the easier it is to imagine what she'd be like under my flogger. Pretty red ropes wrapped around her pale skin. Cuffs holding her arms behind her back, forcing her to thrust her breasts up for my pleasure. Oh, yes. I enjoyed that image. Making her mine would be an exercise in satisfaction. Then, once I put a child in her belly, my reign would be solidified.

"Well?" Raff's voice brought me back from my thoughts. "What do you think? Will either of my daughters entice you to make an old man happy?"

Scoffing, I set the photo down on the desk and leaned back once more. "You may be old, but no less dangerous," I reminded him.

Raffaello shook his head at my comment. My eyes fell back upon the image, in any case. Evangeline Price likely wouldn't know what was coming for her, not until it was too late. It made me a terrible man, but the second I laid eyes on her, I knew. I would accept Raff's proposal, and this was the one I'd choose to be my wife.

I could feel Raff watching me carefully and was thankful for the mastery I held over my own expression. Without batting an eyelash, I reached out and picked up the glossy photo of her.

"Just to be sure," I said, "you're not trying to sell me a child bride, are you?"

Raffaello laughed. "No, my Angel is eighteen. She'll be nineteen in the fall. Even I am not so cruel as to marry off a child."

I pressed my lips together. Eighteen. Yes, I could see that. The expression in her picture is a little defiant. Something I'd have a fantastic time fucking out of her. Barely into her womanhood, but a woman was all I saw. Gorgeous. Voluptuous. Stunning. Her oval-shaped face and small smirk made something cruel twist in my guts, a sinister craving that I hadn't felt in far too long.

I wanted to see what she would look like spread out on my bed, her head thrown back in ecstasy as I drove my cock into her pussy. Would she scream or mark me with her delicate little nails? Would she cry and try to push me away, or would she fight back and force me to hold her down while I fucked her into submission? I knew it was wrong to think such a thing, to find both options appealing as I eyed her delicate figure, but I'd never been a knight in shining armor. I wasn't going to start now. *Mine*. This woman was going to be mine. My bride. My wife. And then ... the mother of my children and the next heir to the Price Syndicate. I would not fail where Raff had. I'd fuck her day and night until I planted my seed and it came to fruition. I wanted this power that Raffaello was offering me. It made me a monster of a man, but then again ... I'd never claimed to be good.

Raff nodded down to where I still held Evangeline's photo in my grasp. "So, can I take it that I have your answer then?"

Had someone told me that morning that I would be offered one of the Price princesses as a bride, I would not only have laughed at the thought, but I might have even killed the bastard for attempting to toy with me.

I was not laughing now.

Damn Raffaello Price. I'd been perfectly content with my bachelorhood, but one look at this one— the softness of her angelic features—and I knew. There was only one answer. I would take her. I would fuck her. I would become the next Price Heir and make one of my own.

"Yes," I said, folding the image of Evangeline's face in half and tucking it into my inner pocket. "I want Evangeline."

2
ANGEL

She's wrong. Insane. Absolutely certifiable.

It was the only explanation. This couldn't be happening. Absolutely not. Not when I was so close to my freedom. The applications were in, and even though my family could afford to send me to any school in the world, I'd sworn to myself that I wasn't going to take blood-stained money. I'd applied for scholarships and I knew I was guaranteed at least some financial assistance in that area.

Confusion whipped through me as I strode out of the library and into the hallway of the Price Estate. While the world had moved on from extensive properties and manor houses, the rest of society choosing to settle into more appropriate apartments and suburban houses, the Price Family had not. We couldn't. Not with all of the enemies my father had made along the way—before my mother's death and since. Thanks to my sister—who enjoyed regaling me with all of the things she'd overheard and dug up because she knew just how uncomfortable it made me—I now knew far more about it than I cared to.

That all slipped from my mind though, the second Gertrude—our longtime maid—had congratulated me on my upcoming nuptials. Nuptials that I hadn't heard about until that very moment. I'd stood frozen in the library as she'd chattered on about how she'd gotten married young too and her husband had been a solid ten years her senior, but an older man always felt a little naughty, didn't it? I could honestly say there were things now I was thinking about Gertrude that I never, in my life, wanted to consider.

"It's not real," I told myself. "She's just going senile. She probably thought I was her granddaughter." God, it was horrible, but I prayed to any god that would listen and even a devil or two that the old woman was just losing her mind.

"Where are you heading?" I stopped at the sound of my sister's voice behind me.

I turned and faced her. There was a kernel of knowledge in her eyes—in the way she smiled at me, which was both amused and smug. I wasn't sure, but from the quirk of her lips and the light of amusement in her eyes that was so rare, I had a dreadful feeling. It was her expression that tipped me off. She always got the same one right before she tormented me.

"You knew, didn't you??" I blurted out the question, hoping against hope that my sister would laugh over this horrible misunderstanding. Is that what she does, though? Of course not. Not my psychopath of a sister.

Instead, her smile widened, and my stomach dropped. "Who finally told you?" she asked.

"Told me?" I repeated, shaking my head. My chest felt hollow and strangely sore, as if something had punched right through me. I rubbed a hand over it absently as I tried to think of something to say, some way to get out of this. "Don't you think I should've been more than told?" I snapped. "I should've been fucking asked! If this bastard has to choose one of us—"

"One of *us*?" Jackie laughed, the sound like a sharp piercing horn in my ear. So loud, it made me flinch away. "No, kiddo, not us—*you*. Congrats, you're getting married before me. Gotta say, I'm a little bit jealous." She didn't sound jealous. Instead, she sounded almost pleased—amused.

Out of respect for our dad and our mom, despite her passing, I'd refrained from being too angry with Jackie in the last seven years, but right now, it was really hard not to want to smack her face. She had a personality and an ever-present tone that made it clear she was laughing at everything and everyone around her. As if the world was a comedy she couldn't help but chuckle at, no matter the circumstances. And unfortunately, most of it had been centered around me, including today.

This can't be happening. But even as that thought echoed through my head, I knew the truth. The fact that Jackie seemed so amused to know something about me that I didn't, made it painfully clear that this wasn't the horrible joke or the ramblings of an elderly woman slowly disintegrating into insanity that I'd hoped it would be.

"How did you find out before me?" I demanded. "If I'm the one getting married, then why wasn't I even involved?"

Jackie shook her head at me. "Oh, sweetheart." The endearment sounded caustic and sarcastic coming from her lips.

I gritted my teeth as she approached. Jackie and I were related by blood, but that was where our relationship ended. Where I preferred to sink into the background, reading books and studying while secretly planning and hoping that one day I could leave the family behind and start a normal life—she was … well, ambitious was a polite way of putting it. For as long as I could remember, and since I'd realized what our family did for money, Jackie had been preparing to take over the Price empire whenever our father finally stepped down. She'd been convinced that because I was so dead set against it all, she would be the only choice, and she'd blatantly said as much.

I loved my father—honestly, I did—and I knew he loved me. Because of that, I had foolishly misled myself into thinking that one day he'd support me in trying to have a future outside of the mob and my role as a woman born into the Price Empire and let me go to college. Otherwise, what was the point of the last seven years?

Is it purposeful? I wondered. *Is he angry with me? Because I told him that I wanted to move out?* The reminder of the acceptance papers sitting on my nightstand stung.

Is this a punishment? Can I talk him out of it? Make him see reason? He wouldn't even have to pay for my tuition. Not that we couldn't afford it, but I'd worked my ass off to ensure I got a scholarship covering everything. He and Jackie might have felt perfectly fine living in the shadow of danger, but I wanted out.

There was only one instance in which I'd been grateful for the wicked men that surrounded my family, and that was seven years ago when I'd asked one of them to kill the person who'd taken my mother from me—the man from the funeral. It was the one and only time I'd allowed myself to ask something of the dark criminal world into which I was born.

"Why?" I shook my head, trying to make sense of it all. "Why would he do this? Why wouldn't he at least ask me?" I repeated.

"*Little Angel.*" Jackie's heels clicked against the rich mahogany floor as she moved closer. The tight, low-cut dress she wore tightened around her thighs with each step. The way she said my name made my insides churn and irritation build. Fuck, she was such a bitch. I wanted to smack the shit out of her every time she said it in that condescending tone. "*Daddy* doesn't need to ask your permission for anything." Her words were mocking. "You should've realized it by now. Men like him can do whatever they want."

She was right. As much as I'd wanted to hide from it, run away from it these last several years, the truth was that my father was no different than any other man in this dark godforsaken world. He controlled. He ruled. He made the ultimate decisions. It was as if I'd been picked up and dropped back a hundred or more years in the past when women were little more than commodities. That still didn't explain why she seemed to be so okay with that, in any case.

Stopping in my tracks, I spun to face her. "Why aren't *you* freaking out?" I demanded.

Jackie came to an abrupt halt and tilted her head to the side as she considered me. Her deep brown eyes were lined with a black that contrasted as much as it could with her olive complexion. She pursed her red lips as I waited for an answer. When it came, though, it wasn't what I expected. With an indifferent shrug, Jackie smiled back at me. "It doesn't really affect me, now, does it?" she said. "So, why would I care?"

A growl rumbled in my throat. Of course, she would think that. The urge to slap her resurfaced, but I refrained from doing so. "No," I said again, shaking my head. "This is a mistake." My hope was a valiant little thing, blossoming in my chest even when I knew, deep down, it was a fragile thing that was easily broken.

"Well, I hope, for your sake, dear sister, that the man Father's chosen isn't some fat, bulbous old fucker," Jackie said, making the light snack I'd had earlier curdle in my stomach. I felt lightheaded and uneasy. I turned away from her, hating the image that popped into my head. Enjoying what she was doing to me, she continued. "Or maybe he's bald and mean. Oh dear, what if he beats you? That would just be *terrible.*" Jackie's slender arms came around me from behind, and she pressed herself against my back.

The expensive scent of her perfume choked me. I said nothing.

"You want my advice?" she asked.

I looked back at her. Jackie was offering me advice? "Why?" I asked.

Jackie pressed her lips to my ear. "Conquering a man is easy business, little sister," she whispered. "Even if he's ugly and old. All you need to do is spread your legs and keep your mouth shut. Don't tell him about your daydreams, don't tell him about that little college you want to go to and how all you want is to be *normal*. Pretend to be interested in everything he says or does. Treat him like a king, and don't complain even if he hurts you."

My hands curled into fists. No. No way in fucking hell would I just lay back and take it. "I need to figure out how to get out of this," I said, mostly to myself.

A chuckle rumbled against my spine as Jackie laughed again. Her arms released me, and she pulled away before stepping around to my front. "You won't," she said. "It's already been decided. Just take my advice. It'll be so much easier for you if you do. The sex is for him, not you. Just stay loyal long enough to give him a son and then you can play around with a man who knows how to truly please a woman."

Her words collided in my mind and the image of some strange man with graying hair and a belly that trembled like jello crawled over me. I tried to keep my breathing even as the thought sent me into a mental tailspin, but it was no use as the fear quickly turned into a physical anxiety attack. Without another word, I jerked away from her and dashed down the hallway, heading straight for my father's office.

Jackie's laugh followed me as I ran, like the horrifying wail of a banshee. I hurried toward the double wooden doors that marked his office as fast as my legs could carry me. As it came into view, I didn't think about stopping or knocking, I reached for the handle, turned, and stumbled into the room.

"Dad! We need to talk, I—" I came to an abrupt halt as I realized he wasn't alone.

My eyes landed on the man looking over his shoulder from where he sat in front of my father's desk and stayed there, unable to turn away.

Even from where I stood, I could tell that this man was tall. His shoulders were wide—wider than the chair he sat in. When he turned to face me, I felt my mouth go dry. Eyes as piercing and blue as the ocean, with a light stubble coating the lower half of his face that matched the same dirty blond shade of his hair—he appeared distinguished in a way that I was most certainly not. Though he wasn't quite as old as my father, he was older than me. Mid-thirties if I had to hazard a guess. Probably twice my age. There were fine lines around the edges of his eyes—crow's feet—but the rest of him appeared big and brawny. Like he was a Viking who had somehow fit himself into the suit of a modern man.

In his gaze, was an intense glimmer of heat. It cut through me as I froze in the doorway, my hand still wrapped around the doorknob and my mouth hanging open. When he blinked slowly, cutting me off from that impenetrable gaze only to return a moment later, I realized that there was a steeliness to his attention. A careful amusement that was only surface deep. The man looked at me as if he had seen or done horrible things, pillaged villages and burned houses, and I—I was the thing he'd been searching for all along. It was … disturbing.

"Evangeline." My father stood from his chair and smiled at me, lifting his arm as he gestured for me to come closer. "Come here."

"I'm sorry," I said, adjusting my silk blouse slightly and tugging it down against the waistband of my jeans as I stepped further into the room and released the door. "I didn't realize you had a guest."

My father chuckled. "Gaven is more than a guest, Angel," he said.

I frowned. His name was Gaven then. What an innocuous name for a man who'd no doubt done horrible, awful things in his lifetime. I could see it in his eyes. No normal man stared at a woman the way he did unless he was a predator seeking something to eat. I swallowed roughly, nervously.

"Who's this, Father?" I jumped as Jackie's voice sounded behind me. I hadn't realized she'd followed me here.

When I didn't move toward the desk, Jackie stepped through the open doorway and around me. She strode farther into the room, her eyes locking on the man as he rose from his seat as well, the elegant cut of his suit jacket hanging open. "Oh, you're a handsome one." Her voice turned sultry as she approached, and I watched with a spark of something dark in my mind as she touched his arm and batted her lashes up at him. "Are you one of the new guards? Perhaps we should spend some time together later."

"Enough, Jacquelina," Dad barked, his expression darkening as irritation took root. "Gaven is not a guard." A sinking feeling took over. If he was warning Jackie away from a man, that could only mean one thing. Dad turned back to me, the cold expression he had flashed to my sister melting away. "Please, Evangeline, come in. I'd like for you to meet my friend, Gaven Belmonte."

"Your friend?" I repeated.

With a hefty gulp, I took one single step further into the room. I didn't trust myself to move any more. Jackie's hand had yet to leave the man's arm —not that he seemed to notice. His eyes were zeroed in on me in a way that could only be described as hungry. My back straightened and I lifted my chin, meeting his gaze head-on.

Even as I glared at the man, I spoke to my father. "Dad, I need to speak with you. It's important."

"Yes," Dad replied. "I have something I'd like to say as well, but first, please say hello. You're being rude, Angel."

His tone was gruff, slightly frustrated and confused—as if he couldn't understand my unease, my impoliteness. I had to admit, it wasn't like me. At least not to outsiders. Years of biting back retort after retort and fiery reactions gave me an air of obedience. I didn't exactly feel like being polite to this man, though.

Something about him put me on edge. Perhaps it was an old memory, something I couldn't quite recall, but I had a feeling it was something more. A premonition of what was to come. Instead of me being the first to say anything, however, the choice was taken from me by the man—by Gaven's deep, precise voice. He looked familiar. Strange. I wracked my brain for the information, but he spoke before I could find it.

"Hello, Evangeline," he said, stepping closer to me, shrugging off Jackie's arm despite her slight attempts to keep hold. A frown curled her lips, but I wasn't paying attention to her because it took every ounce of my will to keep from reacting to the depth of his voice. It wasn't husky like I was used to hearing from my father's men. It was a smooth, rich baritone that seemed to weave its way through me, nestling next to my erratically beating heart.

"Hello, Mr. Belmonte," I murmured, nodding at him, though I made sure not to move closer. "It's lovely to meet you. I apologize for intruding on your meeting."

"It's no problem at all," Gaven said, smiling my way. "In fact, we were just about to invite you to join us."

Fuck. That could not spell good news. My eyes darted to my father, who stood behind his desk, appearing quite pleased with himself. "Why?" I demanded.

"Well, my Angel..." My father rounded his desk until he stood between the man—Gaven—and me. Jackie moved back with a frown, her eyes darting between the three of us. "I was planning to talk to you this evening, but I expect there's a reason you came in here so abruptly. I'm sure you've heard by now."

"Yes." I remembered the reason with sobering clarity. I turned to my father. "Is it true?" My eyes met his. "You're planning to *force* me to get married?" I emphasized the word 'force' to showcase my extreme dislike of this situation.

"Yes." The answer came through loud and clear,

but to my utter surprise, it didn't come from my father. My head pivoted as if twisting on an axis. With my full attention now on him, Gaven smiled gently and continued. "Your father has asked me to join the Price Family and take you as my wife."

Another sliver of shock echoed through me, not because it was happening so quickly, but because I hadn't expected the man before me to be the one I would be forced to marry. There it was, though— that damn premonition. Before I could respond, my father spoke up once more.

"It's my goal, Angel, to have Gaven become the next head of the family. It's time for me to step down and let the business go into younger, capable hands. I'm ready to retire, and I want to make sure that my girls are well taken care of."

Gaven chuckled. "I'm not all that young, Raffaello."

"You're far younger than I am," my father replied with no small amount of amusement.

I was reeling, and I could feel the hope that had bloomed in my chest despite my worst fears dying a slow and painful death.

"You can't be serious." At first, I thought my horror and confusion had all come pouring out in that one word until I realized it wasn't my voice at all.

Father shot Jackie a disapproving look at her words, but otherwise ignored the outburst, taking a step closer to me and reaching for my hands. "Please, my Angel," he said in a low voice. "I hope you understand that this is necessary. For our family to continue, Gaven will ensure your safety and—"

"Is this because of my acceptance?" I demanded, cutting him off. I flash a dark look at Gaven out of the corner of my eye, unsure if I should say anything about the university in front of him, but also unwilling to let my father go without a clear answer.

"No, this is not about the matter of your acceptance to Eastpoint University," my father said. "This is simply the best course of action for the family and for you."

I shook my head. "No, I don't—I *can't* agree to this."

My father's face changed, shifting and morphing into one I knew too well. It was the face of the head of the Price Family—the immovable and unrepentant man who was responsible for things I refused to be a part of. Things that would almost certainly have him arrested and committed to federal prison for life if he were any less careful. And now … I was the next piece of his business plan. A simple pawn, no matter how much I worked on leaving this life behind.

"I've made my decision," he said, releasing my hands, leaving me feeling cold all over as the blood drained from my face. "It would be in your best interest to give Gaven a chance."

"This isn't the medieval ages, Dad," I hissed, my voice breaking when I realized Gaven was watching my humiliation with a curious and analytical gaze.

"No, but you are part of a very old-school family, Evangeline. My marriage was arranged too. You *will* agree to this." It was a command, not a request. I wanted to protest harder, but I knew the truth—no matter how much my father might care for me, he would force the issue. Or choose someone far worse.

Heart hammering against my ribcage, I looked over to Gaven Belmonte. By all appearances, he wasn't monstrous. Appearances, however, could be deceiving. As if understanding that our small interlude had come to an end, Gaven stepped forward and offered his own hand in greeting.

"It truly is a pleasure to make your acquaintance, Angel," he said. "I look forward to our life together."

"Evangeline," I corrected automatically as I took his hand. It nearly engulfed mine with warmth and strength. His palm and fingers were rough with callouses as he squeezed lightly.

He smiled. "I think Angel suits you."

I wasn't sure how to respond to that, so I remained silent, simmering in my rage and desperation. Already, I was trying to work out what would be the best course of action.

How could I turn back the clock?

How could I get out of this?

What did I have to do to get this man to refuse me as his wife?

"I understand you may be a little confused by all this, but I was hoping that you would join me for dinner tomorrow." He smirked. "I think it'd be nice to get to know one another more intimately, don't you?"

My lips parted and my eyes bounced from his to my father's and to Jackie's—who stared at the two of us with a deep scowl on her face. "We don't know each other," I stated. "What makes you think one dinner will change anything?"

"*Angel.*" My father's angry voice was so rarely turned on me that when he said my name in that gravelly tone, it made my pulse jump.

Gaven's hand tightened on mine, and he used his hold to pull me closer until he could lean down and brush his lips over my ear as he spoke. "I promise you won't regret it," he said. "Just one date."

"She agrees," my father said.

No, I fucking didn't, but I couldn't deny it now. Not with his glare burning into the side of my face.

As Gaven backed away and released my hand, the hard, beckoning stare of my father told me what I already knew. This was all a farce. Gavin's request was merely an illusion. The reality was that the choice had already been made for me, so I gave the only answer I could, the words feeling like acid on my tongue.

"Fine," I snapped. "Yes. I'll go to dinner." And that was where I'd start to make him regret his choice.

3
ANGEL

Dreams were fragile creatures, so easily damaged, so easily cast aside. I was beginning to learn that. My dreams of going away to college and leaving behind this life—a life bathed in crime and secrets—seemed as far away as ever as I walked through the estate to the front, where I would wait to be picked up by Gaven Belmonte.

After the meeting in my father's office the day before, Jackie had stormed off, her mood having turned foul for some unknown reason. She'd been perfectly amused to hear of my arranged marriage, but now she seemed more upset by it than even I was. And I was *plenty* upset over it. The man my father had chosen was handsome, and a part of me felt as though I should've been grateful for that small consolation, but it couldn't erase the fact that I didn't know him or that I would forever be tethered to this family and its cruel intentions.

I closed my eyes and sucked in a harsh breath as

I contemplated turning my ass right back around and going back up to my room to lock myself inside. It would be a child's tantrum, but I felt like throwing one right now. All of my carefully laid plans were being ruined, and the man—Gaven—didn't seem all that concerned with the fact that I had no interest in marrying him.

"Miss." My eyes opened as Bruno, one of my father's closest men, approached me. "Mr. Belmonte's here. He's waiting in the sitting room."

"I see.." I glanced down at my dress before smoothing the slightly wrinkled sides, the movement giving me something to do. Unlike Jackie, I didn't wear dresses too often—much preferring jeans and shirts to her tightly fitted designer outfits. Right now, I felt out of place in the dress even though it wasn't nearly as tight and flowed down my thighs in light folds of fabric. I reached up and touched my curled hair. I hadn't wanted to make any more effort than necessary, but Gertrude wouldn't hear of it, so she'd spent the better part of a few hours styling my hair into soft curling waves and painting my face with far more makeup than I usually wore. *At least it was all natural looking*, I reminded myself. I'd rejected any harsh colors and gone for neutrals.

The fidgeting and adjusting allowed me to hide the slight tremble in my hands that Bruno would probably report to my father, to note how the *engagement* was developing. Swallowing the lump that formed in my throat, I forced my gaze back on him. "Thank you, Bruno."

Bruno nodded, his eyes following me as I moved past him. The place where Gaven waited was a room my father often invited guests. Gaven was different, in any case. Just as my father had said, he was no guest. He would soon be the next head of the Price Family. This man knew what that meant. He knew who my father was, knew what he did, and I could only assume that meant he was just like him.

Since my mom passed and I discovered what the family business actually was, I'd kept careful watch over who my father invited into our innermost estate —some he seemed to care for and some he seemed to despise. I'd come to learn that he invited them all, whether they were friends or enemies, because the best way to deal with enemies was to keep them just as close, if not closer. My only question now was …
Which one is Gaven Belmonte to me?

I remembered how my father spoke of him the day before. He'd called Gaven a *friend*, but it was hard to know anyone's true motives in this life. If he was a potential enemy, then he'd just been offered the keys to the kingdom, and I was part of the consolation prize.

As I entered the sitting room, Gaven turned away from the window and offered me a smile. It was a careful smile, one meant to reassure, but the only way he could have reassured me was by calling this whole farce off. I doubted that he would, though. That would be all too easy for me, and I'd come to know that life was anything but easy.

"Hello, Angel."

"Hello..." I let my reply drift as I lowered my eyes. He'd worn a suit similar to the one I'd first seen him in. Dark colors to his lighter skin with a black button down, yet no tie. My eyes scanned even further down to the black box he held in his hand, and a jolt of worry constricted my chest at the sight of the package. "What's that?"

His smile deepened into one that felt more real as he held it up. "I thought it'd be nice to bring you a gift for our first date since your father couldn't be here to see you off."

"He's working. I'm used to it," I said with a small shrug, trying to soothe all the ridiculous ideas my brain conjured that could have been his *gift*. Still, curiosity had me reaching for the box as he held it out to me. "Can I open this now?" I asked, lifting my gaze once more to meet his as I fingered the top of the mysterious package.

He nodded. "I'd like it if you could wear it while I search for something more suited to your tastes." He paused, and almost as if he couldn't help himself, he added, "And mine."

Frowning, I pinched my fingers under the lid of the small box and then opened it. My lips parted when what was inside was revealed. I stared down at the diamond choker with surprise. It was a single slender gold chain so finely woven that the links were almost indiscernible. Every inch or so was a diamond, and from the way they glittered—perfectly clear and unclouded—I could tell that they were real, as real as anything my father might have given my mother.

I glanced back up at him, my chest tight. "This is too much," I said uncomfortably.

More than that, it was clear what this was. A declaration of ownership. I shuddered at the thought but couldn't pinpoint whether or not I was put off by it or intrigued. Perhaps if Gaven and I had met the old-fashioned way, I'd be more keen to accept, but that wasn't how our relationship had come to be. I tried to hand the box back. "I'm sorry, I can't accept this."

"It's not enough," he replied, never losing that careful mask of his as he pulled back without taking the box. "I should have known you wouldn't care for something so simple. Please keep it and I will look for something better." His words were almost enough to make me want to scream. I was being forced to marry this man, an elusive and secretive stranger, and yet he acted as if he'd known me my whole life. Or, at the very least, as if he could guess my likes and dislikes without having spent so much as a singular week in my presence.

"I'm sure it's very expensive," I said, trying again to return the box to him. "But I don't think it's appro—"

"Think of it as an engagement gift." A scowl formed on my face at his words. An engagement gift? He couldn't be serious. "I haven't been able to go shopping for a ring yet," he admitted.

A ring. For me. Because that's what a couple who

were engaged to be married did—they exchanged rings. I'd probably have to look for one for him too. I stopped trying to hand the necklace back to him. *This is really happening.*

Not only was I really going to marry someone who my father had chosen to take over the family, but it was also becoming an inevitability that the rest of my life would likely develop into something like this. This man bringing me gifts, commanding me, watching me with those … penetrating eyes of his.

"Here." Gaven moved closer. "Let me help you put it on."

Without an excuse for why he shouldn't, I found myself standing silent and frozen as he removed the diamond choker from the black box and lifted my hair. His fingers brushed my skin, shockingly warm as he circled my neck with the jewelry and clasped it into place. The gold and diamonds felt cold against my skin. Somehow, it became heavier the longer it rested there—weighted and meaningful.

This wasn't a present. It was a declaration. This necklace wasn't a sweet engagement gift, but a shackle being locked into place. The visual signs that I was now being traded like cattle and my new owner wanted to see his claim upon me.

My insides roiled with uneasiness and something else. The new sensation was so shocking it locked me into place as Gaven's hands moved over the back of my neck. *What the fuck?* The thought of this man—of Gaven Belmonte—laying claim to me when he hardly knew me should not have made me

… excited. Yet, there it was, a telltale pulse between my legs, an abnormal wetness that only ever occurred when I read romance books.

"You should say thank you, Angel," Gaven said lightly. Despite the gentle and calm note of his voice, though, Gaven's words were a command and shockingly, I found myself answering.

"Thank you." The words breathed out of me.

"You're very welcome," he replied before circling me and offering his arm. "Shall we go?"

This was ridiculous. The betrothal, the extravagant jewelry, his offered arm, and that damned gentleman façade he held tight to. It all felt like some horribly dramatic *Downton Abbey* film. Maybe he thought that acting proper was something that might set me at ease, but all it did was make me wonder what sinister aspects he was hiding beneath the surface.

This was it. This was the reason—after my mother had been murdered—my sister ripped away my blissful naiveté, and my father had finally been forced to sit me down to explain what he did for a living and why my protection was so important. Because knowing was better than being kept in the dark. Knowing was safer. Knowing meant I could plan accordingly. Unlike Jackie, though, my father had never gone into detail. He'd only told me just enough to make me realize that Jackie hadn't been tormenting me and making it all up. It was real.

Dad was the head of a large crime family and, as his daughter, I was a connection to that family—a pawn to be used. Right now, I didn't have the luxury of pretending this was all just some sick, twisted prank played on me by my cruel sister. Gaven was just as real as my father's words. His personality, though, was likely a façade. So, I would just have to wait until this man showed his true colors. Only then would I know what I'd gotten myself into and have the means to try to figure a way out.

4

ANGEL

The ride to the restaurant was quiet, and I was a little surprised that he had elected not to have any of my father's men follow us. It was different than I was used to because, whenever I went out with my father, we were constantly surrounded by guards. As I'd gotten older, they'd been smart enough to fade into the background always watching but keeping far enough away that I could at least pretend I had some sense of normalcy. Now though, I realized just how skilled Gaven must've been if he was allowed to go free with me without bodyguards. Or how arrogant he was to think he was untouchable from threats. If my father allowed it, though, then the only explanation was that he trusted Gaven.

"So..." I began, eyeing the passing landscape as Gaven drove the sports car down the road, "what is it that you do?" It was an innocent enough question for a normal person, that is. For me, though, this was a test. I wanted to see how he'd respond. I pried my eyes away from the window to look at him just as his lips twitched as if he were fighting back a smile. "A little bit of everything," he replied vaguely.

I gritted my teeth. "Care to elaborate?" I pressed.

Gaven's eyes slid toward me once before returning to the road. "Not at the moment," he said. "I don't wish to scare you."

It was too late for that. I was beyond scared. It wasn't necessarily him, though, that I feared. It was the quickly disintegrating future I'd planned for myself that he represented. He was a killer; I knew as much. He had to be if he agreed to my request all those years ago, but that didn't mean it was his primary job. Was he an arms dealer? Did he sell drugs? Or something worse ... was he a human trafficker? I shuddered at the thought. There were things I knew my father had done—he'd killed people. He'd stolen. He'd sold illegal items and opened businesses under legal means for money laundering, but he'd never done something quite that vile.

With a sigh, I turned away from him once more. I settled my gaze on the passing scenery again and bided my time as he drove us into the city—far away from the watchful eyes of my father. Perhaps this little date was a good thing. Perhaps I could convince this man that marrying me should be the absolute last thing he wanted to do. I wasn't exactly sure how yet, but I'd think of a way. I had to … or else …

When we stopped in front of a small Italian bistro, I waited for him to get out of the car, hand his keys to the valet, and circle the front of the Aston Martin to make it to my door. I was on autopilot when he helped me out onto the sidewalk and then as we moved into the building where we were escorted to a private eating room with a single table set for a romantic evening. An elegant white table-cloth, a single rose in a crystal vase, and a small flickering candle, only it didn't feel romantic. It felt forced.

Gaven's gaze on me made me shiver. I wasn't used to being watched with this level of interest. Jackie was always the one who'd commanded atten-tion, flirting with whoever my father's favorite of the week was. But now things were different. I wasn't on the outside looking in anymore. I was smack dab in the middle of this whole ordeal. More than just Gaven, others would no doubt start watching me even closer now. There were other families like ours, I knew, and they, too, would be made aware of my presence in their world. My stomach cramped with fear.

"Are you feeling alright?" Gaven asked as he sat down across from me.

Shoving back the sickness that crept up my throat, I reached for my napkin, spreading it over my lap as a method to avoid his gaze. "Of course."

There was a beat and then he sighed. "I'm not a cruel man, Evangeline."

The sound of my full name coming from his lips caught my attention, making me look up to meet his gaze. "I never said you were." Though I wasn't quite sure how much I believed that statement. Who—if not a cruel man—would force a woman to marry him? Worse yet, what else would he do once that ring was on my finger? The nausea that I'd swallowed down gained new momentum.

His brow arched, clearly reading between the lines of what I'd said. "You're sitting there, shaking and shivering as if you're terrified that I'm going to slit your throat at any moment."

I resented his words. I was, by no means, shaking and shivering in terror.

"Are you?" I countered. He blinked as if shocked by the outright question.

"Now, why would you ask a thing like that?" Gaven focused his gaze on me.

I blinked. "You don't think it's a fair question?"

He shook his head. "I have no reason to hurt you, Angel," he replied. "In fact, it would behoove me to keep you very safe. Without you, I'd have no claim to the Price Syndicate."

"So that's why you're doing this then?" I leaned forward, propping my elbows onto the table between us. *Finally*, some sort of answer from the man about this entire ridiculous situation. "Because you want power."

One thick eyebrow lifts. "Everyone wants power."

"I don't." The answer was immediate, without thought or hesitation. I wasn't my sister. Power had never once crossed my mind in the way my father, Gaven, or others in this life craved.

He smiled at that. It wasn't a condescending smile, but it was one that I expected to be given to a child who'd said something ridiculous. I scowled. "What?" Before he could answer, though, a waiter entered the room and set down two glasses of water as well as a basket of ciabatta.

Gaven cut a look my way as if to tell me to remain silent. I ground my teeth in irritation but didn't say a word. We'd actually been getting somewhere with that conversation—or at least we had started to—and I didn't want to have him fall back on his gentlemanly façade. The more I knew about the man, the better I could plan.

Biting my tongue, I sat fuming as the waiter took our orders—or rather, he took Gaven's before glancing at me. "And for the lovely lady?" the man prompted, poised to jot down whatever selections I made.

Before I could even open the menu or ask for something for myself, though, Gaven's rich baritone filled the space. "*Rigatoni Fra Diavolo* with a side salad and a glass of your best Chianti." Gaven gave the order without even looking at me, and my hands clenched beneath the tablecloth. My desire to demand to order for myself was strong, but I couldn't fault the order in itself. How he knew I tended to like a bit of spice with my meals, I had no idea, but I could guess at least a few ways. My father very well may have told him. He could have questioned the family chef. Or he very well could have just ordered without actually *knowing*—or *caring*—what I actually liked.

"I'm not twenty-one," I said quietly long after the waiter had left. "Technically, I'm not supposed to be drinking."

Gaven lifted a brow at me as his lips curved into a smirk. "A glass of wine is hardly a crime, considering the world we live in, Angel," he replied. "Plus, I suspect you'll need it if you're to enjoy this date."

My insides tightened. *Is this what he considered a date?* This was nothing, I told myself. Just a simple meal. I turned my face away from his. Let him order for me then if he so wanted. He was right in his own way. A glass of wine wasn't much to quibble about when he was just like my father. A killer. A monster. A mobster.

It shouldn't have been anything to get upset about, but the thing that truly pissed me off was that this was a stark reminder that my life was no longer my own. This was a look into my future if I couldn't get out of this marriage. As soon as this man slid a ring on my finger and I said the eternal words 'I do,' he would own me.

As soon as the waiter was out of earshot, Gaven's full attention returned to me. I expected him to begin speaking immediately, but he sat back and stared at me instead. "You're angry," he said after a moment.

No shit, I thought, but I merely nodded. "I'm irritated," I clarified.

He tilted his head to the side, and I felt pinned by his gaze. "You're a curious thing." His tone was thoughtful. "What are you thinking?" Gaven suddenly asked, and with the way my thoughts were rolling through my mind, all it took was that one question for them to come tumbling out from between my lips.

"Why me?" I demanded, fixing him with a confused and frustrated look. Frankly, I didn't understand this whole thing. It truly didn't make any sense. Jackie was the one most suited for the life of a mob wife. She was intelligent. Cunning. Beautiful. But no, for some reason, this man had chosen *me*. My father had offered me even knowing that I wanted to leave. I didn't want to throw Jackie into what I was currently facing, but she *wanted* this life. If the way she'd responded to him the first time she met him was anything to go by, she would've been happy to be his wife.

"I'm not sure I understand your question," Gaven replied.

"I'm inexperienced," I pointed out, lifting my glass of water to my lips.

"That's not necessarily a bad thing," Gaven said. "If anything, it's good. There will be no question whose children you'll bear."

Children? I choked and sputtered on my water,

setting the glass back down with a hard thump. "I'm eighteen," I reminded him. Far too young to be considering children.

"Your father told me that you'll be nineteen soon."

"How old are you?"

Gaven leaned forward and steepled his fingers together, resting his elbows on the edge of the table as he considered me. "Far older than you, Angel," he said. "Although you shouldn't worry, I won't let you be completely deprived of your freedom. Once you've got my son in your belly, you'll be free to make your own choices. You can even attend college if you want to. Your father told me that's what you were planning before he made his offer. Though, I recommend you do so from the comfort and safety of our home."

A mixture of horror and an unwanted tightness in my stomach rolled through me. Not only was this man planning to marry me against my will, but he also wanted to impregnate me. "No."

Gaven shrugged. "Suit yourself." He leaned away from the table and reached for the glass of red wine the waiter had set before him. Something that I couldn't drink because I wasn't even twenty-one yet. Too young to drink, only not too young to have his child, apparently.

"I'm not going to have a child," I snapped.

Gaven carefully sipped his wine and waited until he'd savored the singular gulp he'd taken before he replied. "You will." Those two words were spoken so boldly, so matter-of-factly.

How the fuck could he say something so awful?

"Why not Jackie?" I asked. Despite my earlier thought that I didn't want to throw my sister onto this path, the words spilled out. She was far more agreeable and knowledgeable. She was made for this role. I was not. Perhaps my father hadn't offered Jackie … *No*, even as the thought occurred to me, I knew the truth. This man had definitely chosen me on purpose. It was there in his heated gaze, in the way he stalked me with his eyes. The look he gave me sent chills down my spine.

Gaven eyed me, his cool deep blue gaze analyzing me from my head down to where my lower half disappeared beneath the table. All at once, I felt pinned in place. As if a giant predator had found me and was debating on whether to devour me whole or piece by piece.

"You're a beautiful prize, Angel," he said quietly. "You need not fear the things I can give you. Your future is secured with me. I assure you, I will never hurt you."

"You are hurting me," I snapped back. "You're destroying my future, not securing it. Why the hell would you choose me?" Fear surfaces. It washes over me, a tiny whispering thrill weaving through my body. I swallowed nervously as Gaven leaned forward, one elbow resting on the table as he lifted his hand toward my face.

I held perfectly still as that hand of his neared closer and closer. When his fingers touched my cheek, grazing down to my jawline, it felt like a bolt of electricity had shot through me. Awareness, keen and so very fucking there, lifted me out of the fog of confusion and catapulted me straight into unfamiliar territory. *Fuck. No. I cannot be attracted to this man. It isn't possible. He's the enemy.* As if making fun of my thoughts, the place between my legs throbbed. My thighs clenched, and my chest swelled as I unintentionally leaned into his touch.

"Normally, in a situation such as this, I'd simply tell you that the why doesn't matter," Gaven said, his voice low and deep. "The fact is, you are my fiancée, and you will be my wife." His hand shifted as he stood, leaning more fully across the tiny table. *Why is the table so fucking small?* He practically dwarfed it, hovering over both it and me. His hand clenched briefly before grasping my throat and pulling me forward until my face was tilted to meet his impenetrable gaze. My heart thudded rapidly, my pulse speeding up under his palm.

"It doesn't matter to me if you're inexperienced," he said, his voice dropping another octave. Whatever frequency he was speaking seemed to have a direct link to my core. The lower his voice went, the more I couldn't help but feel a wetness forming inside my panties. When I'd told him I was inexperienced, I meant that I was a virgin. I'd touched myself before, and I'd watched porn, sure. About as much as I'd read it, however I'd never even been this close to a man who was looking at me as though he wanted to eat me alive. Their focus had always been on my sister. I blended into the background, forgettable. Exactly where I'd hoped to stay until my wishes came crashing down. "In fact," he continued, "that makes this easier."

"E-easier?" I repeated.

"Yes," he said as his thumb stroked over my thumping pulse. "Because it means I can teach you, shape you, mold you to my specifications and my desires."

That rankled. "What about *my* desires?"

His close-lipped smile widened, parting his lips as he leaned even closer until I could smell the mint on his breath. "Oh, I promise you, my soon-to-be wife, your desires will be well cared for, but if you're worried, perhaps a demonstration is in order."

Demonstration? "No." I shook my head, pulling my face away from his grasp.

"No?" Gaven chuckled. "Then perhaps a bet?"

I froze at that. "A bet?" I repeated. "What kind of bet?"

"If you can resist me, then perhaps I'll free you from our deal." Gaven's words were all I wanted to hear, although the underlying reality warned me that this was too good to be true and he was, after all, a criminal. Could he really be trusted?

Even as I acknowledged that, I couldn't help but respond. "What are the terms?"

Picking up the chair, Gaven set it next to me so that our thighs would be touching when he sat down again. "The terms are simple," he replied. "I ask a question, you answer. You ask a question, I answer. If we can't or won't answer, then we'll receive a penalty chosen by the other person."

My chest ached. I pressed my thighs together even harder. Glaring up at the crystal blue eyes that looked down on me, I had to think that this man wasn't even bothering to disguise the devil inside. He was as wicked as they came. If I agreed to this little bet of his, would I even have a chance of winning? But if I didn't do anything … then, would I just give in and agree to be his wife and broodmare?

It was a simple enough decision. No. I wouldn't give in. Not that easily.

"Fine," I said, my voice sounding odd even to myself, breathless, uneven. "Are there any other rules?"

Gaven took his seat again, his knee brushing mine beneath the table. "Rule number one." He picked up the glass of wine and held it out to me. "You can't refuse anything I give you for the next hour." I took the wine and tipped it back, draining half the glass before setting it down. "Rule two," he continued. "You'll answer every question I ask truthfully."

"Only if you'll do the same," I replied.

He tipped his head to the side. "Of course," he acquiesced after a beat of silence. "Then, onto the game." Heat stole over my body as his hand slid to my thigh, the warmth of his palm burning past the fabric of my dress. "Answer my questions, and I'll answer yours. Each of us gets one per turn. If you take too long to answer, then a penalty is in order."

"Penalty?" My body was winding tighter and tighter with each word he spoke. "What kind of penalty?"

Those full, masculine lips of his twitched again. One corner tipped up, making him seem more boyish than before. "I'll leave that up to each party. You choose your penalties, and I'll choose mine."

I gritted my teeth. "Fine." Reaching down, I gripped his hand and removed it from my thigh.

He didn't respond save for the soft raise of his brow and that twitch of his lips again. Gaven reached for the wine once more and took a sip. "Let's begin then."

5
ANGEL

He *was* familiar. Something about him pricked at the back of my mind. Every time I tried to uncover the memory, though, it would flit away and I was left with the unanswered question: *Who was Gaven Belmonte?*

"Why are you so against this marriage?" he began.

"I want to go to college," I tell him. "I don't want to be a wife … not now."

"So, it's not the choice of groom, then?" Gaven asked.

I shook my head. "No, also, that was two questions." I smirked. "This was your idea, and already you're breaking the rules."

Gaven blinked and then sat back with a grin. "You're right. What's your penalty?"

"I want you to move away."

With a gruff noise, Gaven slid his chair a scant few inches away. I should've told him to go sit at a different table, but it was too late now. Regardless, just those few inches were enough to finally give me some breathing room. "Your turn," he said.

"Why did you choose me?"

"I thought I told you that the why doesn't matter."

"You did," I nodded and reached for my water once more. "But I want to know regardless."

"I'm attracted to you."

Fuck. Liquid shot up my nose. Coughing, I set my glass down hard and glared at him. He shrugged. "You requested honesty, Angel."

"That can't be all. Why the hell would a man marry a woman based on attraction alone?"

"You didn't ask me for a detailed explanation," he replied. "Now, it's my turn."

Before I could protest, Gaven slid his chair closer once more and his hand landed on my knee. I stiffened. "The rules..." My words drifted off as his finger dug into my flesh.

"You asked a second question," he said, eyes gleaming. "This is your penalty."

I had? I thought back. Shit, technically, he was right. I needed to be more careful with my questions and responses.

"You said you were inexperienced, Angel." Gaven's voice moved over my ears. I forced down a shudder. He was so close—too close. "Does that mean this pussy down here is untouched too?"

"I'm not fucking answering that." Hot, molten blood flooded my face.

"A penalty then…" Gaven's hand shot up past the hem of my dress and curved over my inner thigh.

A squeaky noise erupted from my throat as my own hands jerked down and latched onto his wrist. "*What are you doing?*" I demanded, eyes wide.

"This is your penalty, Angel," he replied. "My turn."

"Wait, what? I didn't—" Motherfucker. He was a conniving bastard. "That's not fair."

"There's nothing fair in marriage and war," Gaven stated. "Now, answer me this."

I struggled to listen to him as his thumb began to rub back and forth over my flesh. Sparks danced down my spine. My insides churned and tightened, contracting and releasing as if anticipating more.

"Do you realize how important our marriage will be?"

"What?" Breathing was becoming difficult. "I-I don't—"

"If there is no Price Heir, one must be made," Gaven continued. "In our world, there are few true liberties. If your father were to perish without the next head of the family being chosen, it would spell disaster. War."

Was his hand moving higher? I swore it felt like it. Even as I gripped his wrist, he didn't seem all that swayed by my obvious discomfort. A whimper escaped me, and I wished I could reach out into the air and pluck it back.

"So, my question for you, my sweet inexperienced Angel, is this: Marriage? Or War? Those are your options. Me? Or Death?"

"No one's going to die if I don't get married," I argued.

"Oh, but they will. Men will fall if there is no heir. Your father's death would leave a vacuum in our world and there will be an untold number of vermin crawling out of the shadows to take what he had. They would take you too."

I gasped as Gaven's hand settled over my crotch, his fingers rubbing against the thin layer of my underwear. I jumped in my seat, only to be settled back down by a firm hand on my shoulder.

"S-stop," I begged.

"You haven't answered me yet," he said, watching me with an intensity that I could feel down in my belly. "This is your penalty. Now, sit back and take it like a good girl."

My mind fogged over as his fingers moved to the edge of my underwear, carefully pulled it to the side, and dipped inside. Whatever rejection I could manage evaporated as, before it could be voiced, Gaven's lips descended until they were suddenly on mine.

My eyes widened as his lips parted, his tongue sinking past my defenses. I'd been kissed before. Of course, I had. I wasn't wholly unaware—inexperienced, yes, but unaware? No. Still, those light, childish kisses didn't hold a candle to this. Those were boys, and Gaven was a man. He *kissed* like a man. Then again, perhaps thinking of this as a kiss was wrong too. It didn't feel like a kiss. It felt like a monster devouring its prey.

It was something that I couldn't fight, either. There was no fumbling or sloppiness, no awkward angles or stunted movements of his lips and tongue. Every single move was calculated and smooth. I felt as though any experience I might have had before was dwarfed in comparison to the ministrations of a master.

His fingers moved into my body, sliding through my lower lips, gathering my wetness as he smeared it up to my clit. "*Shit.*" I hissed through my teeth, cutting off the kiss as I jerked at the sharp sensation that spiraled through me.

Gaven hushed me gently, continuing his ministrations. "There, there," he whispered. "You'll like this, Angel. Trust me."

I growled low in my throat, tossing him a glare. "Never."

That response seemed to amuse him as it only elicited a grin. "The choice is yours regardless," he replied. "But I will have this. I will have your juices soaking my fingers, and I will have your body under mine as my ring sits on your finger."

As he spoke, his hand continued moving. He thrust in and out of my pussy, back and forth, dragging his thumb over my clit and circling it with each movement. Panting, I found myself clutching onto him, nails sinking into his arm as my body responded against my will. This wasn't supposed to happen. I wasn't supposed to fall for his tricks. Yet, here I was—legs spread like a whore, letting him fuck me with his fingers and whisper filthy vile words into my ear.

"Your pussy is clamping so tight onto my fingers." His gruff voice rumbled. "I imagine you'd strangle my cock with a cunt like this, wouldn't you?"

A groan worked its way up my throat as my only reply.

"That's it," he urged. "Your hips are moving, do you feel it? Do you want more?"

No. No, I didn't, yet somehow, I couldn't stop. He was right. My body now had a mind of its own, and it was responding to him. I found myself leaning forward into his hand. Gaven knew what he wanted from me and was determined to take it through sheer skill and heated passion.

Panting, mouth open on a cry, I shouldn't have been surprised when he kissed me again. Coming down hard, his tongue twined with mine, touching and teasing me. His teeth scraped against my bottom lip. I shuddered, that place between my thighs pulsing in time with his thrusts. I ached. Somewhere deep within my body, there was a craving that I hadn't known before. Sure, I'd wanted a man before. I'd laid in my bed at night after watching videos no young woman ever should and reading books that would make my nanny blush. I had shoved my hand into my panties and touched myself, slid the pads of my fingers over the wet nub of my clit as I'd imagined some make-believe man bending me over my own childhood bed and sliding into my wanting slit.

This was no imagination, now. This was real. Gaven was too hot to be anything but a reality. He was burning me from the inside out. I reached up and wrapped my hand around his shoulder. I was tilted off balance and needed to cling to him to keep from falling backward. His tongue invaded deeper, toying with my own.

Gaven's kiss was a conversation, but his fingers inside of me were a battle. He was playing with me, enticing me to follow him back and follow him. I did. Touching his tongue tentatively with my own, I responded to the kiss. He made a noise deep in his throat. A guttural sound reverberated through me and, somehow, made me impossibly wetter.

The sounds that emitted from my pussy where he fucked me with his hand made my face burn hotter. Everything in the room was spinning as he shoved me, cruelly, up the mountain toward an impossible valley of pleasure. My hips ground up as he added a third finger, stretching me. Another whimper escaped me. Heat stole across my cheeks as the noise reached my ears. The small accidental sound seemed to make Gaven even more intense though. His head craned closer to mine and he shoved me back further into the chair, his grip tightening. My head was swimming as he took complete and utter control.

"Fuck, you're delicious," he panted, yanking his head back.

I gasped for more breath, black dots dancing in front of my vision. Somewhere in the distance, I heard a knock. Gaven's response was lost to me, however. Whatever he said was swallowed up as the next pass of his thumb over my clit and the next thrust of his fingers into my cunt sent me careening over that mountain and into an orgasm that stole every single one of my senses.

I should have been frightened. I should have pushed him away. I should have done a lot of things. Instead, however, I descended into the madness right alongside him.

It was wet. It was hot. It was indescribably addictive. I lost all sense of myself in that moment, falling deeper and deeper under the spell he had woven over me. When the orgasm came to a slow, languid stop, I found that I was breathing unevenly, my chest rising and falling in rapid increments. My face felt heated beyond a simple blush, and beneath my clothes, my core was pulsing.

"That's it, right there, milk my fingers, *Angel*." A groan reverberated up my chest, unbidden. I couldn't stop it even if I wanted to. At the moment, though, I couldn't want anything else but what he was giving me. Sheer, pure pleasure. "This is only the beginning," Gaven whispered fervidly in my ear. "You coming all over my fingers is only the first step. There's so much more I can teach you."

I gritted my teeth as my body grew hotter. My hips ground down into his hand as my vision blurred in front of me. "N-no," I gasped. "S-stop." This wasn't right. I was meant to get him to call everything off. Not this. This wasn't what I'd intended.

"Shhh." Gaven hushed me gently, his face alongside mine. His stubble scraped my jaw as he leaned down and ran his lips up the column of my throat. "You're going to come for me again, Angel. You're going to let yourself go and release all over my hand in this room and you're going to love how fucking good I can make you feel. Only me."

Sharp knives of bliss stabbed at me, shredding me apart and filling me with warmth. I cried out and pushed my face into Gaven's chest, muffling the sound of my own pleasure as electricity raced through my system.

Faint … I felt faint. How was that possible? How had this happened? How had I let it?

"You're going to be mine, Angel," Gaven said as he gently pulled his fingers from my pussy. Ice washed over me. I had to blink several times and take a few deep breaths before I felt even somewhat cognizant of my surroundings. Once I did, I realized that he was holding up his hand—the same hand that had just been inside me. As soon as he was sure I was watching, too, Gaven brought his hand forward and sucked his fingers into his mouth.

I gaped at him as the wet juices of my pussy dripped down his digits and he tugged each one into his mouth, closing his lips around them and cleaning them with a satisfied groan.

"I always take care of what's mine," he said as soon as he was done. Then, reaching for a towel set on the table, he wiped his hands and called out for the waiter. The door to the private room opened, and the same waiter from before appeared with a tray of food. Gaven looked toward it before smiling at me. "I suggest you get used to it sooner than later."

Gaven is a dangerous man. I knew as much when we'd first been introduced, but now I knew he was dangerous in other ways. Deadly not only to the lives of others but to my own sanity. Even if he hadn't just fucked me with his hand, that kiss of his could have been enough to ensnare me.

He was a threat. With one simple kiss, I felt addicted. Conquered. Even if I were to be Persephone in this tale of ours, Gaven was no Hades. No, instead, he'd be the pomegranate seeds, and I was fucking starving down here in the underworld, trying to find a way out into the light again. I feared, though, that the second I said 'I do' I'd never see it again.

6

ANGEL

I didn't remember what dinner tasted like after Gaven made me come all over his hand. I didn't even remember the drive home. It wasn't until the front of my house came into view that I seemed to return to my body. The second the car was stopped and one of the men always standing outside the front came to open my door, I rushed past him, straight for the house, not caring what I must have looked like. It didn't matter if I seemed crazed or not. All I knew was that I needed to be alone.

I feared that if I didn't lock myself away as soon as possible, I would combust right there in front of my father's men. Moments later, I dashed into my room and slammed the door behind me, turning and placing my back against the solid wood. It kept me steady and grounded as my knees buckled and threatened to take me to the floor.

Gaven Belmonte was twice my age. He was a stranger. A monster by society's standards. To work

with my father, he had to be. Yet, I'd just let him …
no, I hadn't just let him touch me. I'd resisted. I'd
tried to, but he'd forced it on me. The pleasure. The
orgasm. Heat burned through my body, into my
face, and down my limbs. How the fuck had that
happened?

Resistance scorched my insides, but I couldn't lie
to myself. I'd *enjoyed* his touch. I'd responded to him.
In fact, even now, I could still feel the remains of
what that same touch had done to me between my
legs.

Panting, I locked the door and lurched away,
stumbling across my room to the bathroom, needing
to clean myself. However, the second I stepped into
the luminescent interior of my personal bathroom, I
paused as I caught sight of my reflection. Cheeks
flushed pink. Eyes watery and lips pouting, I didn't
look like someone who didn't want to marry Gaven
Belmonte.

What had he done to me?

In my reflection, my hand raised and touched
the side of my face before my eyes fell on the necklace around my throat. The diamond choker glittered against my skin. An innocent person,
unknowing, would naturally assume it was a simple
piece of expensive jewelry, although I knew the
truth.

I touched the necklace, circling the space above
and below it where it connected with my flesh. It
was heavy, an expensive piece, beautiful in its own
way. A shiver stole over me, racking my body as it

slid up and down my spine. This was no gift. It was a collar. A marking. This was an act of possession.

Soon, I was to become Gaven Belmonte's bride. *His wife.*

All of my dreams of leaving this family were dying, disappearing in the face of my reality. College? I could forget it. A life outside of Gaven and the Price Empire? It was fading fast and there was no way out.

I squeezed my eyes shut and tried to think. What could I do? Was there a plan that could get me out? I was smart. Hell, the number of scholarships I'd applied to and the computer science program I was set to join in the fall was a testament to that, wasn't it?

Even if I did manage to call off this wedding, what would that mean for the future? Would I ever be able to see my dad again? Would I ever be able to come back? Or would rejecting Gaven mean I'd have to leave my family behind too?

My eyes opened, but I wasn't focused on the room before me. Gaven had been there seven years ago. He'd been the one I'd sought out, the one I'd looked to for my deepest, darkest desire. Revenge on the killer who'd taken my mom from me. Even if I wanted to reject the cruel dark world of the mafia, I had to admit that everyone—including myself—had the capacity to be a criminal.

There had never been anyone like Gaven before. No one had ever expressed such a singular interest. If I was honest with myself, I had to admit that at least a small part of the reason I was so hell-bent on leaving the Price Family was to leave behind the mark of sacrosanctity that had followed me my whole life. Jackie had sought out affection, but once I'd discovered the truth behind our mother's death, I'd wanted nothing to do with our family's business and life in the shadows. I'd overheard some of the men say that it was because I looked more like our mother, which was why our father had always preferred me. I didn't like the thought. Jackie, despite her shitty personality, was still my sister and my father was fair in his affection. He loved her just as much as he loved me. Still, despite our half-American heritage, both of us were mafia princesses—tied to the world by the strands of our blood. I hated that.

Was it too much to want someone to want me for me, and not because of the power I could give them?

Gaven didn't exactly want me, though. He was practically guaranteed that power the second he married me and it would solidify if and when he got me pregnant. My hands fell to my belly and I looked down as I smoothed the tips of my fingers over the flat surface. I imagined what it would feel like to be swollen with a baby. I was my mom's last child, so I'd never seen her pregnant and there'd been no female in our household who had ever worked or been allowed in while they'd been pregnant. I wondered what it felt like. Would it hurt? Would it feel magical? There were so many differing opinions of it on the internet. In theory, I knew that each pregnancy was different.

If Gaven was guaranteed power, though, so long as he married a Price daughter, he had a choice. He could have married Jackie. She certainly would've been happy about it, but he didn't. Instead, he chose me. Maybe he did it because he wanted me. He'd said he was attracted to me, but that couldn't be enough to build a marriage off of, could it?

With my mind full of confusion and lingering sparks of desire, I turned away from the mirror and headed for the shower. I jerked the handles down, letting steaming hot water spurt out of the shower head before stripping out of my dress and letting it fall to the tiled floor. When my fingers went to the necklace, I paused.

I knew the precious jewelry shouldn't be exposed to the hot water, but as I tried to reach back and around to undo the clasp, I found it difficult to remove without help. Another thing Gaven had no doubt taken into consideration. With a grumble, I left it and finished divesting myself of my underwear and bra before stepping into the already foggy glass stall. Steam quickly filled the room as I let the water run over my scalp and through my hair. When the scalding water didn't assuage the twisting of my insides and the lingering desire, I fumbled with the handles and flipped the water from molten to ice cold.

Shuddering under the downpour as the water slid over my skin, I closed my eyes and pressed one palm into the tile before me as my other found its way over my chest. My breasts felt heavy and I wondered what it would've been like had Gaven taken them into his hands. Would he have been rough, or would he have been gentle? Would he have taken my nipples between his fingertips and rolled them until they were tight little buds like the men of my books did to their women?

I did that now, wanting to remember the feeling of him against me in a new way. Closing my eyes again as I sunk into my imaginary world, I pretended that none of the reality of our situation—Gaven's and mine—was there. I imagined what it would've been like if we were just two people, a man and a woman, who'd met somewhere on the street.

I palmed my breasts, heaving them in my grip, and pinched my nipples as I flipped around and pressed my spine against the tile with cold water raining over me. It did nothing to quell the quickly rising arousal pouring through me.

My lips parted as I pushed my hands further down, over the soft curve of my belly and to the place throbbing between my legs. Just as it had been at the restaurant with Gaven, I found myself soaked through in a way that had nothing to do with the shower. Wetness dripped from my core down the inside of my thighs. My clit fucking pulsed with need. My pussy felt empty without Gaven's fingers sliding into their depths.

Soft panting breaths escaped me as I slowly lowered my hand further and then brought a single finger to my clit, rubbing the little bundle in a circle as I closed my eyes and imagined that it wasn't my hand there, but Gaven's instead. He'd been so hot in my ear as he'd whispered harsh, dirty words to me and made me ride his fingers. I wanted more than to stand here and touch myself to his image in my mind.

If things had been different, I might have let him do more to me than simply shove his hand in my panties. If things were to continue down the path we were careening down, he would inevitably be allowed more liberties. I wondered what it would be like to have him fuck me. In my mind, he would cover me with his naked body, all muscle and tan skin. His short beard would scrape my flesh, making me shiver with anticipation the way his long stubble had when it'd touched my throat. Gaven's body would be weighty as he pressed me back against the tile.

Are you hungry, little girl? I could practically hear him whisper the words into my ear. I'd respond with a whimper. I'd open my mouth and beg for another kiss.

You want something more, don't you? You want my cock to fuck this sweet little pussy.

I'd nod and open my mouth only to be stopped as he slipped two thick fingers inside.

Lick them, he'd order me. *Get them wet so I can put them inside of you.*

My tongue would roll around Gaven's fingers, between them. I'd soak him with my mouth, only for him to pull out and sink down to his knees before me.

Despite the haze of my imagination as it took over my mind, I continued my own movements— fingers practically flying over my clit as I reached for that pleasure again. Gaven's head would disappear between my thighs as he lifted one leg and hung it over his muscular shoulder.

Those fingers that had been in my mouth would slip towards my pussy, spearing into me and then scissoring apart, stretching me open. He'd bat my hand out of the way and dip his head closer until his wicked tongue came out and licked at my pussy. I could picture it now. The way his tongue would flick out and run right up one side of my pussy and then the other, collecting my juices before it slid its attention to the opposite side. He'd make me wait. Cruel man that he was. He would keep me on the edge of release for as long as he desired.

In real-time, I could feel myself getting closer. My body tightened all over. My muscles contracted and released with my movements. I wanted to feel him deeper. As filthy and wrong as it was, I wanted more than just his fingers. He was right. I wanted him to fuck me.

My mouth opened on a fresh moan as it was pulled from me by my own imagination. My fingers moved down and into my cunt, shoving inside just as he had. I couldn't reach as deep though. Gaven's fingers had been far better than my own, thicker, more experienced, as if he knew exactly where my buttons were.

Little puffs of air escaped me as I groaned and shuddered under the water's downpour. The Gaven of my imagination finally sealed his mouth over my clit. He sucked it between his lips and the pulse of his tongue as it flicked the sensitive little bean would skyrocket me into the first orgasm of many.

Ripping one hand from my pussy, I pressed my knuckles into my lips, and shoved them past until my teeth stabbed into my flesh. My thighs trembled as a great pulse sent my mind into a fog. I cried out, twisting against the tile as I came on my own fingers. A gush of wetness slipped from me, further tracking down my inner thighs. I sobbed against my fist as I rode the wave of my release for several more seconds. Once it finally abated, I found that my skin was littered with goosebumps and I was shivering from the cold. I reached for the shower handles and twisted them back to release the hot water once more and sunk to the floor. My legs came up to my chest and I wrapped my arms around them as water soaked into my hair.

"Gaven Belmonte…" His name echoed into the cold, lonely bathroom. I touched my fingers to my lips. "Angel … Price. Angel Belmonte." I shook my head. No. If Gaven married me, then I wouldn't become a Belmonte, *he* would become a Price. Gaven Price.

If he were to join the Price Family, would that mean he'd take my name or would I take his?

Whatever the case, knowing that soon there would be other forms of ownership from the man known as Gaven Belmonte left me with a lingering sense of loss and ... hunger.

It couldn't be worth it. I couldn't give up everything I'd ever wanted for a man like Gaven Belmonte, but I'd be damned if I didn't say he made it difficult to say no.

7
GAVEN

I had never been a good man, nor had I ever been inclined to try to be. I liked the power I held over people's lives, and my dinner with Angel had only proven that I was going to like it even more with my wife. She was more innocent than I'd expected, still feisty and fiery despite the fact. When the word "inexperienced" had come out of her mouth, I'd acknowledged two things: One, she was strangely more outspoken than I think even she realized, and two, when I planned to spread her legs on our wedding night and sank into that tight pussy of hers, it would be utter torture to not come immediately. If I were a betting man, I'd bet my entire life and all of the money I'd acquired throughout it on the fact that she was a virgin.

At the thought of our previous conversation, my thoughts drifted to our *date*. Dinner the night before had gone well, or at least I thought so. Angel had taken over every thought, every waking moment, as soon as she'd been offered to me. The girl she had once been seven years ago had turned into a woman. I wondered if she remembered the request she'd made, spoken with such conviction—to have me kill the one who'd stolen her mother from her. Did she remember me as the man who'd saved her then? Or had it been so fleeting in her childhood memory that I was entirely new to her now?

I certainly didn't think of Evangeline Price as a child anymore. Our little bet and that kiss had been followed by my fingers in her cunt. If that didn't prove my acknowledgment of the woman she had become in the last few years, nothing would. That small taste of her only made my desire for more grow. Once I had her fully under my control, my ring on her finger, my seed in her belly, she would be the perfect wife. Perhaps even … the perfect submissive.

The thought reminded me that there were other things she had yet to know about me. How funny it was that one simple kiss and just feeling her orgasm around my fingers made me want so much more. Cravings that made me ache. To feel her soft curves under my hands, to hear the sounds that she would make as I fucked her, to watch her come, not just on my fingers, but all over my cock as well.

Soon, she would be mine to own. Mine to corrupt. And I knew as I molded her with my wicked ways, I'd get to watch her fall from her innocence until she was *exactly* what I wanted her to be. The thought was enticing, and I had to force myself to not seek her out and taste even more of her.

Thankfully, the echoing sound of my shoes on the mahogany floor of the Price mansion grounded me. The rhythmic noise bounced off the lavish decor and empty space, accompanying my thoughts. But as I turned the corner, hushed whispers sobered me. My senses sharpened, focusing on the private conversation only a small ways down the hall.

I found myself slowing to a stop as I listened to low laughter accompanying two male voices.

Raff's men, of course, but while I had trusted Raff with his deal, his men were another matter. They weren't yet mine, and to them, I was a stranger coming in to take over. There were, no doubt, quite a few of them that were hesitant and suspicious of my arrival, even if they weren't willing to say as much to my face.

"Raff's gone and done it now," one voice said. "Calling in a hired killer? He's a lone man. Men like him are always out for themselves. Raff must finally be losing it."

"Quiet," Another, deeper voice replied. "Be mindful of where you are." At least one of them had something other than shit for brains. His associate, however, didn't heed the warning.

"I'm just saying," the first man replied. "I doubt the other families are going to take this well. Raff should've chosen one of them to marry his daughter.

Bringing in an American?" He paused, and I could just imagine the man shaking his head in mock shame. "It's not going to go as smoothly as Raff is hoping."

"What Raff does with the family is his business, Giuseppe," the second man replied, finally giving a name to the first. "Now, move. We're meeting the others outside for shift change."

"Fuck, Matteo," Giuseppe muttered. "Lighten up—you know I'm right. If Raff isn't careful, then…"

Whatever Giuseppe had been about to say was quickly cut off as the sound of a door closing reached my ears. The conversation had been insightful, at the very least. Some of Raff's men were not happy about having me on board, while others were obviously quietly biding their time and waiting. Either for me to prove myself or for something else—only time would tell.

"Oh, Gaven!" a sickly sweet voice called out, interrupting my thoughts.

I turned as Raff's eldest daughter hurried up the hall toward me.

"It's so lovely to see you," Jackie cooed.

I arched a brow as she stopped before me and settled a well-manicured hand on my shoulder. Her red nails were a stark contrast against the black of my suit. The Price Family was well known to the criminal underground, and unlike her sister, Jacquelina's name was also well known.

Rumors circulated her as well as various words of association; snake, cunning, *whore*. Whispers said she loved this life, the power plays, the games, using anyone to get what she wanted. She wouldn't have been a sacrificial lamb being married to a man like me, not like Angel. Untouched. Sheltered. But no matter how much Jackie thrived on what she got to do as part of the family, her games wouldn't work on me.

"Jacquelina," I greeted coldly, shifting my attention.

She flashed me a sultry smile, sidling up next to me as she lowered her arm and wrapped her hand around my bicep. It wasn't a gentle grasp; there was a hint of steel behind her slim fingers as they held tight to my sleeve. As soon as she latched on, she leaned even closer, rubbing her chest against my shoulder and biting her lower lip. Eyes so brown they were nearly black stared up at me, reflecting my own expression of antipathy. Frowning, I slipped out of her grasp and turned away.

"May I walk with you?" Even though she was no longer holding tight to my arm, Jackie kept pace with me as I strode down the hall toward the front of the mansion. I didn't say anything as I entered the foyer and moved for the front steps and out onto the drive. "Are you going somewhere?" she asked. "Perhaps, if you wanted, I could—"

"No." I stopped and she did as well.

Jackie blinked up at me. "But you don't even know what I was going to say," she challenged, crossing her arms and shoving her cleavage up as I took a few steps away to eye her.

Do people really play these fucking games with her? I wondered with annoyance.

"Yes, I do." I stopped, turning to glare at her. "I have no interest in spending time with you. I'm engaged to your sister." Anger flashed across her expression for just a second before smoothing into a blank mask.

"Hmm." She hummed thoughtfully. "Commanding, aren't you? I like that in my men."

Her arms dropped, her hands propped onto the hips of her tailored slacks. The silken blouse she wore gaped open slightly as she leaned forward, no doubt purposefully. I glowered at her and she eyed me as if I was a glittering prize for her to snatch up. If she genuinely thought that, she'd be wrong. I could squash her beneath my boot without a second thought.

"Too bad for you," I replied testily. "I am not one of your men, Miss Price."

It'd be quick. Just a snap of the neck and she wouldn't be able to annoy me again. Then again, she was Raff's daughter and the sister of my betrothed. So, regardless of her irritating and licentious manner, I clenched my fists and remained still.

"You know, you might be engaged to *Evangeline*." She sneered her sister's name, practically cursing it. "But you should know, she's nothing like the type of woman that can handle you."

"And just what would you know about that?" I snapped.

With a grin, Jackie sauntered forward to close the distance between us. "A man of your experience," she began, "needs a woman who can give you pleasure. Evangeline is hardly a woman at all. She's a virgin, and if you're as good as I've heard you are, then you know very well a girl like her wouldn't make a very good wife to a boss. This business is cutthroat. You need strong alliances. And my *sister*?" She scoffed, waving a hand. "She's going to get eaten alive."

One thing was clear from Jackie's words—she saw the Price Family as something that didn't belong in her sister's hands. Jealousy, pure and simple, swam in her dark eyes. Hunger. Greed. Everything that I could understand. Jacquelina Price desired power of her own and she was bone-deep pissed that her sister had been chosen instead of her.

There was a bloodthirstiness in her. This attempt at seduction reeked of desperation. She was, no doubt, as likely to stick a knife in my back as she would an enemy and I quickly realized just how different the two sisters truly were. I'd seen it before, both during the funeral all those years ago and in Raff's office, but this? This was up close and personal. It was for all the stakes.

"I have no intention of choosing a different wife," I spoke the words slowly, letting each one land as she stared back at me. The rejection was clear and her lips twisted when my meaning hit. I leaned down closer, my hand snapping out when she tried to take a step back. I gripped her wrist, tightening until her lips parted on a hiss.

"I won't let anything happen to her." The words were as much a warning as they were a declaration. "If anyone tries to harm her—to try and take my pawn from me…" I twisted her twist and jerked her arm, spinning until Jackie's back was to my chest. She yelped as I pulled upward, straining the muscles of her arms as I pressed her thumb to her spine. "They will regret it." Her chest pumped up and down as she breathed harshly. "Are we clear?"

A moment passed and then another. Jackie tipped her head back and looked at me. Surprisingly, there wasn't fear in her gaze but more interest. "I would never think of hurting my sister, Mr. Belmonte."

Lie. "Answer me," I commanded.

After another moment, and with a deep breath, she nodded. "Of course, Mr. Belmonte, all clear," she said, stepping back.

I released her abruptly and took my own step back, straightening my suitcoat with a scowl. Her perfume was tingling in my nostrils, too sweet to be attractive. "Good." I turned, not giving her time to respond as I walked away, leaving her standing in front of the Price Mansion. Alone.

THE BREEZE WAS WARM AS IT WHIPPED AROUND ME. Neither Raff nor I had spoken yet, willing to peruse the streets for a while. My gaze was focused on Angel as she scanned the different stalls with a curious gaze and soft frown. As she walked, her hips swayed back and forth. Her round ass was molded by a skirt that swished around her thighs—thighs that I very much wanted to get between even then. Unlike her sister, I found her movements to be naturally enticing. Jacquelina tried hard to be the seductress, but Angel was tempting without the effort. Her brows were knitted together in thought, almost as if she were contemplating each item for sale, but her attention continued to dart back to me.

Good, I smirked, *I should be what's on her mind.*

"So," Raff started, cutting off my train of thought, "you seem to be quite content with your choice." He glanced at me out of the corner of his eye.

"Not sure what gave you that impression," I stated, knowing full well that I wasn't hiding my staring.

He burst out laughing, his left hand pressed into his stomach as if that could contain the loud chortling. "Yeah, you're about as obvious as a brightly painted wall in a funeral home," he challenged. "I am quite glad to see that she will have someone to protect her." His words were so quiet that no one but me could hear him.

"What makes you say that?" I asked, already knowing the answer. It was apparent when I first laid

eyes on her, but hearing it from her father was different. More personal.

"Angel is not like others in our family or those
we do business with. She's soft and caring, and I
know that that kind of innocence can get ripped
away by the wrong people."

"Does that include from her own sister?" I
inquired. Her earlier attempt at seduction was still
seared in my mind, my anger still simmering from
her games. Raff sighed softly, rubbing a hand on
his jaw.

"Jacquelina is ... well-versed in what this family
is and what we do. She's always been ambitious and
she doesn't quite understand why Evangeline tries to
distance herself. Though to be fair, I believe I may
have made the mistake of letting my youngest live as
sheltered as she has in her own bubble. Not only
from the brashness of her sister but for her own
safety as well. It was too difficult after losing my wife
to bring our Angel into such a ... violent lifestyle.
She was pure and unhindered from the dangers of
our enemies, but I think it was more my own selfish-
ness to keep her that way."

"Is that why you chose me?" I asked, a sliver of
anger building in my veins at the thought of
someone putting their hands on *my* Angel.

"One of the reasons, yes. But I also know that
you wouldn't hurt her. Not like a lot of other men,"
he clarified when I cocked a brow at him.

There were sick thoughts that had popped into
my head when I was first offered her; now that she

was mine though, I would rather mold her willingly. To have her crave my cock like I already craved her sweet pussy.

"You know, speaking of being the head of the family," I started, tucking the thoughts about Angel away. For now. "I did hear some gossip from two of your guards when I was leaving the estate earlier." I gave him a run-down of what had happened, recapping what I had heard. "As I'm sure you can guess, I would rather not risk any possible threats to our deal." Raff's lips had thinned the longer I talked, his friendly demeanor vanishing. As soon as I finished explaining, he leaned over, whispering to his bodyguard low enough that I couldn't hear him.

"With a family like this, there are always enemies," he offered after he was done speaking to one of the three bodyguards. The bulky man turned to make a call. "And while I trust my men implicitly, you might be correct in the transfer of power rattling some cages."

"Better to be safe than sorry, I can imagine."

"Don't worry, it will be taken care of," Raff told me firmly.

I nodded and glanced around once more, eyeing Angel's delicate profile as she stared at an advertisement. "So, what exactly are we doing here, Raff?" I questioned after a long pause. Not that the summer shops and farmer's market weren't a pleasant place to spend an afternoon, but I had yet to figure out our purpose in coming here.

"I figured it would be good for Angel to get out.

And for the two of you to spend time together while still giving us some privacy to discuss the wedding and all of those pesky little details."

"Is that it?" I prodded, knowing there was more.

Raff chuckled, smirking at me. "You've always been observant. I'm glad to see that hasn't withered over the years," he joked before sobering. "I also wanted to discuss what to expect when the ceremony is over. For when you take my place."

I didn't say anything, mulling over his words. *Wedding* was still such a foreign concept to me, but the longer I thought about it, the more open to the decision I was.

"I'm assuming that I will be taking over as soon as the wedding is complete?"

Raff sighed before nodding. "As much as I love my family and what I do, I would rather transition everything over before it's too late." I looked at him, noting the deep-set lines around his eyes and mouth. Raff was growing older, one of the oldest mafia bosses in the United States, and I could only imagine what would happen if his family was left without a successor.

"Yeah, I can understand that, although I'm still a little shocked that you would pick me," I admitted. We'd known each other for many years, but I had never truly considered us that close. I was a good pick for Angel, but one thing I'd learned from him long ago was that Raffaello Price always had *several* motives for why he did what he did. Before I could ask, however, his phone started to ring. Holding up a finger, he dug his cell out of his pocket and stepped away. Giving him some privacy, I sought out Angel in the crowd. My soon-to-be bride. My fiancée. Youthful. Innocent. Just one look at her and I already wanted to corrupt her. It was intoxicating.

8

ANGEL

He was thirty-six—exactly twice my age. A 'businessman' according to my father, which was code for he made his money by doing illegal shit. That was it. That was the entire breadth of information I managed to glean from my father. To say I was frustrated would be an understatement.

Even if he didn't voice it, I knew the truth. Gaven Belmonte was a talented man … in the art of killing. More than that, he obviously had my father's complete and utter confidence because it was only a few short days after our little *dinner date* that I found myself striding along the street next to him as we ran errands and did things any normal couple would do to prepare for their wedding. Except we were as far from a normal couple as possible.

"You seem nervous." Gaven's words were lilted with amusement.

I shrugged and lied. "Of course not."

"Oh?" I could feel the burn of his attention on

the side of my face, but I ignored it as I perused the veils and shoes on the shelf of what felt like the hundredth shop we'd visited today.

I scowled at the white lace and the stick heels that would topple any awkward bride and send them straight to the floor. Heels definitely had to be the invention of a man. They certainly seemed to only do two things—raise a woman's ass and keep them from running away. Heat encompassed my back where I stood in front of the stand of stilettos.

"See something you like?" he asked.

Dimly aware that the two of us are being watched by the guards that have followed us this time—due to my insistence—as well as the store clerk's, I tempered my response. "I'm not into heels," I said.

Reaching past me, Gaven plucked a pair of diamond studded stilettos from the shelf and held them in front of my face. "Really? I think these would suit you perfectly."

I gaped at the three-inch spike on the back of the shoe. "No." I snatched it from his hand and set it back on the shelf before turning and sliding past him. I exited the shop and started walking, knowing full well he'd follow. He had no other choice. Halfway up the block, I stopped outside of a jewelry shop, my eyes finding the ad centered in the window. A young woman held out her hand to showcase the beautiful, studded diamond ring she wore.

Bright sparkling eyes, a gasp frozen in time, all expressing how happy she looked while I stood there with a frown. I couldn't help but wonder if it was an actual woman and not an ad, was she genuinely happy or was it all a sham? *Like my engagement,* I thought with a scowl, my own fingers fiddling with the empty-for-now space where a ring would soon sit. Sighing, I ripped my eyes away from the photograph and looked back to make sure I wasn't alone before continuing down the road.

Although this was supposed to be another 'date'—if one could even call these forced outings dates—Gaven was several paces back, speaking quietly to my father as our guards scanned the street.

"Don't go too far ahead, Miss Price," one of the guards called out.

"I'm not," I replied lightly, throwing him a tight smile.

It didn't matter, though, how many steps ahead I took, it wouldn't take long at all for Gaven to catch up with me. Both literally and figuratively, the feeling of his eyes tracking me through the crowd practically burned against my skin. If I ran, he would chase because, for all I knew, these were my last days with any modicum of freedom. Still, I couldn't help but wonder if I could actually do it.

I'd contemplated it before. The thought of being trapped in a world soaked in blood and vengeance was part of the reason I'd gone into computer technology as a major to begin with. There was so much you could do with technology these days—one could even rewrite an existence if one knew how. I could fabricate a completely new identity. To do that, though ... I'd have to say goodbye to everything I'd ever known. My family. My home. My dad...

Despite being a mafia boss, my father had always been good to his family; I'd been allowed to leave the house, study, travel, and converse, *exist* away from the family business—just not without guards. That didn't mean Gaven would be the same though. For all I knew, he'd keep me locked up until he was sure I was carrying his heir.

An heir ... My hands went to my stomach. *A child that I would conceive with him to continue the Price lineage.*

I shook my head. His wants were preposterous. I was too young to have a baby. Hell, I was hardly old enough to be getting married, especially to someone like Gaven Belmonte. I peeked back once more at my forced fiancé. And yet ... I couldn't help but watch him when he wasn't staring at me. His face was so perfectly cut—*almost* the epitome of DaVinci's law of human beauty. I suspect had he not lived a life of crime and blood, he would've been a model or an actor and he would've kept that handsome symmetry. Now, however, his nose leaned slightly to the side, as if it had been broken one too many times, and there was a small scar above his eyebrow that ruined the portrait of perfection. It was that one and another—smaller and slightly curved that peeked out from his collar.

The edge of marred beauty on Gaven was by far even more dangerous. The perfection may have been soiled, but the image of a savage man who hungered for something darker was all too foreboding. From where he stood several paces back among several other guards, Gaven's eyes lifted and met mine. His lips curled up in amusement as if he could sense the direction of my thoughts. A startling amount of heat rushed to the surface of my skin as I whipped around and faced away from him, nearly tripping in my haste to get away from that impenetrable gaze of his.

I could never tell what he was thinking, but I found myself wanting more and more to know what lay beyond his closed mind. The night at the restaurant was fresh in my memory—almost like a haunting nightmare, except … I hadn't exactly resisted as hard as I'd thought I would. His fingers had been expert as they'd plied me open and penetrated my pussy. He'd made me feel things, sensations that no *boy* ever had.

My minuscule level of experience was nothing compared to the apparent knowledge he had of the female body. He'd played me like an instrument. Plucking at my strings with all of the competence of a master. I'd have been an idiot if I didn't at least admit that he was intriguing to me.

God, even after a few days of thinking about the deal my father had struck with him, I still couldn't believe it. Ever since, too, Jackie had been in her own bubble of silent and petty rage. She acted as if this was all something I *wanted* when that was the furthest thing from the truth. My father didn't even seem to care much that he was ruining all of my well-laid plans. The sickening sensation of betrayal flared, and I bit the inside of my lip to keep my face flat. I was being watched, constantly under scrutiny, not just by my father and his guards, but now Gaven too. The thought only made the emotions build and I was struggling to keep a hold of myself, so I forced my attention on the nearby storefronts.

Don't lose your calm, I commanded myself, taking a deep breath. *You can play the part.* At the very least, until I made the ultimate decision on what I wanted to do. If I wanted to follow through with this or if I could manage to make my getaway. With the silly pep talk over, I felt the tumultuous emotions inside of me ease just as a bright array of pink roses caught my attention. Following the sight of it across the street, I was hyper-aware that Gaven and company were trailing behind. In the back of my mind, I was watching them even as I moved toward the flowers. I wondered if I could grab a few to take back to the house or even ask the florist for samples. *What kind of flowers do I even like?* The silly, simple question made me pause as I stared at the array of bulbs.

For some reason, it seemed like such a ridiculous question, but it made the image of myself dressed in white, walking down the aisle on my father's arm burn brightly in my mind. It could happen, I realized. I could actually end up following through with it all and marrying Gaven Belmonte. *Would it be such a bad thing?* I asked myself. I didn't know him well enough to know what he would expect. An heir, for sure, apparently. But after that … would it be a decent relationship? My father wouldn't ever force me to marry someone who would hurt me. That much I knew for sure.

Over the years, I had tried to separate myself from my family, burying myself in daydreams and passions, into my studies. Yet ... at that time, that had been my only focus. There were no real hobbies or likes, hell, even *dislikes* that I'd discovered about myself. While Jackie had been learning the family ropes to become a perfect mold of our father, I'd become the exact opposite. Turned to anything that wasn't my family with such intensity, that now I wondered if I really knew anything about myself at all outside of the future 'what ifs' that would now never happen.

Nausea rolled over me as I brushed my fingers over the soft petals; four weeks seemed too short. That was how long they'd given me. Not only to get married but to relearn everything I'd ever known. Maybe it was something about the realization I'd had about myself or about the way that I, again, felt Gaven's gaze on my spine—ever penetrating—but perhaps it wouldn't be so bad to marry young? My father wouldn't even have considered him if he was going to just lock me up after the deed was done. I was just a tool, I knew, to hand over the Price empire to someone my father trusted, and if he was happy enough knowing that I'd be cared for regardless of what happened to him, maybe I should just accept it.

There was still online schooling. Maybe if I just

shut my eyes and pretended that Gaven was nothing more than a businessman, things would be—

My thought was cut short as the sound of tires shrieking against the pavement reached me a split second before a loud burst went off—a car backfiring or perhaps a wheel popping? The back of my heel clipped the sidewalk, and as I stumbled and tried to right myself again, something whizzed past me a moment before a motorcycle tore up the shoulder of the street, damn near popping onto the sidewalk.

"Angel!" My head turned at the sound of my name being yelled, except it was too late. The man riding the motorcycle swung his arm out, and my eyes zeroed in on the gun in his hand with realization. That sound earlier had been a gunshot—one intended to kill me, and now he was going to ensure he didn't miss again.

My lips parted on a scream, but it got caught up in my throat as someone slammed into me from the side. The pavement rushed up to greet me, and I closed my eyes tightly as my hip hit the sidewalk and then we were rolling. Body on top of body, black coat swirling in a mess as legs hit mine, and we tumbled out of the range of the motorcycle as it sped up the road away from us.

Heart pounding, head aching, my eyes sprung open again, only to find myself staring straight up into the face of the man I'd been thinking about all afternoon. The harsh set of his jaw was taut as he ground his teeth together, glaring first at me and then to the side as he pushed off the ground and off of me.

Just before Gaven's body leveraged away from mine, though, I'd felt it—the length of him inside his slacks. Long and thick.

What kind of woman did it make me that I was thinking of nothing but my future husband's dick when really … I'd just almost died? Maybe I'd sustained brain damage on the way down.

"What the fuck do you think you're doing?" Gaven barked as several guards came rushing up only seconds later. "You were supposed to be watching our surroundings! Your incompetence nearly got her killed. Get the SUV. We're leaving. *Now*."

No one could manage a word as he began snapping orders and growling at everyone approaching us. Almost as an afterthought, Gaven reached down and helped me back to my feet. I wobbled on one leg, gasping as I nearly went down once more. Glancing down, I realized that one of my low heels —a choice on Gertie's part rather than mine—had snapped in the scuffle and I was uneven.

"For fuck's sake," Gaven muttered, and I briefly wondered if he was about to turn his anger and frustration on me. Before I could utter an apology, however—for what, though, I wasn't even sure—he turned and swept me into his arms.

Blinking, I settled against him without a second thought, feeling small against his broad chest and muscled arms. *I'm definitely brain-damaged,* I thought to myself as my arms twined around his neck. An SUV came screeching up to the corner and he hustled me toward it, sliding in and letting someone shut the door behind us. Only then did he look down at me, and surprisingly there was no anger when he spoke. Instead, there was only concern.

"Are you okay, Angel?"

"Yes, of course." The words came out before I was even really sure. I *felt* okay. A little dazed, but I wasn't harmed.

Gaven narrowed his eyes on me as the SUV pulled away from the sidewalk and slid back into traffic. The driver was a known employee of my father's and remained silent as he drove. His companion in the passenger seat, however, glanced back.

"I want a physician standing by when we arrive back at the house," Gaven commanded.

"Of course, sir," the man replied.

"I don't need that," I said quickly as my mind swam with shock. "I told you I'm fine."

Gaven's hands tightened around me when I moved to release him, and his head jerked down. "I want you looked over by a professional. You were nearly shot to death; there's *no* fucking way you're fine."

Shot to death … yeah, he was right. I'd nearly been killed. Someone had shot at me and damn near took my head off speeding past on that motorcycle. That thought catapulted me back in time to another day when I'd almost died. Another shooter.

Another man who had saved me. My head lifted and I stared at Gaven as if seeing him again for the first time.

No, I realized. Not another man. The same man.

"Angel?"

"You…" My voice escaped me. He'd saved me seven years ago—at my mother's funeral. Did he remember? If so, why hadn't he said anything? Confusion fogged my mind. I felt cold. I pressed a hand to my forehead. I didn't know what happened seven years ago—all I knew was that after several months of tight security, my father had suddenly relaxed. As if his anger had dispersed. No, that wasn't possible. He'd loved my mother so much that he had sworn to never forgive the ones responsible for her death. The only excuse left was that … the ones who'd killed her were dead.

Did that mean Gaven had done as I'd asked? Had he found them? Killed them? My head throbbed.

"Angel." Gaven cupped my face, bringing my eyes back up to meet his. I hadn't even realized I'd lowered them. "Tell me the truth."

The truth? I thought bitterly. The truth was that I hadn't wanted this marriage. I didn't want to be any more involved in my mafia family's business than I already was. I was Alice falling down the rabbit hole, desperately trying to claw my way back to the surface.

I shivered in his arms, wincing as the strap of my heel scratched the back of my ankle. He cursed, dropping his finger away from my chin. Gaven's gaze examined me, and after finding the issue, he reached down and slipped a warm finger between my skin and the strap, sliding first the broken shoe off and then the unbroken one.

"Angel—"

"Thank you," I muttered, cutting him off. Gaven's head came up and his eyes focused on my face once more, lips parting in surprise even as his gaze hardened in careful consideration. "I didn't say it, but thank you."

Without him, I might not have been sitting there. Seven years ago, he'd saved me; today, he'd done so again. I might've been bleeding out on the street, and though a part of me hated him for his role in forcing me away from my dreams of normalcy, I had to admit, he wasn't exactly acting the part of a hitman and future mafia boss. His gentle touch and unexpected affection … it was as though he genuinely cared about me. It was silly and childish to think that way, knowing who and what he was, but I couldn't silence the notion no matter how hard I tried.

Once more, his finger found my chin and lifted my face. He stared at me for several seconds before dipping his head. My heart thundered against my ribcage, threatening to race right out of my chest as he neared. I could smell the scent of mint on his breath. Gaven brushed his full, masculine lips against mine, sparking something inside of me that had been there ever since I'd first laid eyes on him. It was only growing, and if I wasn't careful, it would completely consume me.

Marriage? To him? I was already fucked. Already trapped in this world I'd been born into, but perhaps … just maybe, it wouldn't be so bad if I was trapped in it with him.

His kiss overtook me, his mouth slanting over mine and his tongue delving deep. The world disappeared as I reached up and sank my fingers into the wickedly soft strands of his dirty blond hair. They called me Angel, but he indeed played the part. The savage passion in his kiss speared me. He was a fallen divinity being here to wreak such terrible havoc and all I wanted was for him to destroy me before the terrible things in our world did it first.

Because I *was* scared. Terrified that one day I'd end up just like my mother. Left bleeding alone in a pool of my own blood with no one there to hold me as I left this world. It could've happened today, and maybe that was the reason I caved to my desire to return Gaven Belmonte's kiss. Maybe I needed this physical connection to bring me back to the real world.

Our story, I realized, hadn't started that day in my father's office. It'd begun seven years ago when I'd asked of him the darkest thing a person could ask from another.

I'd asked him to kill for me, so now I had to wonder … *had he?*

9
ANGEL

They were arguing, my father and Gaven. I'd never heard my father argue with anyone before. He was a commander. He gave orders and his men saw them through. There was no back and forth, no resistance. But Gaven was not like other men. He was my father's equal in every way — in strength, in mannerisms, and in control.

"She could have died," Gaven gritted, his voice lowering until it was almost impossible for me to hear.

"I'm well fucking aware of that!" My father's tone was brisk and angry, but deeper than that, he was scared. I rarely ever heard the emotion coming from him, but now I did. My heart stuttered in my chest.

"You know what this is — it's a fucking scare tactic," Gaven snapped.

"It's jealousy," my father replied, his voice even

despite the tightness of his clipped words. "It must be because of the wedding."

"Of course it is," Gaven growled back. "They don't like that you've chosen me or what this union will mean. Angel damn near—" He cut himself off, but he didn't need to finish for me to know what he'd been about to say.

Why I was standing out here like this, pressing myself up against the door like a child wanting to know what her parents were getting her for Christmas, I wouldn't have been able to explain. It didn't feel right to barge in, even knowing I was the subject they were discussing. As far as both of them were concerned, I was simply a woman in need of protection. This, though ... this felt necessary. I had to know what they planned to do about what had happened on the street.

Just how close had I come to ending up like my mother? Dead before my time.

A sinister part of my mind reminded me that despite Gaven's protectiveness, his true anger must have been because his ticket into the Price Family had almost died. Ours was not a match made for love. He'd never mentioned what happened seven years ago. The thought that he didn't remember me was growing in credibility.

Still, the gravelly way he spoke, the cutoff curses, and the rage burning off of him in waves—even through the door—was enough to make my insides flutter like some schoolgirl without a brain. It made me want to take a knife to my stomach and cut all those feelings out.

"But she didn't," my father replied sharply. "For which, I cannot thank you enough. Angel is…" My father's voice trailed off. "Very precious to me." My heart thudded against my ribcage. My father was not an emotional man, so hearing him speak candidly was rare. "I don't know how I would handle it if I lost her after already losing my wife. I am grateful that you were there to protect her."

"Your guards are not enough," Gaven continued. I winced at that comment, knowing that some of the men in question were in the room with them, likely taking the brunt of Gaven's anger as well as my father's. I'd only just come from the doctor's a few minutes before, so I was sure there was more I'd missed. And I had no doubt that Gaven had laid into them—maybe not physically, not yet anyway—but certainly verbally. "They weren't paying attention. She would've been gunned down in the street and left to bleed out on the fucking pavement had I not been there, Raff."

I swallowed roughly, knowing he was right. Turning and placing my back against the door, I released a breath. Dead. Gunned down in the street. The understanding of just how real that might have been slammed into me.

"I don't need you to remind me what could've happened," my father bit out in response. "I know very well the dangers of this life. Why do you think I selected you to marry one of my daughters? They both need a protector."

A protector, I thought, *as if this is the middle-ages and he's a king bestowing me to some ruling warlord.* I shook my head in disbelief. This was ridiculous. And yet, I didn't march in there and say so. No, instead, I remained right where I was, listening in on their conversation. It might have been the lump in my throat that warred with my agitation, knowing my father wanted to protect me instead of tie me here to the family business. Or perhaps it was because, deep down, I felt as though my father wasn't completely in the wrong. I knew next to nothing of the mafia world. Only it was dangerous and it had gotten my mother murdered.

Staying here—marrying Gaven Belmonte— might mean that the exact same thing was bound to happen to me. I'd be taking up space in a casket right next to my mother. I shook my head. I couldn't let that happen. *I wouldn't.*

"Then let me protect her," Gaven's response echoed from the other side of the door. "Move up the date."

"What?" my father sputtered. "It's already happening quickly. We've got everything set up and scheduled for a month out."

"Move it up," Gaven said, his voice hard, "to the end of next week."

Shock and horror warred within me. Was he serious? Move up the wedding? How would that solve anything? Panic encroached on my mind. No.

I wasn't ready. I hadn't yet figured out an escape plan.

"The end of next week?" my father repeated. "Are you insane? Do you even realize how expensive that will be? It'd be better if we simply held Angel here at the estate for the time being. She'll be safe under constant guard—"

"Not safe enough," Gaven interrupted with a growl. "I want her to be my wife, Raff. *Now*. Fuck the money. I'll pay for it."

Suddenly, I felt lightheaded.

I shoved away from the door as quietly as possible and turned, racing back up the back corridor the same way I'd come. They likely thought I was still with the doctor. They couldn't know that he'd released me early. I still had time.

A plan began forming in my mind. If they were moving up the wedding that meant I was out of time. I couldn't stay here and just let this happen. I had to escape. I had to get out of here.

I made it back to my room without running into anyone else, and it was a blessing. I did not doubt that if someone had come upon me with my mind in such turmoil, I wouldn't have been able to hide the fact that I was up to something. The second the door was closed and locked behind me, I dove across the space, ripped open the closet doors, and began yanking out supplies. A duffle bag. A small bag of money I'd saved up—pocket money my father had given me that I'd never spent. It amounted to quite a lot, considering I rarely ever spent it.

Would it be enough? I worried.

Underneath the bed, I found my computer bag tucked neatly away. I pulled that out and cracked it open. For now, all I needed to do was find a suitable place to hole up while I planned the next part of my escape.

A quick search brought up a cornucopia of available places to stay. None of them were high class, but that was good. My father wouldn't expect me to stay anywhere that he wouldn't approve of. Then again, he certainly wouldn't expect me to actually follow through with this plan either, but there was no other choice. I was out of options and out of time.

I selected a shady-looking business hotel that was more of a pay-by-the-hour place and scanned the address to keep it fresh in my memory. I thought about writing it down, but I couldn't risk someone finding it before I was gone. Heart pounding in my chest, I snapped the computer shut and tucked it into the duffle bag before I began going through my clothes and picking out the least ostentatious pieces.

As for the shooter from this afternoon... my hands slowed as I folded a t-shirt and put it into the bag. It would be stupid of me to leave my family's mansion without at least a plan to deal with them on the off chance that they came after me.

Though I hoped that with me gone, whoever was angry enough by the idea of me marrying Gaven would just fade away, I couldn't rely on hope for survival. There was only one person I knew who could help me with that—someone who I was sure would be happy to see me go.

I finished packing and then hid my supplies in the bottom of my closet before I slipped back out of my room and headed for *hers*. I knocked once, twice, three times before she finally opened the door.

"What?" Jackie snapped, propping herself against the doorframe.

There was no "Oh, dear, are you alright, baby sister? I heard about what happened." I knew she had. There was no one else in this house that knew everything about every-fucking-body save for our father and my sister. It was not lost on me that she didn't even seem to care. Which was why she was the perfect candidate for my escape plan.

"I need your help."

She scowled, the expression drawing lines down the sides of her face. "Fuck off." The door swung towards me as she stepped back and I jammed my foot into its path before it could close.

"I'm leaving," I hissed into the crack of space, leaning closer as I lowered my voice. "You want me gone, right? Then help me."

Silence and then ... the door opened again and Jackie's face appeared, a sparkle of curiosity in her gaze. "Well, then…" She grinned, swinging the door open. "Come on in."

I swallowed roughly as I stepped into her room and spotted the wrack of weapons hanging on her wall. It was a definitively masculine aspect to her bedroom, but I'd long since stopped wondering about the strange curiosities of my sister. To know would be to put myself in danger, and it was hard enough to live with her, knowing her inclinations with the bloody world we were born in.

When running from a monster, though, one needed to use all of the weapons in their arsenal. Jackie could be that weapon. She could tell me how to protect myself. She could tell me how to get out, and in the end, we would both get what we wanted. Me, my freedom. And her ... the sole line of succession.

10

GAVEN

A darkness was stirring within me. Something I'd always known had been there, but until that moment—the moment when Angel's life had hung in the balance—I'd never realized just how deep it ran. I'd raised myself up from nothing—little more than an errand boy to the one who cleaned up the messes of others. Recovering bodies and wiping a crime scene down to hide the disappearance of yet another enemy of whichever family I was working for at the time.

I'd seen more money in being the actual killer than cleaning up their messes. It was simple, profitable work. One bullet could garner me half a million. All I had to do was give up a soul that hardly existed in the first place, and my lack of background made it all too easy. There were no parents or siblings—no connections beyond the foster system and juvenile detention hall I'd been raised in. Killing became my business, and I was damn good at it. I'd never actually considered it evil. Just a job.

I'd made my fortune on death and destruction and had nothing to risk. Nothing that could be taken. Not until now. In the split second when I thought my prize was about to be ripped away from me, a crashing wave of rage hit me.

Her wide eyes. The air of innocence that radiated from her. Her very fucking existence was mine. And to think that someone had plotted to take it away from me...

Anger was not a worthy description of my emotions. Untamable. Dangerous. Ready to commit the vilest of acts merely to ensure that what was mine remained alive and within my grasp. Those were closer to the truth, though even they struggled to convey the rage inside.

I inhaled and lifted my gaze to meet Raffaello's as he sat across from me in that giant wing-backed chair of his. *He wants a protector for his daughter?* I thought. *No problem.*

"Then let me protect her," I said. "Move up the date."

Raff's face went slack with shock. "What?" he sputtered, shaking his head as he glanced from me to the door and back again. I knew why. Because somewhere on the other side of that door, my future was being taken care of. The Price Family's private doctor was treating her, but soon, no one would have the right to touch or even look at her without my permission. Raff shook his head again. "It's already happening quickly," he continued, his tone placating. "We've got everything set up and scheduled for a month out."

"Move it up," I ordered. "To the end of next week."

"The end of next week?" he repeated. "Are you insane? Do you even realize how expensive that will be? It'd be better if we simply held Angel here at the estate for the time being. She'll be safe under constant guard—"

"Not safe enough," I snapped, cutting him off. "I want her to be my wife, Raff. *Now.* Fuck the money. I'll pay for it." It wasn't like I didn't have the fucking money.

The unease of the other men in the room filtered toward me. As mercenaries and mafia men themselves, they likely felt the shift in power. Raffaello wouldn't have survived this long in such a bloody criminal world without strength and money, but there was a reason he'd chosen me for this proposal, and I was determined to exceed those expectations no matter the price.

I was just as powerful. No, I didn't have the background of a respected and feared mafia family to back me without conditions, but I had the next best thing—the connections to one. More than that, I had connections to multiple people of similar backgrounds. A laundry list a mile long of favors they owed from things I'd done to earn them over the years. And when I would come calling, they *would* act. The power of one family was great, but the power over many was even better.

"You're sure about this?" Raffaello asked, eyeing me with quiet scrutiny.

"Yes," I answered without hesitation.

Raff released a breath and nodded. "Fine then, we'll move it up."

"Good." Now that we had that out of the way, we could move on to another important matter. "Tell me about the motorcyclist."

He snapped his fingers, and one of his men stepped forward, producing a folder and handing it to him. Raff flipped it open and began to speak. "The man we traced using the license to the bike lives several states over—he's not involved. The bike was reported stolen last week."

I wasn't surprised. No one who went after the daughter of Raffaello Price was stupid enough to use a bike registered in their own name. "What else?" I prodded.

The man hovering at Raff's back flicked his eyes up to me once. By the pinch of his mouth and the cut of his gaze as he glared at me, he wasn't happy with my tone. Tilting my head back against my seat, I stared at the man for a long moment. I hadn't yet been given the opportunity to say something to the guards that had been with Angel and me when she'd been attacked. It was something I knew I shouldn't do in front of Raffaello since he might object, but it was something I would ensure happened. They needed to understand just where they'd fucked up and just what I would do to them if they fucked up again. The sooner they got that, the sooner I could lessen the risk to Angel.

"We're tracking the true culprit," Raff said, his voice hardening as he snapped the folder shut. "We'll have the bastard soon."

"Good," I said. "As soon as you have him, let me know." I pushed to my feet, and the man at Raff's back tracked my movements with his gaze, narrowing his eyes on me. I smirked.

"Where are you going now?" Raff asked.

"To deal with a little problem." Though my tone was light, I could tell by Raff's thinning lips that he understood what problem I was talking about.

I moved around the chair and eyed the men in the room. Each one stared back, but only two were blatantly displeased with my presence. *Displeased for now, at least,* I considered thoughtfully. *By the time I'm through, though, I'm sure they'll all be more than simply displeased.*

"What happened out there today?" I demanded. No one responded. Heads moved down. Eyes sought the floor. Not a single one of them opened their fucking mouths. It would seem I wasn't being forceful enough. I moved towards the center of the room and slowly turned in a circle. "Perhaps I wasn't loud enough," I stated, raising my voice. "I believe I asked *what the fuck. Happened. Today?*"

"We were ambushed by an attacker on a bike," one of them finally answered. His tone was sharp and monotone.

"Ambushed," I repeated, approaching the speaker and stepping closer. His head lifted and his eyes met something behind me. He refused to look directly into my face. Smart man. He assumed if he did, I'd finally lose my temper. He was right. I was very close to it already. "Tell me something," I said. "Would you ever be ambushed like that or let your charge get so far away from you if it had been Raffaello Price, himself?"

The tension in the room racketed up another notch. "Of course not, sir," the man in front of me replied.

"Of course not," I repeated the man's words, nodding. "Then that means today was more than just an ambush." My tone lowered. The rising tide of my anger moved through me. Calmly, I turned from the man and scanned the room.

"Today was the day that you almost let the next Mistress of the Price Empire die." Several of them stiffened at my words, and even though they were far better trained than to move, I could sense the unease that swept through them.

"Evangeline Price—your charge," I reminded them, "nearly died today because of your incompetence." The more I spoke, the deeper my words came out. I strode down the line of men, feeling my blood twist and turn in my veins. As if it was alive, curdling beneath my flesh at the very idea of something that we owned being taken from us against our will.

Never. I thought harshly. I stopped before the

head guard and before he could say anything, my arm snapped out, my hand wrapping around his throat. Raff watched with a keen gaze, not saying a word.

"It won't happen again," the man wheezed in my grip. I squeezed tighter, feeling my rage bubble upward.

"No," I agreed. "It certainly won't."

With my free hand, I reached beneath my jacket and withdrew my gun, flicking off the safety before I settled the barrel beneath his chin. The guard's eyes widened and his nostrils flared as he realized how serious I was.

"As of right now, Evangeline Price is more precious to you than your own fucking family, do you understand?" My words were clear. Succinct.

The guard in my grip nodded sharply, his breath disappearing as I tightened my grip. I spun my gaze down the line and the rest nodded as well.

"Evangeline Price is more than your charge," I continued. "She's your future queen." I released the man in my grip and turned slowly to meet the other guard's gaze. The man bowed his head, coughing and wheezing for breath.

"She is going to be my *wife*," I murmured, moving with silent steps away from the guard. "And she will carry the next Price Heir."

Raff watched me, his eyes cool and dissatisfied. Even now, I could tell he wanted to step. His fists clenched at his sides. After so many years of being in charge, it was hard for him to let me take control, but it was better now since I would soon be the head of the house. It was already rare enough for a mafia head to retire in a way that didn't end at the wrong end of a bullet. He knew that as well as I did. It was why he was letting go—he had to or this would never work.

As it stood, his men all stared at him as if waiting for him to speak up. Smart of him, though, he never did. Instead, Raff merely folded his arms across his chest and waited. He watched. Observing me. I wasn't so naïve to think it was out of support —no, this too, was a test. To see if I was worthy to rule.

"It was *your* job to protect her, and you failed," I said to the line of men. "If something like this ever happens again, it will be your lives on the line."

The guard standing slightly behind Raff eyed me with a narrowed look. I arched a brow his way. "Something to say?" I challenged him.

Finally, Raff spoke. "Giuseppe?"

The guard circled to the side of the desk, squaring off with me as his eyes darkened. "Yes, if you will allow it, Mr. Price."

Raff waved his hand toward the two of us. Giuseppe faced off with me, glaring. "You are not yet the head of the Price Family," he snapped. "You have no power to command us."

I tilted my head to the side, my finger flicking against the gun in my grip. It would be so damn easy to just put a bullet in him and prove my *power*. In this world, it was 'might makes right,' and I had it in spades. I waited, though, curious to see if anyone else would step forward.

"Is that how you all feel?" I demanded.

No one said a word. Good, I thought. Smart men. All save for this one.

Returning my attention to Giuseppe, I stepped forward until we were chest to chest. He was a shorter man but stocky—barrel-chested and gruff. His dark beard covered most of his lower face, but it didn't completely hide the disdain in his expression.

"An American such as yourself wouldn't understand this world," he snapped, growling. "You may think you have some ability—however, Master Raffaello has not yet stepped down. Until he does, you haven't earned our loyalty."

I nodded as I slid my gun back into its holster—an action he noted as his muscles relaxed just as I'd expected. "You're right," I said. His eyes widened in surprise. "I haven't earned your loyalty, except I don't have to. You belong to the Price Empire and soon, I will own that Empire. Evangeline Price will be mine."

Without giving him a moment's warning, I shifted—moving quickly before he could react. Out of instinct, he reached for his weapon, but it was too late. I had already withdrawn a blade I always kept hidden at my side. A bullet wouldn't earn their respect, but proof that I had more than ability … that would do something. If a Master couldn't contain his subjects, then he was worthless.

Gripping the man about the waist, I turned and

slammed him down against the surface of Raff's desk. He cursed and threw his first punch, I dodged it—letting it fly over my shoulder as he struggled against my hold. A moment later, he froze as I dug the tip of my knife into the fleshy side of his abdomen.

"Careful," I said slyly. "One wrong move, friend, and I might just disembowel you."

He cursed again and bucked against me. "Fine," I replied. "Have it your way." I shoved the blade home but didn't twist or slice through his stomach.

A pained grunt filled the room as I pulled the blade back and let the man slump forward, going to his knees between my legs and the desk. Blood seeped over his fingers as he pressed against the wound. The room was frozen.

"Let this be a lesson," I stated, holding up the blood-soaked blade in my hand. More blood dripped over my fingers as it slid down the metal and handle of the knife. "Fail at your duties again, especially when it comes to Evangeline Price, and you will pay dearly."

One of the guards reached for his gun with shaking hands. "You can't just—" he started, only to freeze as Raffaello held up a hand.

"Enough," Raff barked, his eyes shutting for a brief moment. When they reopened, they were blazing with fiery anger. "Gaven's right. My daughter, *the Price Heir*, was almost murdered today. You don't have to agree with his methods, although you do need to accept the consequences of what happened and the lack of respect the rest of you have shown him. It won't happen again, am I clear? Because if it does, then Gaven will handle the punishments."

Silence echoed back from the guards at Raff's statement.

I slid the knife back into the sheath without caring to wipe the blood from the blade. The guard's quiet groans of pain filled the room as I twisted my shirtsleeves around my forearms. "I'm going to check on Angel," I informed Raff as I headed for the door, "and then I'll be making the arrangements to have the ceremony moved up."

My sentence ended as I turned the handle to the door and pulled it open, storming from the room without glancing back. Anyone I passed within the halls stiffened and shifted out of the way, even if they were a distance from me. They sensed the dangerous predator in their midst and were quick to keep their heads down and stay out of my way.

After finding one of the maids to direct me, it didn't take long for me to arrive at the wooden door to Angel's room. Crushing the urge to storm in and ensure she was alright, to inspect each and every part of her despite having her looked over by the physician, I didn't. The few raps of my knuckles on the door were sharp and loud within the quiet hall, but the silence that followed seemed to be even louder. My eyes narrowed. I knew she hadn't been okay after what happened, and I wondered if she had tried to sleep off the shock and adrenaline of the day.

Not waiting any longer, I shoved the door open. It only took a moment for my gaze to sweep over the large bedroom and the scathing anger of the day pulsed deep within my chest when I found it empty. It wasn't that she wasn't in the room that fueled my rage, it was what caught my attention in the simply decorated space. The closet door hung ajar and hangers, clothes, and dresser drawers littered the area.

I closed my eyes and inhaled sharply. That darkness I was so accustomed to swarmed my blood; it lit me up from the inside out. She was gone. The evidence was clear. I'd seen this plenty of times before when tracking down my targets. She thought she could escape me.

Angel had *run*. From me. From our engagement. *Our future*. She had run from the one person she should have trusted to protect her. The key to everything I wanted had taken flight, and my path to power was quickly dissolving. The anger I'd held toward the guards and the asshole who thought they could touch what was *mine* shifted.

Angel would be found, and she'd be punished for thinking she could escape this—for thinking she could escape *me*.

She belonged to *me*, wedding or not, and once I found her, I'd be sure she never forgot that. If I had to clip her beautiful wings to make her realize there was no way she could crawl out of the hell she now found herself in, well, so be it. She was the angel to my devil, and now it was time to corrupt her. To damage and stain those pretty white wings until she couldn't fly away from me ever again.

I swept from the room and withdrew my phone from my pocket. There were only so many places she could go. Only so many ways to travel. Where would she have hidden? How long had she been gone? I couldn't have been far behind. Did she have connections? Someone to help her escape? If so, I'd kill them. I was already prepared for as much.

A sickly sweet voice pulled me out of my tunneling focus. "Oh, Gaven, I heard what happened—" Jackie's words abruptly cut off when I whipped around and my glare landed on her. She stared back at me, stopping in the middle of the corridor with her eyes widening. *Would Angel have gone to her sister for help?* I twisted fully as the thought occurred to me.

My arm lowered back to my side as I advanced on her. "*Where is she?*" I growled. Jackie's brows drew down as confusion covered her face. A trick? Potentially. There was something beyond the confusion— pleasure. Try as she might, she couldn't hide it. She was more transparent than she realized. I stalked forward until there was only a breath of space between us. "I won't repeat myself again. Where. Is. My. Wife?"

Jackie tipped her head back and, unlike most, met my gaze head-on. There was no fear in her eyes, just excitement—like a bloodhound scenting prey.

She paused for a moment before a small, impish smile appeared. "She's not your wife yet, now, is she? As for where she is, I don't know."

My fingers curled around my cell. The sound of cracking reached my ears. The urge to grab her by the throat and strangle her surfaced, a familiar feeling, but I tampered it down.

"What *do* you know?" I demanded.

"That she's a little dove who finally wanted to spread her wings, lest you clip them. Or lock her in a gilded cage," Jackie answered. "Outside of that, I know nothing. As I'm sure you're aware, *Angel* and I have never truly seen eye-to-eye." The bitter vindictiveness in her murmured words was cutting, but I didn't press her further.

I sensed that Jackie was smart enough to be telling the truth now. Either it was by design or something else, but she likely didn't care to know where her sister had gone, and I was wasting precious time. I had to wonder if her mocking taunts were meant to be a distraction. The idea that Jackie wanted Evangeline gone couldn't be ruled out.

I turned away from her and kept moving. The phone's screen had a singular line through it, but thankfully it still worked, and I used it to call in every fucking favor I had. It didn't matter where Angel had gone—soon she would be back in my grasp and I would ensure that she would be too wary to try and leave again.

Within hours, Raff had been informed and the

entire estate was turned on its side. Guards combed the grounds, but I knew the truth. Angel was too smart. She wouldn't hide in the manor. No. She'd left completely and likely thought she'd never see me again.

Raff barked orders at his men as I stood by a set of computers that had been set up. I watched the last bit of the security feed containing Evangeline Price as she walked down the path with a suitcase in hand, looking back every so often. Her brows were pinched and her lips were chewed to hell. She had to have known I would catch her. She wasn't a dumb woman. So, why now? Because of the attack? It was a scare tactic. No doubt the family who had ordered the assault had never really intended to harm her— they were just expressing how angry they were at our upcoming union. That was all.

My phone rang and I answered it before the second shrill sound could reach my ears. "Speak," I snapped.

Archer Petrov's voice came across the line, and never before had I been more than relieved to hear the hacker and mercenary's tone. Though not quite what I would consider a friend, Archer was a damn good contact to have and if he couldn't help me find my bride, he'd know someone who could. "I've got a bead on your girl," he said. "Caught her face on CCTVs a little over an hour ago in Danover."

Danover. The small city popped into my head. It was only a few hours from the Price Mansion. How fast she moved. A small part of me was proud.

Another much larger part was enraged that she managed to get so far so quickly.

"Belmonte." I lifted my head as Raff called my name. The older man met my gaze with a stern look of his own. "You got something?"

I nodded. "I do," I said.

His face hardened and he looked away towards the men in the room with a sneer of disgust. A moment passed and then he returned his attention to me. "You have twenty-four hours," he finally said. "I won't ask any fucking questions. All I ask is that you bring her back within that time frame. As she's to be your wife, I understand a man such as yourself needs time to … clear the air with her. No more than that, though. I want my daughter home."

I understood what he didn't say. He knew what kind of man I was. Hell, he was the same. Men like us craved control in every aspect of our lives. He knew what kind of leeway he was giving me. He was old school and that meant that his ideals were old school. Raff might have given his daughters the liberty to learn of modern customs, but at his core, he was still the same man who had said fuck it to the Prezzo ancestors and married an American woman. It hadn't just been because of her beauty, but because of her submission.

Angel would learn, too, that submitting to me would make her happy. Everything I did would, inevitably, lead her to happiness. At my side. At my feet. Taking my cock in her tight little throat.

"Yes, sir." I gritted the words out and then swung

away as I put the phone back to my ear. "I want fucking details, Petrov," I growled into the receiver. "I want to know the time and exactly where she is."

"According to the CCTV footage," the man replied, "Evangeline Price is still in Danover. She wasn't as easy to find as I anticipated. She was clever. After the withdrawal a few miles outside of the Price Mansion, she's been using cash."

"Do you have eyes on her right now?" I demanded.

Silence met my question, and that itself was an answer. "*Shit.*" I hissed the curse as I took the stairs two at a time until I reached the foyer. I bypassed Jackie whose gaze was locked on me. Whether she wanted her sister gone or not would have to be a problem to solve later.

I snatched the keys out of the hand of the man coming in the door, ignoring his call of surprise. I hit the button on the fob and followed the sound to the row of black sedans along the side of the entryway.

"There's another guy I can call," Archer said. "Goes by Hadrian—he's a better hacker than me. He could probably—"

"I know the man," I cut him off. "I'll call him. Send the coordinates you have to my personal cell." With that, I hung up and popped the respective sedan's driver's side door open.

Shoving the key into the ignition, I twisted and reversed out of the spot, sending a spray of gravel flying behind the wheels. A moment later, my phone beeped, and when I bluetoothed it into the sedan's system, a GPS screen appeared. Three hours to Danover. I'd make it there in half the time, I knew. My foot pressed down harder on the gas as I dialed a new number—one that I knew wouldn't exactly be receptive to my attention.

Unlike Archer, Hadrian answered much later. "What the hell do you want, Belmonte?"

I wanted a pretty little brat over my fucking knee as I pounded her ass red with the flat of my palm. I wanted her on her knees between my legs; her lips stretched tight around the base of my cock as she showed me just how remorseful she was for disobeying me. I wanted a fuck of a lot of things, but from him, I *needed* more.

"I have a missing woman," I stated. "Evangeline Price. Last known location was Danover, New York."

A beat of silence passed, and then, "Evangeline Price? As in of the Price Empire?" Hadrian's curiosity was clear in his tone and likely the only reason he'd picked up my call. God knew that he and his partner and their shared wife wanted very little to do with me. They weren't enemies, but they certainly hadn't appreciated my own part in bringing the three of them together. It didn't matter that I'd been acting as a proxy. I'd been the face of the man who had threatened the three of them. To them, I was a liability.

I didn't care about any of that. I'd owe them a favor if he managed to help me, and I'd repay that favor in blood if they so requested. "Yes," I cut the word out.

"The very same. I need you to find her. I need you to hack more than the CCTVs. Private computers, cars, anything you can to get a bead on her."

"Hmmm." Hadrian hummed in the back of his throat as I sped out of the Price Mansion's gates and down the long winding road toward Danover. "Let me get this straight," he said. "You want me to help you? Hack into the privacy of an untold number of American citizens all for … a mafia princess?"

Biting down on my tongue, tasting blood in my mouth, I spoke the truth. It was a rare occurrence but lies wouldn't help me here. "She's my fiancée," I said.

A bark of laughter met that comment. "No shit!" Hadrian chuckled. "You? Married? Never thought I'd see it happen."

I repressed the urge to crush the steering wheel beneath my grip. "Can you do it?" I demanded.

"Oh, I can do it," Hadrian replied. "You do understand, though, that this means you'll owe me, right?"

"I'll be at your disposal," I reply. "*If* you can find her and bring me to her location, I'll kill whoever you ask."

Hadrian continued to chuckle as the sound of movement echoed from the other side. Fingers clicked across a keyboard. "I assume you're on the way to Danover now?" He didn't wait for an answer. "How far out are you?"

"Less than two hours," I replied.

"I'll call you back in an hour," he said. "I'll have more information then."

With that, he hung up and I was left with my thoughts. As I drove, I found myself refocusing on Angel and what her punishment would be.

Angel was smarter than most would give her credit for. Already, I knew any expensive or higher profile hotels would gain her unwanted attention and she wouldn't want that. Whatever her plan may have been, it was likely that she'd go to a cash-only, cheap, remote, and out of the way motel. Hadrian —like Archer—would figure that out faster than even me. If CCTV footage couldn't be found, then he would go further. Everyone had a cell phone with a camera these days, and they had computers. No matter how remote a place was, there was always some sort of technology. It didn't matter how safe or protected she felt, I would find her. That was a given.

Fifty-three minutes after he hung up, Hadrian returned my call and proved my assumptions correct. "Faraway Inn," he said. "Address 659, Yvera Drive. Room: 47. It's just outside of Danover. Seedy. Cheap. She was smart. There's no security footage. It's one of those places businessmen fuck their STD-riddled and questionably gendered hookers. I had to hack the front desk's computer system. Easy enough, but—"

"Thank you. I'll return the favor," I said, interrupting him as I steered the sedan off the highway and followed the new path set by the GPS. With that, I ended the call and stomped on the gas.

So fucking close.

Just under thirty minutes later, I was pulling up outside the Faraway Inn—a stretched-out, two-story building half hidden by an old factory that likely hadn't been used in over a decade.

She'd had her few hours of freedom, but that was all about to come to an end. Fury simmered as I turned off the car. My long legs ate up the distance between me and the grimy door—one with no peep-hole or window for her to see who was at the door. After three sharp knocks, I waited.

"Who is it?" Angel's voice was sharp, mistrustful.

I inhaled sharply. "Open the fucking door, Angel," I ordered through the thin wood.

"Gaven?" Her voice grew closer. "What are you doing here?"

"I'll tell you … as soon as you open the door."

There was a pause, and then, "I don't know if I should," she admitted. Smart girl. She had to know I was angry.

My fist landed against the door and I laughed, the sound low and anything but amused. "I assure you, sweetheart," I said, "if you don't open this door for me of your own free will, when I do get to you— and I will, make no mistake—you'll regret it. Now, be a good girl and open the door before I kick it in."

More silence followed my threat and I was preparing for what I would have to do to break the door down when finally, I heard the tremble of the chain lock unhooking.

Wide eyes peeked out from the sliver of the door Angel opened, coated in shock, a hint of anger, and more than a little fear.

Good, I thought. *She should be afraid.* I looked forward to more of it, but first … it was time to deal with my wayward bride.

I smiled wide, all teeth filled with *promise.* "Hello, Angel."

The charming façade had fallen away, revealing once again the true Gaven Belmonte, and this time the greedy monster was here for me. My heart pounded a rapid beat in my chest and sweat slid down my spine as I took a careful step back. His eyes followed the movement forcing me to freeze in fear that he would give chase.

"Gaven…" I stumbled away from the door as it swung inward and he stepped into the dark interior of the shitty motel room I'd rented for the night. *How the hell had he found me so fast?* I'd been careful. I'd only used cash. I'd caught the first bus I'd been able to. I hadn't even really planned—thinking that if I planned too far ahead then he could predict my movements. Yet here he was. I swallowed roughly. "I-I can explain," I started.

"No." He shook his head at me as he reached up and unbuttoned the single button holding the lapels of his suit coat together. "No more talking, Angel. You've lost the right to speak."

"Excuse me?" He shut the door behind him and flicked the lock back into place. My heartbeat picked up speed. More sweat coated the back of my neck.

Gaven shrugged out of his coat before tossing it across the room as if it wasn't thousands of dollars worth of designer material. My eyes trailed the path of the black suit jacket before reluctantly and nervously returning to the beast that stalked forward. With a yelp, I stumbled backward and slammed into the wall as he came down over me.

He snatched my hands up and slammed them both over my head, holding them in place at the wrist with one of his while his free hand reached up and gripped me by the throat. My widened eyes turned upward and I met the gaze of my soon-to-be husband. His nostrils flared and his eyes were ablaze with dark fury as he glared down at me. His face was shadowed like this, making him appear even more sinister, and his hair was in wild disarray as if he'd run his fingers through it several times instead of its typical slicked-back style.

"Do you know what a man like me does to those who betray him, Angel?" His question filtered into my ears as he leaned forward and the softness of his breath touched my neck. A shiver stole over me.

I gulped. No. I couldn't let him have this kind of control over me. I needed to be stronger than that. Inhaling, I bucked against him. The attempt to force him a step back, however, did nothing. It was as if I were trying to shove a brick wall.

"Stop it," I snapped.

"No." A gasp escaped me as Gaven's response was quickly followed by teeth sinking into my earlobe, biting down hard. Blood rushed up through my body and dispersed into my limbs. So fast, so suddenly, that it filled my mind with horror. Yet, deep inside, I couldn't deny I felt something else too. Excitement.

The sharp pain of Gaven's bite made another part of me soften. My thighs rubbed together as wetness leaked from between them. I closed my eyes as the pain blossomed and I felt it as something wet dripped onto the top of my shoulder. *Blood? Had he bitten me hard enough to draw blood?*

I didn't get the opportunity to look. Gaven released me for a split second, but in the next breath, he dragged me away from the wall, turning and lifting me off of my feet. Fear erupted within me and I jerked against his hold, struggling within his arms as I shoved the flat of my palm up his chest and into his jawline. "No!" I screamed. "Stop!"

Gaven didn't speak. No words left his mouth as he reduced my struggle to nothing. Twisting one way and then the other, I cried out and cursed as he carried me over to the bed in the center of the room and tossed me upon the mattress. Stripping off his necktie, I half expected him to tie my hands, but instead, he surprised me. The necktie was yanked down around my own neck and then tied into a series of strange knots to the metal headboard.

"What the hell!" I fumbled, feebly to try and undo the knots he'd created, but the more I tugged, the tighter the fabric squeezed my throat until it grew hard to breathe. Spots of black and white danced in front of my vision as I gasped for breath. "Gaven … please." I was beyond being too proud to beg. This had gone too far. "Let me go."

Again, Gaven refused to reply. His jaw was tight, a vein throbbing in his throat as the dark look he gave me bore into my very soul. He gave nothing but utter silence. Instead, his hands moved to the button of my jeans. He popped the closure and then unzipped me. "No!" I screamed and kicked. A mistake on my part, because all the kicking did was make it easier for Gaven to remove my pants and underwear in one quick sweep.

Pressing my thighs together, I growled low in my throat, sure my skin was turning a molten shade of red as embarrassment spread through me. Gaven Belmonte might have been acting the gentlemen for me before, but the fact was … he wasn't. He was a mobster. A killer. Why would a killer respect a woman's wishes if he could take her regardless? He was caustic. Selfish. Cruel. Controlling. And at the end of it all, I was just a means to an end.

My heartbeat—which was already racing fast—picked up the pace. The necktie around my throat cut into my flesh, making me wince. I opened my mouth to talk once more, but before I could say a single word, my own underwear was shoved between my lips.

Gaven's gaze met mine. "Spit them out and you'll regret it, Angel," he warned, his voice low and dangerous. I contemplated doing it anyway, but I was already tied to a bed and at his mercy. There was no telling what else he would do.

Gaven waited a moment—I assumed to see what I would do—and when I didn't immediately spit the thong back in his face, he went back to work. His movements were meticulous. Lifting a knife from his pants, he set the cold metal to my lower stomach. I sucked in a sharp breath at the icy feel of it as he sliced upward, cutting my shirt straight up the center and in half.

Tears gathered along my lashes, but I blinked them away—not wanting him to see as he carefully ripped my shirt to shreds and then used the pieces to tie my hands to the headboard as well. Finally, he was left with two long black strips of fabric of what used to be my favorite t-shirt.

One hand gripped the underside of my thigh, making me jump, and a muffled sound escaped past the underwear in my mouth. He shoved upward and then used one of the strips to bind my leg together, my calf to my thigh. Gaven turned and repeated the process with my other leg until it was clear that his objective was to keep me from closing my legs.

Closing my eyes, I turned my head to the ceiling as a tear broke free and then trailed down my cheek. Heat burned into me. I'd never felt so humiliated, and it had nothing to do with my nakedness but the fact that I knew he could see the ripeness between my legs. With the fresh air brushing over my pussy, I could feel just how wet I was.

It was wrong. It was disgusting. How the fuck could I be attracted to this? How could my body betray me like this?

"It seems you don't mind a little punishment, Angel…" Gaven's rough voice penetrated my ears a split second before I felt him drag a single knuckle up the center of my pussy and right through the soaking wetness that was revealed to him.

I shook my head back and forth, my thighs tightening instinctively. Try as I might, though, there was no closing them. Tingles raced through my trapped limbs.

"No?" I reopened my eyes and met Gaven's gaze as he withdrew his hand and then licked his knuckle free of my juices. Gleaming eyes touched mine.

His hands fell to the buttons of his shirt and with each one he undid, a broad, muscular chest smattered with light hair was revealed. The small scar I'd noticed always peeking out of his collar was much larger and longer as it curved down over his collarbone in a wicked angle that still looked painful even though it had long healed.

Gaven was big—bigger than I thought beneath his clothes. He was also marked by scars, some more extensive and frightening-looking than others. Some were thin lines crisscrossing in random areas, and then there were the puncture holes that I knew only bullets could have left behind. As if being bound before him, at his mercy, didn't make me realize seeing those scars of his reminded me that he was no regular man.

His scars were the markings of a man who'd carved through hell itself. I wasn't numb to that. The knowledge that this man had felt pain and inflicted it made my insides tighten and convulse. My brain knew that he was dangerous and warned me away, but my body was an entirely different being—a hungry, needy thing that was helpless to the physical sensations of attraction seeing him like this elicited.

"A wife is supposed to obey her husband, Angel," he said, unbuttoning his cuffs before stripping away the shirt and sending it the way of the floor. "Even if we're not yet married, the fact is … you attempted to run from me, and as your future husband, it's my duty to make sure you understand your mistake."

Forgetting that there was a ball of fabric in my mouth soaking up my saliva, I tried to speak, only for the sound to come out in a garbled noise. I blinked and then shoved the underwear to the front of my mouth with my tongue. Before I could spit it out, though, Gaven jerked forward, bending over me as his hand gripped my face hard. He hovered over me, dark eyes glaring into mine.

"Remember what I said, Angel," he hissed. "You spit that out and you will regret it."

I narrowed my eyes on him. *Fuck him*. Rage and irritation slammed through me, and I shoved my tongue under the underwear spitting it out right in his face.

"Fuck you!"

The thong fell between us, right between my bared breasts, but a bit of my spittle landed on Gaven's cheek. With his free hand, he reached up and swiped it away with his thumb before tucking that same thumb into his mouth and sucking my saliva free. I waited. My chest pumped up and down as I gasped for breath.

Inhale.

Exhale.

Inhale.

Exhale.

He smiled. He fucking smiled and I realized how wrong I'd been. There were worse things than being fucked by Gaven Belmonte. And he was about to show me just what they were.

12

GAVEN

She was trembling beneath me, and all it did was make me want to take this further. I wanted to scare her. I wanted to make sure she understood the consequences of her actions. Not only had she run from me, but she'd run from safety. What would have happened if one of those fuckers who resented the very idea of me marrying her to take over the Price Family had gotten ahold of her? They would've ruined her. Driven her to the brink of insanity and then slaughtered her.

I knew it all too well. I'd seen it time and time again. She had no clue. She wanted normalcy? She was born in this world of darkness and blood. She needed to accept that there was no leaving, not unless she was willing to get her own hands dirty.

My cock throbbed within the confines of the pants that I'd yet to undo. I knew what she was thinking—I could see it in the nervousness of her gaze. She thought I was going to fuck her here and now, and I wanted to. She was ripe and ready for the taking; her legs forced open and bound for my pleasure as much as her humiliation. The stain of her blush quickly moved over her features as she shivered under my gaze and shifted from side to side as if she was trying to figure out how to regain control of the situation. There was no regaining control for her, though. I was the master here.

Turning away from her, I strode around the bed and then opened the top drawer of the hotel nightstand. She was so innocent, she didn't even realize the type of place she'd rented for the night. I knew it well enough, however. This was no ordinary hotel. It was why instead of a solid flat wooden headboard, the metal twists and turns had been so easy to use to restrain her.

I reached inside and pulled out everything I needed. A vibrator still in its packaging, a bottle of fresh lube, and … *yes, I'll definitely be using these,* a pair of metal clamps. They were cheap and certainly not what I would have preferred, but my own toys were miles away and I'd yet to go shopping to select the perfect ones for my wife.

"G-Gaven, what are those?" Angel's voice squeaked as she stumbled over my name.

"Hush," I commanded as I tossed my supplies toward the end of the bed. She craned to try to look at them, but every time she pulled against the necktie wrapped around her throat, it cut into her. I could have felt sympathy, but the easiest solution for her would have been to stop moving.

Ripping open the packaging on the clamps, I pinched one on the end of my finger as I adjusted the tightness of it. Once I was sure it wouldn't do any lasting damage, I moved to the upper part of the mattress.

"Gaven, please, let's just talk about this."

I arched a brow down at the doe-eyed woman under me with her limbs bound and her cheeks flushed. "Sure," I said. "We can talk after you've had your punishment."

"No—I—" She cut herself off with a gasp as I bent down and took one pebbled, rosy pink nipple into my mouth. Curling my tongue around the hardened nub to entice it to tighten even more, a rumble of a groan reverberated out of her throat. Lifting my head, I turned the same attention to the second nipple. When both were hard and wet, and she shuddered each time I plucked at them with my thumb and forefinger, I set the clamps to her pretty nipples.

"*Ah!*" A sharp cry echoed up from her parted lips as I released and tightened the clamps. I closed my eyes, relishing in it. It was a beautiful sound—a woman realizing just how pinned she actually was. "*Gaven!*" I tightened the clamps until her nipples became puffy little bullets at the tips of her breasts, reddening further as they reached upward, begging for release the same way she would be soon.

"Shhh."

Her body was flushed all over. Tears shone in her eyes and I wanted to see more of them. I desired to see them streaming down her face with her lips parted on cries of both pain and pleasure as she took from me everything I wanted to give her. No matter how disgusting, no matter how vile—as my wife, it was her duty.

I would not be an entirely cruel master, though. I would allow her the pleasure of orgasm—over and over again, until the mere thought of me, of my hands on her body, made her insides tremble with need.

Seeing her like this—tied down in makeshift bondage wear—made me want to open the door to darker desires. Soon, she would know what it meant to be my bride, to be my wife. She would find that I could do so much for her. I could take her to heights she had no knowledge of.

As if she sensed the direction of my dark thoughts, Angel's mouth trembled before she sank her teeth deep into her lower lip. She hated showing her fear—I knew that from watching her. In fact, it seemed she hated showing anything too deeply, especially to me. Sparks of resistance danced in the depths of her gaze even now as she was splayed out and bared before me.

I moved back to the end of the bed, looking up at her as I crawled onto the mattress. The shitty ass bed sunk beneath my weight, causing her body to shift slightly and the tie around her throat to tighten as it was pulled taut. I watched her face carefully. There would likely be a bruise around her neck before the night was through, but so long as she could breathe, all would be fine.

Lifting the unopened bottle of lube, I popped the cap and then peeled the layer of plastic off before returning the cap to its place and quickly squirting a dollop onto my fingers. What I planned for her punishment would take time and infinitely more patience. I'd once waited forty-seven hours before getting my chance to take a target out through the scope of my sniper's rifle. Patience was something I had in spades.

"Gaven…" As I took the cool lube and spread it over her pussy, she jumped into my palm. I smiled wickedly as I smeared it up and down her lips, avoiding her clit as it pulsed in need. Her inner thighs were wracked with tremors, muscles bunching and jumping beneath her flesh as she panted for breath.

"You're going to learn, Angel," I said, "that naughty girls don't always get what they want." But they did get what they deserved and she had earned this fucking punishment.

Once I was done smearing the lube over her opening, I reached for the vibrating dildo and ripped open the packaging. Her eyes widened further as I held it up. The toy was slender, tiny in comparison to my own anatomy, but it would do for what I had planned. Thankfully, the cheap ass motel she'd rented at least managed to prepackage batteries to go with their other amenities, and I inserted them before settling the narrow end to her cunt and pushing.

She groaned and arched her hips up as if to avoid the penetration.

"Ah, ah, ah," I warned her gently, placing a hand on her hip bones, carefully sliding my palm up and away from the bruise forming on her side. My lips pressed together as I stared down at the dark splotch of skin, a pang of regret filling my chest. I'd been too rough with her when I'd tackled her to the ground earlier, but if it was between bruising her and risking her life—I'd do what needed to be done. Every time.

Pushing the thoughts of regret away, I thrust the dildo the rest of the way into her pussy and spoke. "There's no escaping from this, Angel," I said. "I recommend you stop trying and just take what you're owed. It'll make the punishment much easier, I promise."

Above, Angel hissed out a slow breath and growled at my words. My smile stretched out further. As angry as I was with her, now that she was here in my grasp, I found that my fury had waned. She was so fun and amusing to play with. I wondered if I would feel this way once we'd had years together. Would it be the same when her belly was round and swollen with my seed as she grew our child inside of her?

Only time would tell. For now, I had her discipline to see to.

I switched the vibrator on, eliciting a sharp cry

from Angel's throat as she bucked automatically. Her body bowed under the quick movements of the toy. Anchoring it into place with two fingers, I held it inside her for a moment before I began using it. Pulling it halfway out and then pushing it back in. Wetness gushed around it as she shuddered under its vibration.

My eyes were locked on the place between her legs. It was a small toy, not nearly as long as what I wanted to put inside of her. The smallest bit of blood stained the toy. The sight of it made me grin. Emotions could be faked. Orgasms could be fabricated. But this—*blood*—was the ultimate truth. The one thing I could rely on.

Raff had given me twenty-four hours to get to her and return her to her place in the Price Manor. I would use that time to its fullest potential too.

With the clamps biting into her tits and the vibrating dildo thrusting in and out of her cunt, I looked up and watched as Angel's face brightened further. She bowed her head back and her body rolled into the thrusts of my hands as I fucked her with the vibrator. Back and forth. Pausing and then repeating the motions.

I could tell she was getting closer and closer to the edge of release. She stopped talking and started to groan, the animalistic noises like music to my ears. In this moment, she was no longer Evangeline Price, but a submissive under her Dom's clear command. Soon, she'd know what that truly meant. Soon, there would be more—there would be a contract detailing exactly what she was allowed and precisely who she belonged to.

I continued my thrusts. Twisting the toy in her cunt, more of her juices squirted out around my fingers as I pushed it all the way to the hilt, shoving my fingers in alongside the plastic shaft.

"This is only the beginning," I said as I watched her tits rise and fall as she panted, gasped, and whined. "Before the night is through, love, you'll be begging for my forgiveness."

And if she accepted her Master, maybe … just maybe, I would give it to her.

13
ANGEL

I lingered on the edge of something great and terrible. It was different from that night in the restaurant. It was more. My insides were a swirling mass and I shuddered beneath each thrust of the vibrator that fucked into me. Gaven's hands were consistent, never letting up, never stopping, and never easing the bundle of nerves that was my clit.

If my hands were free, I knew, beyond a shadow of a doubt, that I wouldn't give a single shit that he was sitting before me. I wouldn't have cared who watched. I would have fumbled for my clit and rubbed it until I could finally touch that bit of heaven that waited for me.

Unfortunately, though, even as I crested towards it, my orgasm was denied. Gaven's hands slipped away and the toy was removed. I cried out and whimpered—uncaring how wicked it was, uncaring that I was acting pathetically in need. I'd never felt this way before and was lost to all the sensations that now coursed through my body. I wanted—no, I fucking *needed* him to release me from this hell and I was afraid that I would do anything to achieve my liberation.

"Please…" I rasped through a voice nearly gone. The tie around my throat wasn't quite enough to cut off my airflow, but it did make me feel dizzy. I had to work at breathing and it was difficult to do that as well as focus on the rest of my body.

My breasts felt heavy and tight. My nipples which had, at first, felt sharp pains at the clamps placed upon them, were now tight little buds of nothing but *feeling*. They ached and I wanted him to repeat what he had done earlier. I wanted his mouth on me. All over me.

"Do you understand what's going to happen, Angel?" Gaven asked as he set aside the vibrator and then reached up for my breasts. I pushed them out and into his hand, begging silently for him to remove the painful rubber and metal that held them imprisoned.

His fingers lightly played over my nipples, teasing them with the prospect of freedom. I whimpered low in my throat when he didn't immediately let them go, but that only made the fire in his eyes heighten. I could see it—the way he enjoyed what he did to me. His cock was straining against his pants as he watched me wriggle like a worm on a hook, caught in his trap as he tormented me. The devil got off on his sexual torture. He liked giving me pain, and somewhere deep down in the recesses of my mind, I had to admit—if only to myself—that I kind of liked receiving it.

The smile that played upon Gaven's lips as he was arched over me was like that of a hungry animal having found the perfect feast and that was what I was, I realized. I was his feast. Except there was no more hunting. He'd captured me and now, I was about to be eaten, consumed by his lust.

"Do you want something, Angel?" he asked teasingly.

I nodded sharply. "They hurt," I replied, craning upward to try and get him to release me from, at the very least, the metal and rubber teeth biting into my tits.

"What hurts?" he prompted me. "Your breasts hurt? Your nipples?"

"*Yessssss.*" My answer turned into a hiss as he unclamped first one nipple, taking it between his thumb and forefinger and rubbing away the sting of the restraint before he did the same to the other. The clamps landed on the bed at my side as he took the full weight of my breasts into his palms. He thumbed my nipples causing sharp spikes of agony to slide through them, making my eyes glaze over with tears.

A part of me wished I were stronger than this, but he was impossible to resist.

I wanted him. I wanted this.

Even if only for tonight. Even if I still wanted to run from what we were meant to be.

"You look beautiful like this, you know," Gaven

said, his words hoarse as he stared down at me. "A pretty little girl bound under me, your body mine to play with, to toy with. Are you my toy, Angel?" My nipples were tight little beads, a darker, angrier color than normal. They were swollen and felt more sensitive to the touch. He leaned down and closed his mouth around one, tongue lashing against me with a violence that sent electricity racing through me.

My pussy pulsed with need. The only thing that could have made the sensation of him licking my nipple better would have been feeling something hot and hard inside me. Now, the thought of every backseat stolen kiss from high school faded. Every secret fondling from a school boyfriend felt like another lifetime. Nothing could compare to this.

Gaven's lips popped off of me with a sharp noise that had me yanking my head up once more. He pressed a finger over the now-wet tip of my breast with a grin. "So hungry, aren't you?" His eyes settled on mine. "Answer me, Angel. Are you hungry?"

I bit my lower lip, not wanting to admit the truth. I *was* hungry. A beat passed and then another. Finally, a chuckle rumbled through him.

"No matter," he said. "You'll still get discipline, love. I'm sure you expected your virginity to last until our wedding night, but I have other plans now."

"Are … are you going to fuck me?" I asked. Nervousness pooled in my belly. Did I want him to? Yes. The answer was yes.

Gaven shook his head, though, surprising me.

"No," he said. "You haven't been a good girl. You've been a very, very bad girl. Good girls get fucked. Bad girls get spanked."

"So ... you're going to spank me?" I asked, confused.

"Yes," he said. "But not tonight. Tonight, I have something else planned for you."

"What—" My next question was cut off as he pinched my nipple sharply and twisted until my insides reacted. I cried out and arched into his touch to try and ease the pain. As soon as it'd come, though, the pain receded. Gaven leaned down and I closed my eyes at the wet feel of his lips and tongue once more. He laved each nipple with deliberate attention before he released me and moved back to the edge of the mattress. The pain and the pleasure he gave were his weapons, and I found myself trembling at the effect they both had on me. Gaven lifted the bottle of lube again.

A panting, sweating mess, I watched him as he opened the cap and squirted a hefty amount onto his fingers. My eyes widened as more and more poured out into his hand until he was practically slathered in it. What could he be planning with that much lube? He was emptying the entire container.

"Mafia families are traditional," he said as he moved back and bent over before me, sliding right up between my tied-open legs once more. His un-lubed palm touched my thigh, pushing me open farther than ever before, until I felt stretched to the point of snapping in half. "Just like the Kings of old, most family heads want to marry virgins," he continued. "For good reason too. They want to ensure that any children their wives have belong solely to them as she will carry the future heirs of their lineage."

The penetrating blue steely ice of his gaze landed on me briefly before his fingers pressed into my opening. Two at first, sinking deep and quick, eased by the amount of lube coating them. It was an odd sensation but not uncomfortable. I squirmed beneath his attention, feeling something inside of me catch fire. I was burning—burning alive, and the only thing that could both stoke and release the flames was him.

"That was another reason I chose you," he said. "I knew your sister would not be untouched, but you … Angel. You have the look of a virgin. Innocent. Inexperienced, as you admitted before. You have the heat of a woman in need of pleasure."

"What—" *What did any of that matter anymore?* I wondered, swallowing the words as his fingers penetrated me. *Why was he telling me this?*

"You might not be getting fucked by me tonight, Angel," Gaven said. "But I will ensure that no other man will ever be your first."

Confusion rippled through me. A third finger joined the first three, stretching my channel open. I winced as he fucked into me with his hand. Back and forth. I was too tight for this and his hand—his fingers, they were massive as he invaded me. His eyes remained trained on my face, watching … for what, I couldn't say. He was absorbed, though, solely focused. The discomfort became more pronounced as he added a fourth finger, spearing all of them into my cunt as his thumb rolled over my clit—finally giving me a hint of that pleasure ... and the pain.

"Ah!" I arched against the tightness and the stretch. I swore he was trying to drive me to insanity. That was what his punishment must've been. He wanted to see me lose complete and utter control, to hand it all over to him. Somehow, I wondered if I wouldn't like that.

Would it be easier, in the end, to just give him control?

I shook under his hand, wanting to press my thighs together as the burn of the stretch made me crave more. I pulled against the bindings keeping me tied to the headboard. My throat closed briefly as the necktie tightened impossibly further. Dizziness swam through me. It wasn't enough and it was too much all at once.

My lips parted, but no more sound emerged. I wanted to cry and beg. I wanted to sob for my release, but I doubted he would ever give it to me. After all, as he'd said, this was discipline. A punishment.

Did it make me an absolute deviant to admit I liked it? I couldn't stop my body from responding the way it was, but my mind ... I should have been able to hold off my thoughts. *Should* have ... but couldn't.

My insides flooded with wetness. My pussy clamped onto his fingers, sucking them in with each pass of his hand. I was so full. So incredibly full, it was a wonder that I hadn't already shattered into a million pieces.

I groaned as my eyes rolled back and I undulated against him. He wasn't giving my clit enough attention. Only every few seconds would he press his thumb to it and circle—just enough to keep me from screaming from the twinges of pain between my legs as he forced my pussy open for him.

"You're taking my hand so well, Angel." Gaven's praise seared my mind. "Maybe just … one more…"

One more? One more what? I was so overwhelmed by what he was doing, it took several seconds for my thoughts to catch up with his words. Before I could make sense of them, I felt it. The thumb that he'd had gently rubbing against my clit, moved downward. My eyes popped open. I hadn't even realized I'd closed them. Leaning up, I gaped down at him and started shaking my head. *No. Oh, no. Nonononono.* I couldn't do that. It was impossible. I was too small. I was still, by technicality, a virgin.

"G-Gaven." His name came out on a choked cry. "Please … *no.*" It was too much. He was insane. Absolutely deranged if he thought my pussy could take his full hand.

"Yes," Gaven replied. "You'll take it, Angel. Trust me. I know what you can give me."

That was just the thing though. I didn't trust him. In fact, I hardly knew him. We were arranged to be married. He was far older than me, far more experienced. Had likely fucked his way through a harem of women. But this … he couldn't truly mean to do this to me, could he?

Whether he could or not wasn't going to be decided by me though; that much was clear. His gaze was focused on the place between my legs, his brows low and his eyes glittering with the intensity of his task. He didn't stop. He pushed forward, edging his thumb against the seam of my cunt. I choked again as the pain spread outward. The agony of him spreading me open for his pleasure, for this punishment, made me strain upward and then back. There was nowhere I could go. I was trapped, pinned beneath him, and beholden to him and his attention.

Gaven continued to fuck my pussy with his fingers, in and out, slicked with lube, stretching my hole until I swore he was going to rip me apart. Tears flooded my eyes, watering the world around me until I couldn't see anything. They streaked down my temples and slid into my hair. All I could do was feel. Feel the pain, take it, accept it, and become one with it. My insides cramped, but somehow all that did was make it easier on him. My muscles gripped his fingers, dragging them back into me with each withdrawal.

My body was a needy bitch. A greedy creature that refused to let him back away even when my mind couldn't take the duress. The tears trailed down my cheeks as I continued to shake my head. "Please," I begged him. "It's too much. It hurts!"

"You'll take it," he growled as his thumb slipped against my stretched hole, pressing against the side of his fingers as he curled them together. First, it was just the tip, lingering at the outer curve of my lower lips and then it was the whole pad. "You'll take everything I have to give you, Angel. Your body was made for it."

"It hurts!" I cried out again. "You're going to break me."

His eyes flashed back to mine. "You won't break," he assured me, "and it's supposed to hurt. It's a punishment, after all." Then he thrust, fucking into my pussy with his hand—his thumb and fingers all together as he pushed into my insides.

I cried out, my back bowing as I thrashed against the pillows against the headboard. His free palm landed on my lower belly, keeping me pinned as his hand turned inside of me. It was a strange sensation, but I could feel it. My pussy tightened around individual fingers—five of them inside of me. His fist moved into me. His whole fucking fist ... was inside of me.

I was so startled by the fact that he'd been so cruel to do this that it took my mind a beat to catch up to the fact that I was in a new kind of pain. A sob slipped free of my lips as a sharp agony ripped through me. Was this how it felt for normal virgins? I doubted it. Normal virgins got love—or at least the facsimile of love. They didn't get a madman's fist shoved up their pussy as punishment for running away from their arranged marriage.

Despite myself, I couldn't stop crying. I gritted my teeth, forcing back the curses that threatened to fly out from between my lips. There was no telling what other cruel punishments Gaven would plan for me. After several moments, I managed to breathe through my mouth—in and out—and I started to realize that he wasn't moving. In fact, he merely held still. His body hovered over me, hot flesh before my eyes as sweat clung to my body. Sweat and other slick liquids—my own wet juices were still leaking out of me, dripping down between the cheeks of my ass. My face was practically on fire from the knowledge. I was a virgin no more, but I was most certainly *owned*.

Still, Gaven waited. It was as if he were letting me grow accustomed to the massiveness of his hand in my cunt as I panted and wiggled under him. It was too much. I was too full. Sharp, biting cramps overtook my stomach. The lube, I realized. That was why he'd poured so much on himself. He'd been planning this from the beginning. The fucking bastard.

"There, there," Gaven said, his voice rumbling with approval. "Look at you now, you've done it, Angel. You've taken my whole fist into your pretty pussy. It's so swollen around my hand, red and begging for relief."

A moan of shame overtook me. How dare he say such disgusting things to me when all I wanted to do was wrap my hands around his throat and strangle him the very same way he had me choking on his necktie. Bastard. Asshole. Prick.

As if he could hear my thoughts, Gaven grinned. "You're going to be such a filthy little bride, Angel," he whispered, bending down so the heat of his voice and breath was right against my ear. I stiffened. "Your pussy is begging for more pain, you know. I can feel the fluttering of your muscles squeezing me so tight. You want my cock, don't you? Perhaps if you're good for me and do what I say, I'll give it to you. I'll fill you to the brim with my cum and even let you suck me off afterward. I bet you'd like that—a dirty girl like you."

With a groan of disbelief, I arched up against him and glared his way when he finally pulled back enough to peer into my eyes. "Fuck … you…" I seethed.

His low rumble of amusement slid over my ears in the nearly quiet room, penetrating through the pounding of blood rushing through my head. I felt sore down there, my nipples fucking hurt, and yet, he was amused.

"You might say that, love," he replied. "But your pussy very much wants me to. You're squeezing my fingers inside of you like you want me to fuck your insides with my hand. Is that what you want?"

"No!" My scream was hoarse due to the tie around my throat. Much more, and it would make me pass out, but I couldn't let that happen. There was no telling what else this man would do to my body if I was unconscious.

"Oh, I think your body is much more honest than that pretty, lying mouth of yours." Gaven chuckled.

"I'm not—" I tried to tell him that I was not a liar, but the words were cut off as he began moving his fingers inside of me. My inner walls contracted as he pulled until the largest part of his palm was nearly out of my insides before thrusting back inside.

"Ah!" Stars danced in front of my eyes and my breath left me in a rush. I could feel where his wrist was against my opening, stretching me. I was afraid to look down, afraid to see just what he'd done to my body.

"So tight," I heard him mutter to himself, eyes centered on my pussy. "So perfect. It's too bad you had to be such a naughty girl. This could have been so much easier on you."

I gritted my teeth, wanting to thrash and curse him but afraid I might rip if I moved too quickly.

"Have you learned your lesson, Angel?" Gaven's question was nearly lost on me as my entire mind was focused on the tightness of his fist in my cunt. It took a moment for the words to catch up with my consciousness.

Unable to even resist, I replied quickly. "Yes!" I snapped. "Yes! I've learned my lesson!"

"Will you accept my ring?" he asked, thrusting his fist against my insides again.

"Yes!" My head turned back and forth as more

tears leaked out, streaming down my face, sticking to my cheeks.

"Will you marry me?"

"Yes!" It was all I could say. Yes. Yes. Yes. Anything to stop this madness. Anything to free me from the agony.

Then, as if he could sense just how close to the line I was, his free hand moved down and his fingers plucked at my clit. Suddenly, a rush of fresh slick wetness gushed around his hand. It had nothing to do with the lube that eased his passage. It was all me.

Humiliation burned through my mind and body.

No, I didn't want to like this.

He'd taken my virginity in the worst possible way. Forcing his hand into my body and ripping it from me like the monster I'd always suspected him of being. I couldn't ... I couldn't get off on that. It wouldn't be right.

Yet, the reality of pleasure was right there. He thrust into me, spearing my pussy with his fist as his fingers tortured my clit, sending me up a cliff so steep, the way back down would shatter me into a million pieces.

"You'll be mine, Angel," he growled out through gritted teeth. "You'll take my seed and only my seed, bear my children, and then offer your holes to me for pleasure or pain. Do you understand? Say it, tell me yes."

I couldn't deny him. Not anymore. Not like this. So, as I next parted my lips and the orgasm that had been just out of reach earlier finally crashed into me like a tidal wave. I screamed out a broken, "Yes!"

As I did, Gaven pinched my clit between his fingers, sending me ever higher until the world faded into blackness. Oblivion opened its arms and took me into its bosom.

When I finally came to, I found that my pussy was sore, but empty, open and gushing wetness onto the mattresses. Gaven stood over me, quickly wiping his fingers clean. There was blood too. I saw. On his hand. My virginity was now gone—taken, not by a man's cock, but by his fist. I shuddered. He reached forward and untied my neck from the headboard. His fingers smoothed around my throat as my lashes fluttered.

Exhaustion weighed into me, taking me further away. Lifting me into a sea of sleep and carrying me far, far away. In a world that had nothing to do with mafia men or bondage or even hated marriages.

Just before I was completely lost, though, I heard Gaven's voice. "Sleep, Angel … tomorrow things will be different. The punishment is over now. You're back to being my good girl, and my good girl will be well taken care of." As if to prove his words, a few moments later, I felt a warm washcloth slide over my skin. He was cleaning me—as if I were his doll.

Taken care of, my ass, I thought snidely. Still, I had to admit … that … had been an experience of a lifetime. The orgasm had been stronger than any I'd managed to get on my own. It'd been terrifying. It'd been overwhelming. But now ... it was over, and I was slowly drifting back to the harsh reality that made this man more than just a fucked up sexual deviant but my future husband.

To have and to hold ... until death would we part.

14

ANGEL

My throat was sore, but more than that, my nipples fucking *hurt*. They were aching, puckered little things and every scrape against the inside of my bra made me wince even days after Gaven had tracked me down and thoroughly violated me as punishment for running away.

The trip back to the Price Estate had been a silent one, and no one said a word when I was brought back. They didn't even glance at the faint ring of reddened skin around my throat from Gaven's necktie. I was so humiliated by them, that I doubled the layers of my makeup to cover them. Thankfully they were lightening faster than I anticipated, but I expected I'd have to wear foundation on the wedding day as well. That was, unless I was expected to wear his first gift—that stupid diamond collar. It would just be another way to cover them up.

The only person who seemed just as upset at my

return as me was Jackie who glared at me as I was led inside with Gaven's hand tight around my arm. My father had been disappointed. That much was clear from the dark look on his face, but other than thanking Gaven for finding me and bringing me home so quickly, he hadn't said more than a few words to me.

And just like that, the days began to pass in a blur. The wedding approached and I was under constant watch. Even the guards seemed more wary of me. What little room I'd had to escape before had evaporated. It was only a few short days before the ceremony that it all came to a head—my own internal riot of emotions manifesting in the worst possible way. My dreams ... or rather my nightmares.

It began with a feeling—happiness. It spread throughout my body. A sensation that filled me as I lay on a cushion so soft it made me want to roll back and forth like a cat. It was my own bed, I realized. The one from my childhood, though, surrounded by fluff and pink ribbons and white lace.

I sat up and stared around my bedroom, curious and confused. The longer I sat there, the more the happiness swelling inside of me disappeared and new, darker emotions took its place. The thread of anger, hurt, and betrayal grew in the pit of my stomach. I wasn't entirely sure why, but it was there nonetheless, and no matter how I tried to push it down, it kept coming back with a vengeance. Cramping my insides until

I swore I could feel Gaven's fist inside me again—reaching up through my pussy, pounding my insides so harshly—far more harshly than he'd done in reality—I swore I was being ripped to shreds from the inside out.

Jerking up from the bed, I stumbled forward and nearly went down on my knees. Looking down, I gaped at the ground beneath my feet. Not the soft carpet of my bedroom floor but dirt.

"What the…" I murmured, looking back up.

My room shifted, the walls around me falling away and changing. I spun in a circle and stopped when a shadowy figure emerged from the darkness. Gaven.

He didn't seem to notice me, though, and instead, strode forward, yelling at men that began to creep out of the shadows as well. My father's men. Soldiers—their faces etched with impassivity even though blood stained their clothes.

How many of them were killers? I'd always wondered and always shoved down the question. I opened my mouth to say something. To call out to Gaven. To try and get a sense of where I was and what was going on, except no words escaped me. It was as if my voice was locked inside my head.

A void was left in the wake of my confusing emotions and I turned, stumbling again as the dirt beneath my feet grew darker—stained. Wet.

When I blinked, my surroundings transformed again. A bit of white caught my attention out of the corner of my eye and I looked up only to freeze where I stood. My mother's body. This time, though, when she lay in the casket I remembered from seven years ago, the top remained open.

I'd never seen her corpse. Not when I was young, but I'd always hoped she would look peaceful. She didn't. Not now.

There was blood dried everywhere, with several bullet wounds in her chest. Her nails had been ripped free and red stained her fingertips. Gasping at the sudden tightness in my chest, I glanced around for someone—anyone—to help ground me.

Vomit threatened to spew out of my lips. I spun in a circle. Seeking. Searching. For someone. Anyone.

"Little sister." Jackie's voice taunted me and I whirled around as she appeared before me, her signature smirk and cruel gaze centering on me. She stood over our mother's body but never once glanced at it. "Did you really think you would escape?"

My chest tightened, coiling until not an ounce of oxygen was left in my lungs. I wheezed out my response. "I-I tried," I said. "I don't want this."

"You don't want what you are?" she asked. "You're a princess, Angel. A doll. A pawn to be used."

A princess? No. A doll, though? A pawn? Yes. I could imagine that was exactly what I was. A Mafia Princess. Soon to be a Mafia boss's wife. With no freedom of my own. Gaven Belmonte would own me the second I said 'I do,' and if I didn't give him what he wanted... would I be any safer?

"Everything you thought you could have? College, a life away from crime ... there's no way you can have it. Any of it, Angel," she whispered.

Gaven and my father appeared, right behind her. Their faces were masks of rage. My father's mouth opened and he shouted though the words were lost on me. All the while, Gaven merely stood there and stared back at me. His cruel, dark blue gaze promised an untold number of punishments if I didn't conform.

My insides softened. Against my will, I felt my body grow

lax. Why did he do that to me? *I wondered. He was a monster. I should've wanted to run as far and as fast as possible, but what if... what if, instead, I could make a deal with the devil?*

What if I gave him what he wanted, and he gave me what I wanted? This didn't have to be the end. Jackie didn't have to be right.

Every breath I attempted to take was a struggle, my sister's chuckles echoing around me. I tried to hold onto anything I could reach, to stay steady, but everything disappeared when I touched it. Swaying back and forth, I watched as the space around me constantly changed. Different places I'd been, people I knew, everything spinning around with a life of its own.

"You'll never be free again," Jackie cackled amongst the chaos.

No! *I screamed in my head.*

No matter how much I tried to stop it, to change what I was seeing, to have control, none of it worked. All I was left with was the empty void and panicked breathing...

GASPING, I SHOT UP IN BED. SWEAT COATED MY BODY and my heart thudded so loudly in my ears I couldn't hear anything else. Panic and fear iced my veins as I sat there, still stunned from my nightmare. But the longer I sucked in air, the less the emotions affected me until my heart rate had calmed and my chest wasn't tight. I tossed the blanket off of me and slipped from between the sheets, my focus falling immediately onto my laptop that sat closed on my desk. Sinking into the chair, I took a breath, reached for the computer, and opened the top. I needed some semblance of control, even if it was only an illusion.

I'd been allowed to keep the laptop, but not before it'd been thoroughly gone through by my father's men and Gaven's too. Intelligent men, for sure, but also underestimating. None of them had ever considered that I knew the back route into the darkest of internet places.

The dark web. Where identities could be traded, bought, and stolen as easily as walking into a store and picking up a pack of gum. Before I'd been captured, I'd been working on this. A new person— a new me. Freedom.

And I probably wasn't the only person who wanted freedom from this life. I bet hundreds of people were out there, just like me, trapped in the cruel underground criminal world. The government couldn't help them, just like it couldn't help me. Even knowing what I did was a crime, I'd—in essence—become an accomplice. I'd known that from the moment my father confirmed all of Jackie's claims.

The dark web had been my way of fighting back. My knowledge of technology and what it could accomplish was a skill they couldn't take away from me. Maybe someday it would be my salvation.

Taking a deep, steadying breath, I leaned back in my chair, slumping against the worn cushions. I couldn't risk it. Not now. Not so quickly after I'd been caught, but at least I knew I had a chance. Maybe. It wasn't much, but knowing the option was still there finally calmed the remaining worry.

Still, I might not even need it. The dream—for all the hellish emotions and worries that had tried to plague me from it—had also given me an idea. A deal with the devil. Gaven Belmonte wanted a child, and I wanted freedom of choice. Getting up from my chair, I shut my computer and headed into the bathroom. I bent over the sink and splashed a handful of cold water on my face, relishing in the refreshing sensation on my sweat-coated forehead and flushed cheeks. When I stood back up, I found my own tired, haunted eyes staring back. Dark circles were forming, and my skin was a sickly pallor. Grinding my teeth, I straightened my spine and strode from the bathroom.

All Gaven wants is an heir, I reminded myself, *and he'll do anything to get what he wants.*

I could give him that. It would be easier, no doubt, if I were willing. I could be convinced to be willing too. All I needed in return was a promise. College. Normalcy. It wasn't everything I wanted, but it was something. To elicit such a promise, though, I would have to face him again. After everything Gaven had done to me, after all that he'd made me feel … I would have to stand before him and offer myself and sign the paperwork that would officially make him my husband.

The alarm on my bedside buzzed, announcing that it was time for me to get ready. Wanting to get ahead of the game, I rushed through my routine. Today was the day I'd be looking for my wedding dress—a dress I was shocked they were letting me select myself—but it was also a day I'd be forced to be near Gaven. It was perfect for what I had planned.

I found Gaven in my father's office. The door was open, but I still knocked softly on the rich wood and waited for an answer.

"Come in," my father called out. I pushed the door wider and stepped inside. Gaven's ever-vigilant gaze found mine, his lips tipping up slightly.

"You called for me," I said coolly. Try as I might, I couldn't stop the downward turn of my eyes as I looked him over. He was dressed pristinely today. No suit coat but a dark button-down and slacks. His sleeves were rolled up to his elbows, revealing thick forearms that reminded me of the things he'd done to me. I shivered and yanked my attention away.

"Yes, I did." My father lifted a brow as he looked back at me. "There will be no more running away, Evangeline," he stated. "Gaven will be going with you to your fitting."

I nodded. Just as I'd anticipated. "I understand, Dad. I know you're upset, but I promise I'll be good."

He narrowed his gaze on me—as did Gaven, though I ignored him. After a moment, though, he merely nodded and then waved a hand as if dismissing both of us.

"Keep me updated on the Bertellis," Gaven said,

glancing at my father as he spoke. "They will likely still be upset by the marriage, but with things this close, there's no stopping it now."

My father scowled as if reminded of something awful. I stood by, silent and patient, but still listening in. *Could the Bertellis be the family that had tried to kill me that day on the street?*

"They will be dealt with," my father sneered. "You keep her safe."

Gaven nodded and stood from his chair. "Angel." I looked up as he approached and didn't shy away as he stopped at my side or when he took my hand. "Shall we?"

If he was surprised by my lack of hesitancy, he didn't show it. In fact, he didn't say a word as he led me out into the hallway, down the corridor to the staircase, and into the foyer. We were met by a small battalion of guards who lined our sides, front and back, as we left the mansion and got into a town car.

"You're being quite good today, darling," Gaven commented as he released my hand and the car moved forward.

Folding my hands into my lap, I turned and met his gaze. "Yes, I am," I said.

"It makes a man think you're planning something."

"I am," I agreed.

His gaze lit up and then narrowed. "Oh?" He arched a brow. "Do tell."

I inhaled sharply. "As it stands," I began, "you want something from me."

"I want a lot of things from you, darling," Gaven replied with a cruel twist of his lips. "But do go on."

"What if I stopped fighting it?" I said.

"Yes?" His head tipped in curiosity.

Heart thudding wildly in my chest, I pressed on, taking it as an opportunity. "If I can't get out of this marriage, then I want some freedoms."

"What kind of *freedoms*?"

"College," I said. "I want to go."

"No." Gaven's word was followed by a head turn as he glanced out the window.

I bit down on my lower lip, but I wasn't going to stop there. "Yes," I snapped. "It doesn't have to be in person. I can take classes online and you can get what you want."

"What is it, exactly, that you're offering, Angel?" Gaven asked, looking back at me. "I've already got your hand in marriage."

"You might have my father's agreement," I said. "But you don't have *mine*."

"I don't need it."

I gritted my teeth at that statement. "You think that only because you don't know how stubborn I can truly be," I replied.

His lips twitched. He hummed deep in his throat for a moment before speaking. "What's flitting through that head of yours?"

I ground my teeth, not trusting myself to say anything. I wanted to tell him it wasn't any of his business. Because the fact was, it was his business … and mine.

The landscape whooshed past, startlingly close to my dream and I felt myself quickly losing hold of that sliver of control I'd found. I wanted to keep a portion of myself secret. A piece only for me, but with a man like Gaven, I already knew he'd know every part of me inside and out.

"I won't fight you anymore," I said. "I'll sign the marriage certificate. I'll do everything you ask of me. I'll…even get pregnant." I paused before that last one, but the fact was, it was his desired outcome. He wanted me pregnant with his child to ensure that he would be the next head of the Price Family Syndicate. I could give him that. I was willing to bind the two of us with more than just a marriage, but a child, so long as I got something out of it.

"I can take all of that from you, you know," Gaven pointed out, his voice calm as if he were discussing something as simple as the weather versus my enslavement.

"You could," I admitted, "but it would be easier for you, wouldn't it, if I simply gave in?"

He contemplated my words. "Yes, I suppose it would be easier."

"It means nothing for you to allow me to have a life outside of all of this," I said, leaning towards him even as I gestured around us. "I promise, if you give me this, I won't run away again. I'll do everything you ask." I arched my brow at him.

"Everything, hmmm?" The corner of his mouth tipped upward, a sure sign that I was getting through to him. I had to believe that. Hope rose within me.

"Well, I suppose I could offer you some incentive to be a good girl."

I held my breath as he seemed to contemplate my offer further. A beat passed and then another and another until finally, he nodded. "Yes, alright," he said. "I'll allow you your sense of normalcy, Angel. I'm not completely disagreeable. I do believe in rewards as much as I do punishments."

"You will? I mean—thank you." For the first time since I'd met him, the weight inside my chest eased. "Thank you so much. You have no idea how much this means to me."

Gaven leaned forward, capturing my chin as he held my face between his thumb and forefinger, angling me so I was face-to-face with him. "Remember, love," he said, "that this deal of ours stipulates that you do everything I say."

I nodded. "I will."

He grinned. "We'll see about that," he replied enigmatically. "Only time will tell." Releasing me, he reached into his pocket and pulled out a small box. "But we'll start now, shall we?"

"Now?" I frowned as he lifted the box and handed it over. Hesitation and curiosity warred within me, but sensing his attention, I bit the inside of my cheek to keep my face void of emotion.

"What is this?" I asked.

He chuckled. "Why don't you open it and find out?"

Concerned, I slipped the lid open and stared at the black tissue paper inside for a moment before removing that as well. My eyes widened at what was inside. Within the box was a scrap of lace, a dainty pair of white panties.

"Panties?" I asked.

"Yes," he answered. "A gift to my bride. Put them on."

I looked around the very small backseat of the town car. "Here?" He couldn't be serious.

He shrugged. "Did you not say you would do whatever I asked?"

I bit down on my lip hard. He was right. I had. Gingerly taking the gift, I set it in my lap. My eyes shot to the driver with concern, but Gaven snapped his fingers, dragging my attention back to him. "Don't worry about him," he said. "I want those panties on you before we arrive at the dress shop. You'll wear them for your dress fitting."

I swallowed against a thick throat. He always managed to humiliate me, but we had a verbal contract. This was nothing compared to receiving some of my freedoms back. Taking the fabric the rest of the way out of the bag, I held it up for my view and then set it on the seat next to me.

Thankfully, I'd worn a dress out today. It wasn't as difficult as it could have been to unbuckle my seat belt and reach under my skirt, hooking my fingers in the waist of my underwear and slipping them down my legs before I reached for the new lingerie. As I lifted it again, though, I felt something hard in the center.

"What—"

"Now, Angel," Gaven insisted, "my patience is wearing thin."

With a grunt, I snapped a glare his way and then bent over, fitting the leg holes to my feet and pulling them up. I winced and tugged. They were the right size, but something wasn't quite right with them. They felt heavier than regular underwear. I shifted uncomfortably in the seat, and when I reached for the old pair, his hand made it before mine.

I watched as he lifted my panties to his face, turning the crotch—which I knew would be slightly wet because, in spite of myself, it always was around him—to his mouth and nose. He inhaled deeply, closing his eyes with the movement, and then they reopened, centered on me.

"Aren't you going to thank me for your gift?" he asked casually as if he hadn't just done something so embarrassing as sniffing my underwear. He tucked the small scrap of fabric into his pocket and then looked at me expectantly.

"Thank you," I bit out, glaring at the lace as if it was the cause of my entire situation. It was suffocating in the small interior of his car, especially with the intensity of his focus centered squarely on me. The longer I sat there, the more unusual my thoughts became. I squirmed as images flashed into my mind. I tried to force them away, but it was difficult. He was so close, so near, and he smelled ... like something wild and deadly.

A deal with the devil ... had it truly been the right choice?

15
ANGEL

I stood in the bathroom of the bridal shop and shifted restlessly as I washed my hands. The underwear Gaven had given me molded to my pussy and cupped me in a way that made me viscerally aware that I was wearing something a little bit different than usual. I couldn't quite pinpoint the reason why they were so heavy by comparison. Whatever it was, it felt like a little bead between my legs, nestled right against my clit, and I had no doubt it was purposeful.

Asshole, I thought to myself. At the same time, a shiver chased down my spine as I shut off the tap, dried my hands, and headed for the exit. Every step reminded me that they were there. I accepted it, though, because in the end, I'd elicited that promise from him. It couldn't be all that bad—I was attracted to him, after all, and I wasn't adverse to children. I just … wanted a bit of normalcy too. If he was willing to give me that, then I could conform for now.

Wearing Gaven's gift as I strode through the bridal shop made me feel deviant, almost as if I were walking naked down a sidewalk. I doubted that others realized just how dominating and possessive Gaven Belmonte truly was. I bet he liked knowing that I was wearing something he'd purchased for me. More than that, I think he liked the idea that it was such an *intimate* piece of clothing.

The constant sensation against me made the memory of his *punishment* that much more prominent when I'd been trying my damned hardest not to think about it. My pussy and nipples were still sore. Maybe another woman would have been cowed, but I couldn't be. I refused.

"Dear, are you feeling alright?" I stopped in front of the attendant as she frowned my way, examining my face. "You appear quite flushed."

I coughed, my face heating even further. "I'm fine," I lied. "It's nothing."

"Are you sure?" She was an older woman with graying hair at her temples pulled back into a tight bun on her head. Her demeanor made it clear that she'd likely mothered many young women who came into her shop. She didn't hesitate to step forward and lift a hand to lightly touch the top of my forehead.

Behind her, I saw Gaven's smirk as he took us in, and I glared at him as I stepped away from the attendant and nodded. "I swear," I insisted, forcing a smile. "I'm fine."

"All right, well, you let me know if you're feeling dizzy. This is a lot to take in, and I hear that you'll be married quite soon," she replied. "Let's hurry and find that dress. The dress of your dreams!"

I marched after her as the attendant flitted forward, glancing back when Gaven withdrew his cell from his pocket as it rang and put it to his ear. Even though he was barking into the phone, his eyes followed me the entire way, making me hyper-aware of every move I made. As if I needed another reason to be so fucking conscious of him.

The attendant—Marie as her name tag read— helped me sort through various dresses. I stood stiffly at her side as we rifled through the backroom racks. She chattered on, looking me up and down as she tried to select dresses—according to her—that would flatter my figure. I didn't care if it flattered me at all. In fact, if I had my way, I'd wear the most hideous dress known to man as I was forced down the aisle into Gaven Belmonte's arms.

I wanted other men to pity him for having to marry me. Unfortunately, I knew with him here, that wouldn't be allowed. I had to pick my battles, and a dress was not one I was willing to waste energy on. Finally, Marie decided on three pieces to take back to the dressing room—one in cream, one in white, and one in off-white lace.

"Alright, you go ahead and try those on," Marie said as she hooked them on the tops of the dressing room door and the hooks placed around the room. "Give me a call if you need help lacing up and we'll go from there."

"Thanks," I muttered as she left the room and I was alone to face the reality I found myself in.

With a scowl, I grabbed the first dress on the hooks and flopped it across the lounge at the back of the room before I stripped. I shifted uncomfortably at the weird sensation of my new panties but grabbed onto the dress and slipped into it anyway. It was pretty, though slightly plain. Turning this way and that, my head tilted as I eyed the dress in the mirror. The fit felt awkward on my waist and hips, so I quickly stripped out of it and shoved it onto the lounge before reaching for the next.

I was halfway through getting the third dress on after the second one wouldn't even make it up my hips when the doorknob jiggled. Without thinking, I reached up and turned it as I pulled the short straps of the dress up my arms.

"Can you tie the strings at the top, Marie?" I asked, turning away as the door swung slightly inward. My whole body tightened a moment later when masculine fingers brushed against my spine, finding the nearly invisible zipper instead of strings, and pulled it down.

I gasped, jerking my head up, and was caught by a pair of startlingly deep blue eyes as Gaven moved farther into the dressing room and shut the door behind him. "What are you doing in here?" I hissed as the dress slipped off my shoulders. I tried to yank it back up, but his hands gripped the fabric and pulled it back down, right off my arms, until the material was pooled on the floor and I was left before him in nothing except my underwear. "You're not supposed to be in here!"

Rather than answering, he flipped the lock on the door, and my heart began to beat double time. I swallowed roughly. "You can't be in here," I repeated, hoping I sounded stronger than I felt. I lifted my arms and covered my chest, but his eyes sparked with irritation and his hands reached around me, gripping my wrists and pulling them away as he spun me and pushed me back against the mirror.

The cool surface made me shiver and I was forced to crane my neck back to look up at the wicked man pinning me in place. Gaven loomed over me, a hulking mass of male beauty and dangerous intentions. "You're not as traditional as your father, Angel," he said, "but I thought you might like another lesson in what it means to be my fiancée. Tell me something, do you like the present I gave you?"

"No." The word snapped out of my lips as I narrowed my gaze on him. "I'd like it if you would leave me the hell alone." My thighs rubbed together as I tried—desperately and in vain—to look at anything in the small, cramped room other than him. His skin was so hot against me, my body felt as though it were being lit on fire. His eyes were like twin orbs of hypnotic ocean and I was viscerally aware that I was bare before him once more.

I knew he'd already seen everything. He'd had his fingers—his entire fist—inside of me, but still, I hated the sensation of his eyes roaming down my naked body. It made me feel hot, out of control. It was ridiculous.

"No?" His voice was tinted with amusement. "I think you'll like it much better after this," Gaven whispered as one of his hands left me and reached into his pocket.

I frowned as he lifted a small remote no longer than my pinky and pressed the black button in the center of it. Immediately, all of the breath in my lungs left my chest as the crotch of my underwear began to vibrate. I arched my spine, confused and utterly stunned, as the buzzing reached my ears.

Gaven smiled as I squirmed under his gaze. I whimpered when he spread my legs and shoved his knee between them, grinding the little rounded bullet that had been expertly hidden within the fabric of my underwear right against my clit.

"Ah!" I cried out and then pressed my lips together, eyes sliding to the door worriedly.

"That's right, sweetheart," Gaven said, breathing into my ear. "Better be careful how loud you are. You wouldn't want the nice sales associate to hear you come all over your fiancé's knee, would you?"

I shot Gaven the deadliest look I could manage, but he merely smiled at me. His hands moved to my hips as he pulled me forward, forcing me to ride his thigh, pressing the pulsating little thing against me over and over until I was nearly sobbing with the need for relief.

My nails sank into the fabric of his sleeves. I wanted to beg him to end this unnecessary torture. My lips parted, and I cried out again as the little bullet hit my clit once more at just the right angle and a burst of white overcame my senses. I squeezed my eyes shut, clutching onto him and praying that he wouldn't let me go because I knew without a shadow of a doubt that if he were to release me now, I'd fall to my knees.

Gaven waited, however, until the orgasm had run its course. Only then did he take a step back and let me sink down to my knees. Panting and trembling, I could feel the wetness leaking from beneath my underwear, running down my inner thighs as I looked up at him through a blurry gaze filled with tears as he finally hit the button on his remote once more and turned off the resonating vibrations.

I knew he and his damned 'gifts' couldn't be trusted. With a scowl, I reached between my legs to pull the strange object away from my clit and then take off the offensive underwear, but before I could manage it, Gaven captured my hands and yanked them up to waist level.

"We're not done yet, Angel," he said, his voice growing deeper. His eyes were darkening by the second. Something sinister was building within their depths as he hooked my hands at the sides of his hips. "Let go," he warned me, "and you'll regret it."

I swallowed roughly but needing a moment to ground myself, I let my hands remain where they were on his hips. His fingers found the front of his slacks and slowly lowered the zipper. My lips parted in shock as he freed himself from the constraints of his pants and then held his cock before me, mere inches from my face. "One more lesson today," he said. "Open your mouth."

I flinched back. "Fuck you," I snapped. He was fucking massive. I knew he would be. I'd felt the evidence of his cock against me enough times to know, but it was different seeing it in person. The width of him was wide, and the length … it was frightening. I had a moment to think that perhaps taking my virginity by fisting had been a kindness from him instead. With how hard he was now, practically pulsating in front of my face, he looked ready to tear me apart all over again.

Gaven stroked himself once, moving his hand up and down the length of himself squeezing as he neared the head before taking the shaft in one hand and palming the back of my head in his other. My eyes jerked up to meet his, and he smirked as he pressed the tip of his cock to my lips. "I intend to fuck you, Angel," he said. "Now, open those pretty lips of yours and take my cock or I'll shove it in, and believe me, I'll be much rougher if you make me fight for it."

Gaven Belmonte was a certifiable monster. A cruel man. It was my fate, now, to be taken by him. That much was clear. I shivered at his words. I wanted to push back, to fight, but I knew he was right. He would make me regret resisting him. He already had. Call it self-preservation or maybe even a bit of curiosity, but I had no other recourse. I gave in. I let my lips part, accepting the head of his cock into my mouth. He pushed forward, stroking himself over my tongue as he released his length and reached up to grip the back of my skull with both palms.

Rough, masculine hands slid through my hair, unleashing some of the strands from the bun I'd tied it up in to get into the wedding dresses. They fluttered down to my neck. A groan rumbled up from Gaven's throat as he pushed further, the underside of his cock sliding over my tongue as he moved steadily toward the back of my throat.

"That's it, sweetheart," he said through gritted teeth. "Suck me deep."

Heat danced along my cheeks. I could only imagine what I must have looked like. A whore on her knees for a tall, powerful man, using her mouth as he wanted. I'd never felt so fucking degraded, and yet, as I shifted my weight on my knees before him, I also couldn't deny that there was still wetness leaking from my pussy.

I'd never done this before—a fact I was sure he knew—but he didn't act as though he cared. No, in fact, he continued to thrust himself back and forth until I'd taken over half of him into my mouth. I gagged as his tip brushed against the back of my throat, and he sighed, stopping and holding himself there.

He stretched my lips open until the corners burned. I looked up at him through a watery gaze and found him staring back, the glitter of something in his gaze—hunger. "Let this be your next lesson, Angel," he said quietly, one hand coming around to cup my jaw as he stroked my skin with his thumb. "The first step to pleasing your husband is to suck his cock like a good little slut. All the way."

My eyes widened, and I jerked my gaze down to where a good three more inches rested outside of my mouth. *There's no way.* If I took any more of him into my mouth, he'd go down my throat. I couldn't. I would suffocate.

As if sensing the direction of my thoughts, he smiled down at me when I once again lifted my gaze to meet his. "You'll do it," he said. "Now, hold your breath. I'm going to fuck your mouth. I want you to swallow what I give you. That's your duty now. I'm going to come down your throat, you'll swallow it all, and when I'm done, you'll thank me."

I glared at him. The fuck I would. Before I could pull off of his cock, however, he was already moving forward. He didn't give me a chance. His hands locked onto my head as my nails scored his hips.

It was apparent that once Gaven decided to do something, he was secure in knowing he would. He said he would fuck my mouth, and that was exactly what he did. I squeezed my eyes shut as he held me still and pulled himself out of my mouth, only to sink back in a moment later. He repeated the motions over and over, thrusting back and forth over my tongue until something salty began to leak from the head of his cock.

Shocked, my eyes widened as it poured out onto my tongue and soaked the inside of my mouth with his precum. Salty and thick as it eased his passage. I wondered … Gaven was such an in-control man. Dominant. What would he do if I actually tried to make him lose his cool? On his next withdrawal, I opened my eyes and looked up as I flicked my tongue, curious to know what it would do. I lapped at the liquid spilling from him and found pleasure in the stuttering of his hips as he jerked—as if he were oversensitized.

"Fuck," he growled.

With a mouthful of cock, I grinned. Yeah, he wasn't as composed as he'd like me to believe, and certainly not as much with my lips sucking him deep. Ice-blue eyes glared down at me as he shoved harder on the next thrust, choking me with his length.

My eyes widened as I coughed and sputtered. He merely kept going, not caring if I was suffocating. *What if I vomited on him?* I breathed through my nose, in and out, harshly.

"Did you like that?" Gaven asked, his tone tight. "Licking my cum off the head of my cock? I didn't know you'd be so pleased by it. Perhaps, I'll let you do this again if you're so enthusiastic."

My hands anchored at his hips tightened and

this time, when my nails scored them, I pushed them deeper into the revealed flesh on purpose. I was angry. I wanted to draw blood.

The pain only made him hiss as he forced himself farther into my mouth and held still. "Yes," he huffed out, head tilted back. "Every morning, I'll wake you with my cock. Sometimes, I'll shove it into your warm and waiting pussy, soaking your cunt in my cum and making you walk around with a little piece of me in your womb. After you're too pregnant to take me, though, that's when I'll use your mouth. Every. Single. Fucking. Morning." His words came harsh and angry, yet they somehow only made me wetter.

It was embarrassing to admit, but I could picture exactly what he was saying. Waking up with a big man like him over me, shoving his cock into my pussy at the very moment I'd wake, shuddering around him as we both came apart.

"You'll be round with my fucking child," he continued, painting the picture of *his* perfect life. "On your knees before me, completely naked so I can see it all as you part these pretty lips of yours and suck me clean. Maybe I'll make you clean my cock after each time I take you, licking your own juices and cum off of me."

That heat in my face from earlier spanned downward, moving over my bare chest as my nipples tightened. I hated that he was filling my head with his depraved fantasies. After all he'd done to me, he knew he had me trapped. I knew it too. My pathetic attempt at running away had been ill-exercised at best. We were too close to the end now, to the actual ceremony, for me to think of another way. Because of that, too, I was being closely watched. Monitored by not just my father and his men but by Gaven himself.

Otherwise, why else would he be here? Fucking my throat like a man who was confident that his claim was sealed? He was reminding me that I was a butterfly trapped in his web. I squeezed my eyes shut as his hips continued to thrust. His cock powered into my mouth, over and over again. He fucked my lips like a pussy, fast and hard until I knew that they, too, would be sore after this. A moment later, more of that salty fluid came over my tongue, filling my cheeks and slipping into my stomach. It came in spurts, shooting against the back of my throat. I choked, but he tightened his hold when I tried to shove back.

"Swallow. It," he snapped. Tears leaked from my eyes as I looked up. His expression was hard, unforgiving. "Swallow my fucking cum, Angel, like a good girl or I'll do something worse than fist your pussy. I'll fuck your ass raw and force you to walk out of this fucking shop with it dripping down your legs."

Unable to do anything else, I obeyed him, swallowing as more of that liquid filled my mouth. Once he was sure I was submitting, his harsh grip relaxed slightly. Strong fingers touched my hair, sifting through it far gentler than before, and when he finally moved back, pulling his cock from my mouth,

I found myself gasping for air, coughing, and reaching up to wipe beneath my eyes.

"If you listen to me, then this will be much easier," Gaven said as I heaved for more breath, inhaling and exhaling rapidly. "My wants are quite simple, after all. You will obey me and bend to my will, and I will treat you like the queen I expect you to become. You will be showered with gifts and given everything your little heart desires."

"*My heart desires freedom*," I hissed back, coughing still.

"Everything but that, then," he amended.

I glared up at him as I tried to catch my breath. Gaven met my gaze as he tucked himself back into his slacks and zipped up. "This doesn't have to be awful for you," he said, reaching down for me and pulling me to my feet.

I was still mostly naked before him, standing there in the vile underwear he'd forced upon me with the weight of the bullet he had complete control over, buried right next to my clit as a constant reminder.

"The relationship you have with your father is far different from most other women in your position," he says, cupping my cheek. "You love him, and he you. I can see that."

I stiffened at his words but merely glared back at him without a verbal response. *What would be the point?*

"Think of it, Angel," he urged. "You have the

opportunity to give a very powerful man something he's always dreamed of."

I scoffed. "You being that powerful man?"

"Yes," he said honestly. "Imagine how grateful I would be to the woman who made me a king and gave me an heir."

"You aren't acting fucking grateful," I snapped.

He arched a brow. "That's because you're fighting me," he replied. Gaven leaned forward and delivered a light kiss to my cold, uncooperative lips. I held perfectly still, waiting for the moment to end, but he wasn't done. Not yet. "Remember, love," he whispered against my mouth, "you give me what I want, and perhaps, I'll allow you to taste that freedom you crave so badly—with conditions, of course."

When he pulled away, I stared back at him, full of confusion. He'd let me taste the freedom I wanted so badly? What did that mean? Did that mean, if I obeyed him, if I married him, and gave him a child … I would be allowed to leave? If I did all of that … could I?

Gaven didn't allow me more time to think about what he could mean. He stepped back and removed his body completely from mine. "Think about it," he prompted as he turned towards the door, straightened himself, and then unlocked it and walked out.

Think about it? The words repeated over and over again in my mind. *What was there to think about?* In the end, he would still always get what he wanted.

16

ANGEL

Despite Gaven's interruption at the bridal shop, we managed to select a dress. Now, several days later, I stood at the foot of my four-poster bed, staring at it. The extravagance of the gown was a stark contrast to my simple comforter as it laid flat upon it. It wasn't what I would have chosen for a supposedly 'joyous' occasion, but for this, it felt appropriate. Plus, with the row of beaded buttons at the back, I felt a minor burst of pride at how irritated Gaven might be when he had to get it off me later tonight.

My lip tucked between my teeth, I bit down hard as my gaze refused to leave the image of the soft fabric and delicate lace before me. This was it. I was about to become what I'd never wanted to be. A mafia wife was precisely what my sister wanted. It seemed like a cruel joke that I would live out her dream rather than mine. I crossed my arms.

As if I'd conjured her from my thoughts, a voice

spoke from behind me. "Are you just going to stare at it all day, or are you actually going to put it on?" Jackie's catty tone filled the room, bringing with it a fresh wave of irritation.

I'd been so focused on my thoughts that I hadn't heard her come in. Glancing over, I found her leaning against the open door frame with crossed arms and pursed lips. The tone of her words and stance wasn't lost on me; she'd always seen situations differently than me. There was always an angle to use to her advantage. No matter how convoluted or difficult, she'd make the most out of it and come out on top and this was no different.

"I'm waiting for Gertie," I explained, facing her fully. I didn't want to think about the monumental moments I'd be enduring in a few short hours.

"Of course you are," she muttered, sighing.

"Is there something you wanted?" I asked, wondering why she'd come if she had nothing to say.

"Not particularly. Just wanted to see if you had any questions. You know, about what will happen after the reception is over." A cruel smirk curled her lip. "I'm sure you know what comes after getting married, right?" Swallowing the lump in my throat, I forced myself not to rise to the bait.

"Sex, yes, I'm aware," I stated, forcing my back straight. I uncrossed my arms. "Thanks, but I'm good." Far from good, I think I knew a little too much about it at this point. I pressed my thighs together at the memory of that night in the hotel. I reached up and rubbed my throat. The bruises—which I'd been hiding since with makeup—had faded enough to not need more than a thin layer now.

"Are you ready for it? It's okay to be afraid," she murmured, sauntering forward. Her dress split open, revealing a long expanse of thigh. She pursed her lips and smirked at me, the red lipstick making her lips look thin. "A man like Gaven whose tastes I'm sure are more … violent than you're expecting."

She had no fucking idea. A shiver worked down my spine, but I refused to acknowledge it. I'd seen more than a hint of Gaven's tastes, but she didn't need to know that.

"I figured," I told her. "I'll do what needs to be done." I wanted it to be a lie, but I knew it would happen whether I wanted it or not. I was still angry about what Gaven had done—both in the hotel and in the dressing room. He was quickly filling up my thoughts, day in and day out. He was vicious and, yes, he was violent. What was worse, though—more so than anything he'd done to me—is what I had to admit to myself. A small, dark part of me *liked* it. I couldn't deny the power that Gaven seemed to wield over my own body. The speed with which he'd made me come on his fingers that first night, our first date, and then the night in the hotel when he'd punished me for running away by making me come around his fist as he stood over me and showed me just how dominant he could be. It was impossible to refute the influence he had on me. While I couldn't stop the strange desires building toward Gaven Belmonte, I could pretend that piece of me didn't exist. For now, at least.

Chuckling, Jackie started to circle me, and my focus pulled from my internal crisis to her. "Really? Precious little Evangeline Price is going to satisfy the needs of a violent hitman?" When I didn't answer, she continued to prod me. "He's not going to be nice or gentle. I've seen the two of you together, the way you react to him. How he watches you like an animal prepped for slaughter. Any hint of sweetness or tenderness? Ha!" She waved a dismissive hand in front of my face. "This may be your first time, but it's not about you, *little sister.* This is solely for him, and if I'm going to be quite frank"—*as if she would be anything else,* I thought—"he's going to *destroy* you. Rip that virginity of yours to shreds right before he takes you apart. Mind, body, and soul." She finished with a shrug and a "That's just what men do."

I didn't say a damn word. She had no idea that Gaven had already done all of that and more. He *had* ripped my virginity to shreds. Pulled the safe and protected insides of my mind apart, and now he had me questioning everything I'd ever wanted.

Stopping before me, Jackie stared at me. Her expression was cold. She cocked a brow. If she expected me to respond with fear, she was going to be sorely disappointed. I was beyond fear. Anything I could've kept from Gaven was already taken, gone. But she was doing what she always did; trying to get into my head and make me second guess.

Normally, I fell for it. Every. Time. But not this time. I steeled myself, shoving the doubt away. *She won't get the pleasure of watching me spiral from her words,* I vowed.

"I know what to expect," I told her.

Her brows arched. "Oh, so you're ready to give up on your dreams then? No more college for you? After your sad little runaway adventure, which you couldn't even manage, you're just going to roll over and spread your legs?"

"I didn't say I was giving up on my dreams," I snapped, crossing my arms once more.

This time she didn't chuckle or smirk; she fully laughed in my face. Grinding my teeth, I continued to stare at her instead of looking away. We'd always been at odds, two sides of the Price Family coin, but after everything I'd dealt with that week, I wouldn't let her undercut me. Not without pushback.

"Your naiveté is astounding," she scoffed. "Don't you get it? Unless you leave this life behind. The family. Gaven. *Everything.* There is no future for you, not in the way you want. You're a simple broodmare that father offered up to someone he thinks is worthy of taking over his position." There was hatred in her voice, her expression twisting into anger before smoothing out once more. I didn't need to ask to know that she was bitter that he hadn't offered it to her. As much as our father's misogynistic views hurt me; they also hurt her. "You need to get that through that pretty little head of yours before you end up with a bullet in it."

My fists tightened, hidden beneath my crossed arms, and I had to blink back the burn in my eyes at her harsh words. I hated it, but she was right, there was no going back after today. Still, I latched tight to my dreams, and no one—not even her, our father, or Gaven—would take them away. *I could be a boss's wife and still have freedom,* I told myself.

Gaven had told me to think about it, and I had. If I gave him something he wanted, he would give me something I wanted. Perhaps, I couldn't be one hundred percent free, but that didn't mean I had to be wholly chained down and miserable.

"Aww, precious princess, don't cry," Jackie cooed, patting me on the shoulder.

I shrugged her off. "I'm not fucking crying," I growled.

She merely blinked at me, feigning innocence. "I'm sure you'll have plenty of opportunities to spend time away from the family. Perhaps after you've popped out a few heirs, Gaven will release you from your chains and let you go to a spa or something." There was no hiding the mocking tone in her voice, and I refused to rise to the bait again, glaring at her as she leaned forward. "Have a good afternoon, Angel," she whispered. "It'll be the last one you have for a while, I guess. You'll be too sore after your wedding to enjoy much of anything, I'm sure. And afterwards…" She drifted off with a faraway look in her eyes. "Well, I suspect you'll be on your back for a while. Enjoy the dick. Hopefully, he's not a selfish man. Most are."

With that, she spun on her heel and strutted out, Gertie stumbling out of the way as she swept through the door.

"My, my, someone sure is in a hurry," Gertie muttered, eyeing down the hallway where Jackie had stalked off. There was a moment of silence, and then Gertie turned back to me, a bright smile plastered into place. "Suppose she's going to prepare for the wedding herself. Are you ready to get into your dress, Miss?"

I wasn't. Not by a long shot, but there was no fighting back now. So, instead of voicing the truth, I merely nodded. Whatever worry and doubt my sister had attempted to weave over me was shoved into the recesses of my mind. I stepped towards the bed and Gertie shut and locked the door as I began to undress. She helped me into the gown, both of us moving and working in silence. As kind as she was, she was even more powerless than I over my fate.

"You look beautiful, Miss," Gertie said as we finished buttoning up the back and arranging the dress into place.

I stared at myself in the floor-length, tri-fold mirror in the corner of my bedroom. It showed all sides of the wedding dress save for the back. I took a shaky breath and gave her a tight smile. "Thank you, Gertie."

"You make a stunning bride," she gushed.

Normally, I wouldn't think anything of her compliments—I was so used to hearing them from her sweet lips—but right now, I had to admit she was right. This dress. The makeup she'd put on me accented my skin tone well. It made my eyes look bigger, rounder. My lashes were longer and darker. My hair had been curled into the waves Gertie seemed to prefer and pulled away from my face, arranged so that the veil could fit at the back of my head. The entire look—the makeup, the dress, the veil, and the jewelry—turned me from merely adequate to extraordinary.

And last, but certainly not least, the necklace that Gaven had originally gifted me sat at the base of my throat flush against my skin. Reminding me physically, with its glittering jewels and weight, that my body was about to become owned by him. I turned slightly, the skirts clinging to my legs swished with the movement.

"Gertie," I said, throat growing tighter the longer I stared at myself in the mirror, "can you give me a few moments alone?"

The older woman tilted her head back, her all too-knowing gray eyes likely recognizing the riot in my mind. She nodded and then quietly left the room. As soon as the door shut behind her, I stepped off the dais that had been placed in front of the mirror and turned away from it. My chest felt tight.

As strong as I'd tried to be, it was this moment—the dress and Jackie's fucking words—that were finally getting to me.

My gaze fell to the table that had been set up to display all of the useless items brides needed for a wedding day, something old and new, borrowed and blue. My lips thinned as I eyed each object before, finally, I glanced down at the ring on my finger. It'd been delivered by a man I hadn't recognized not long after the dress shop trip. A single gold band with a cluttering of diamonds that glittered every time I moved my fingers. It was gorgeous. It was ostentatious. It made the rock sitting at the bottom of my stomach feel that much heavier.

"What the hell am I doing?" I asked myself, pressing the back of my hand to my forehead. My skin was clammy.

"That's what I'm wondering." The familiar baritone was so sudden and startling that it nearly made me trip over my own skirts as I whirled around too fast to face the man who'd—once again—snuck up on me.

Gertie had evidently not locked the door when she'd left, and I hadn't heard him come in. Gaven stood there, just inside my bedroom door, his hands in the pockets of his black suit. Far be it for him to dress for a wedding. He looked like he was dressed for a funeral. Black shirt, black jacket, black slacks, even a black tie. It was always the same with him. I wondered if there was even a single spec of color in his closet. Still, he was handsome. Entrancing. I couldn't pull my eyes away from him. My breathing sped up. Steel blue eyes moved down my body, examining, analyzing, heating.

"What are you doing in here?" I asked. "You're not supposed to see me before the wedding."

"It's in an hour," he said with a shrug. "And I'm not one for waiting. What are you doing?"

My hands found the skirts at my upper thighs, my fingers digging into the fabric. "Getting ready." It felt like the lamest thing in the world to say, but that's what I was doing, wasn't it? Preparing myself to marry the cruelest man I'd ever met, and the most frustrating.

"Are you admiring your dress?" he asked.

I frowned at him before I shrugged. "I suppose."

"Yeah?" He arched a brow. "Usually, when one admires something, they have to be looking at it. Why aren't you looking at yourself, darling?" Heat rose to my face, and I had no response to that. He pushed away from the door and approached. "Well?" he prompted when I still hadn't answered him. The closer he came, the faster my heart beat until I swore it would leap right out of my chest.

I moved away, but he came forward. It was as if we had this constant push and pull between us. Whenever I would pull away, he would push forward. Whenever I'd push back … well, sometimes, I wondered if he actually liked that. It wasn't until the backs of my legs met the table that I realized he'd been steadily directing me. By then, though, it was too late.

Gaven's arms came down on either side of me, and he leaned in close enough that the scent of whatever cologne he'd chosen for today's special event was all that I could smell. It was something spicy and it enticed me. I hated that.

"Are you having second thoughts, Angel?" he taunted. "Are you wanting to run away again? You remember what happened the last time, don't you?"

"You're not doing that to me again," I replied tersely. Both he and my father had made it all too clear that regardless of my wishes, this wedding would come to pass. There was no way out.

He chuckled, the sound reverberating through his chest and into mine. "You act as though you hated it," he said, leaning closer. "I distinctly remember your wet cunt gripping me so tight, not wanting to let my hand go. I remember your body rolling against me, your hips thrusting onto my fingers and fist as you came apart."

Why is he always trying to humiliate me? I wondered. It was as if he got off on the degrading words that came out of his lips. *No,* I corrected mentally. *He is getting off on them and more so on what they do to me.*

Gaven dipped his head as one of his hands came up and swept my hair back. My pulse throbbed in my veins as he leaned down even further, pressing a chaste kiss to my throat. Right where he'd tied a fucking noose around my neck. I parted my lips to speak, except the hard bite of his teeth shocked me mute as they sank into my skin. I gasped, and without thinking, my hands went to the waistband of his pants, gripping onto him there but not quite pushing him back.

The sharp pain of his bite slipped through my senses and traveled downward, lighting a fire within me as the place between my legs softened.

"Gaven..." I whispered, both a plea and a refusal. I wanted him to release me almost as much as I wanted him to give me more of those sensations. My brain lit up with the pain as it morphed and shifted, changing into a distinctly wicked kind of pleasure.

"You have no clue what I'm going to do to you tonight, do you, Angel?" he said, but even as he asked the question, he kept going, pressing himself more firmly against me so that even through the copious fabrics of my dress and his pants, I could feel how hard he was. The thick length of him throbbing against me. "I'm going to mold you, sweetheart. I'm going to teach you exactly how to please a man like me, and I promise you that you're going to like it. You'll like everything I give you and ask for more. You'll beg for it, and as it's your duty to submit to me, it'll be mine to give you all that pleasure and maybe just a little bit of pain."

I pulled my head away and glared at him. "It's always more than a little bit of pain with you," I reminded him.

Gaven grinned and twisted his head as his gaze roved over me. Sweat popped up along my spine. "You like the pain I give you, sweetheart," he replied.

I didn't say a thing in response. I knew any denial would be a lie, and fuck him, but so did he. I licked my lips and moved my head back so I could look into his perfect, devious, blue eyes. Reckless. He made me want to be so fucking reckless. "You said that if I gave you what you wanted, you might give me something I wanted," I reminded him instead, lifting my hand to his chest. His body tightened against mine and a flare of something wicked entered his eyes. "Is that still true?"

"Yes." His answer was quick.

"What do you want now, Gaven?" I asked.

He hadn't been planning to do anything to me now, I realized, but my words changed something inside of him. My readiness, my willingness, had shown him that I was contemplating something dangerous, a place at his side. I wanted to know what it would be like if maybe I actually stopped fighting him and instead joined him. Waiting for several more hours to find out seemed like a hellish pursuit.

"Oh, Angel." The sound of my name rumbled in his chest. "You're going to wish you hadn't asked me that."

"Are you going to hurt me?" I challenged him. "*Make* me like it?

He smiled. "Yes," he admitted. "I'm going to rip you open and get myself inside of you, sweetheart. I'm going to tie you down and fuck you until you can't breathe."

"You've already done that." My voice was already breathless, as if all the air had been stolen from my lungs.

Gaven moved even harder against me, thrusting his already hard cock against my belly as I stared up at him in my white wedding dress. "I'm going to do more," he promised. "I'm going to shove my cock so far between those pretty lips of yours that all you'll know is the taste of me. I'm going to fall asleep tonight with my cock in your pussy, wake up, fuck you again, and then do it all over the next night."

"What happens if I let you this time?" I prompted. "What if I were to stop resisting? What will you do if I become the queen you're looking for?" Will it be better for me in the long run to just give in? To use him and let him use me?

Ice-blue eyes locked onto my face. "I'll make it worth your while."

"How?" I demanded.

A finger touched the side of my face, the slight touch gentle and so damn contradictory to the pain he'd given me before. "Our relationship doesn't have to be one where you get nothing but protection," he said. "We can both get something out of this."

"Why tell me this now?" I asked. "You're going to get what you want regardless; you've made that clear." Could I trust him? Could I trust the words of a monster?

"You're right," he said, nodding. "After today, you will officially belong to me."

"A pawn in your blood games," I murmured thoughtfully.

It was curious that Jackie wanted that so damn bad. Why? Because she liked being a beautiful woman on the arm of a powerful man? I shook my head, accidentally removing his finger from my face.

His hand came back quick enough, though, and he tipped my chin up again so our eyes were locked together. Gaven's expression was thoughtful, considering, as his steel blue gaze roved my face. His brows pinched together, creating a v.

"I've never owned anything I couldn't bear to let go," he finally said after a moment. "When you grow up with nothing, you learn not to get attached."

"You grew up with nothing?" I repeated his words, curious at the hint he revealed of the man behind the mask.

Gaven chuckled, but the sound was dry. "I grew up hopping from one shithole to another, Angel," he replied. "Meth labs, crack houses, you name it. I've lived in it. Crime is a way of life for men like me. It's the easiest path to take. I've built myself up good and well from the things I've done. I don't regret any of it."

"There's never been anyone you've killed that you later wished you hadn't?" I frowned. Did that mean he didn't have emotions? No, that wasn't right. He obviously did. I'd seen him intrigued, angry, and even curious. Gaven Belmonte might not have acted like the average man, but he still had emotions—no matter how deeply buried.

"I've never looked back," he answered. "The people I've killed, I forgot as soon as the job was done. Just as I try not to think about my past, I don't want you to think about yours."

"Then what do I think about?"

"Your future." My skin tingled as he stared down at me. "Evangeline Price," he said, his lips forming my full name. "If you give me what I want, then I swear to you there will be no regrets. But you should be warned—once you're mine, there will be no going back, and there's nowhere you'll be able to run that I won't come hunting for you."

Perhaps it was curiosity—Gaven's words, the small tidbits of information about him slowly revealing the insides of a profoundly secretive man —or perhaps it was reckless hope. Whatever the case, I doubted there was a way to stop my fate now. So, I nodded. Silently, I agreed to his proposal. He would use me, but I would use him too. Two players in a fucked up game of chess, both needing the other and hating them too. I only hoped that the game would end with both of us alive.

17

GAVEN

Stronger women have bowed to me. More fierce women. Women who wouldn't hesitate to put a bullet between my eyes. This one, though, this one is different. In a few short hours, Evangeline Price would become my wife.

Her big, hazel eyes gazed up at me. She looked like her namesake—an angel waiting to be defiled, an angel ready and willing to take that leap into the dark abyss of hell if it meant she got what she wanted. I liked that about her. It made her predictable.

The more and more I got to know her, though, the more she surprised me. I'd chosen her because I thought she would be the easiest to control and over the past few weeks, I realized that my initial impression of her had been wrong. It was rare for me to admit a mistake.

Now, it was too late.

She intrigued me too much, and who would

want a wife that cowered before him anyway? Certainly not me. I'd seen far too many bow their heads, either in defeat or in false loyalty. I want to see her bow hers in true submission. I had come to crave that sight. To see her bare before me, not because I forced her to be there, but because she *wanted* to be. If she never wanted to be, well … I'd take what I could get, even if I couldn't have what I wanted.

"I can never tell, Gaven," when Angel spoke my name, it made my insides twist—like vile snakes slithering over one another, excitement boiling beneath their scales, "whether or not you're threatening me or propositioning me."

A smirk rose to my lips. "Both," I informed her, moving closer. "Always both, love."

Her breath hitched as my cock pressed against her. Her eyes widened and her nostrils flared. All telltale signs of a woman tempted. Good. I wanted her to feel that. Hungry. Curious.

Where I was drenched in blood, no matter how unseen, she was as different from me as a person could get. It was laughable that I was thinking of tying her to me for the rest of her life. Marking her as mine. But I wasn't just *thinking* about it; I was going to make it happen.

The quiet perfection in the photograph Raffaello had shown me when he'd made his initial proposal had been fleeting. The reality was something else altogether. I was becoming obsessed with my soon-to-be wife. Every fragile, breakable inch of her. I wanted to shatter her into a million pieces and then put her back together and pour gold between the cracks. I wanted to see if I'd even be capable of breaking her. So far, she'd proven to be far more durable than I'd ever anticipated.

Angel's lashes fluttered, and with a movement that was absent of any intention, her tongue swiped out. Her teeth immediately followed, digging down into the fullness of her bottom lip. It was that look, that one small movement, that sealed her fate.

"You—" She didn't get another word out. My hands dug into the backs of her thighs and lifted her, cutting off whatever she might have said in an instant as she gasped in shock.

Those hazel eyes shot to mine, and she yelped as I deposited her ass on the table at her back. One quick swipe of my arm sent all the little items that had been displayed there skittering to the floor. Pushing her legs apart, I reached down and began lifting the folds of her dress.

It took a moment for her to realize what I was doing. Once she did, though, she didn't disappoint. "Gaven!" Shock and fury flooded her face as she gripped her dress and tried to shove it back down; her little movements of resistance made my smile widen even more. "Stop it," she hissed.

"No." I wanted her fury. I wanted to see her innocence bleed away into something new. I wanted to shred her to pieces and remake her into my perfect queen. I meant every word when I told her I wanted to fill her stomach with my seed and watch her grow round with my child. I wanted so much more than that too. I wanted to tie her up and fill her to the brim with my cum. I wanted to see her choke on it, her eyes begging me for relief. Relief I had no intention of giving.

Soon she would realize that everything I wanted was something she would crave. I would peel back the petals of her innocence, ripping them to pieces so they couldn't be put back together. Then and only then would she finally reveal her deepest, darkest desires to me. Already, I could see the change overcoming her as my fingers brushed her inner thighs, while I shoved her skirts up her hips, and her body swayed towards me.

"Spread your fucking legs, Angel," I growled.

She glared at me and pressed her knees together in response, forcing me to grip them and shove them farther apart. She winced as I spread her open impossibly wide, my hands gripping her under her knees. I pushed up, the crinkling of the soft and delicate fabric of her dress crunching under the movements.

"You're going to ruin the dress," she snapped. "Everyone will know."

"Does that embarrass you?" I mused aloud.

Bright pink touched her cheeks. "Yes," she hissed back.

"Good." More, I pushed her legs until she was entirely on her back on the table, nearly folded in half. "Hold your legs."

Angel shook her head back and forth. "We shouldn't be doing this," she replied.

"Who gives a shit what we should be doing?" I couldn't help the growl in my voice. My cock was pounding in my slacks and her delicate little pussy was so close. I was close to losing my control, something even rarer than a woman who intrigued me the way she did. "I do whatever I fucking want," I informed her as I shoved her legs even farther apart despite her half-hearted resistance.

My fingers left the white stockings she had on underneath her gown and moved upward until I touched silky flesh. A groan bubbled up my throat as her gaze darted to mine. There was a flush on her beautiful face. It trickled down from her cheeks and spread across the skin of her upper chest that was rising and falling, pressing her breasts up and nearly spilling them out of the heart-shaped neckline of her dress.

"I can fucking smell you, Angel," I whispered, relishing in the spark of humiliation that lit up her gaze as it bounced down to my face and then away as if she could hide it if she didn't look at me. Stepping closer, I moved my hips between hers, keeping her legs pressed open.

Panting, she glanced up at me from beneath her lashes. "Why are you doing this?" she asked.

I hooked my fingers in the thin lace of her underwear and pulled the tiny white thong up her thighs until they were hooked at her knees. She looked like a feast spread open before me, surrounded by all this innocent white lace, her pussy on display.

"Because..." My eyes were locked on her flesh. "I can, Angel." I grabbed the fabric of her skirts and shoved it up further, leaving her with the several thousand dollar gown bunched around her middle.

Her breasts were still bound within the bodice, and as much as I wanted to free them—to bite and lick at what I was sure were tight, pointed little nipples—her pussy was my goal. I slid two fingers between her bare folds, and when they came away, the truth of her feelings became clear. Shoving my hand in front of her face, I held my sticky fingers before her, the evidence of her arousal on display.

"Someone's not a very honest little girl, is she?" I taunted her.

A faint growl escaped her as she glared back at me. "If you're going to fuck me, then just do it, Gaven. Don't torment me like this."

"Oh, but that's what I love, sweetheart," I replied. "I love tormenting you. Making you question … will he fuck me? Will he put his fist back inside of me?" Her whole body went rigid at that last comment and I chuckled.

"Don't worry, love," I assured her. "I have no intention of making you walk down the aisle after having taken my fist in your pussy again."

"I don't trust you," she shot back.

I returned my fingers to her cunt, sliding through her folds once more before pushing them into her entrance and feeling her tighten around me. "I don't care if you don't trust me," I said.

Her eyelids slid shut, but that wouldn't do. I withdrew from her pussy and reached up, tweaking her clit between my thumb and forefinger. A delicate squeak escaped her mouth, and her eyes shot back open.

"Keep your eyes open and on me," I ordered.

Angel bucked against the strength of my fingers as I shoved them back inside. She whimpered, the sound going straight to my cock. "Gaven," she whispered. "Please—just let me go. People are waiting..."

I lightened my touch, but only by a little. It was enough for her to breathe a sigh of relief and relax in my arms. "Do you want something else, darling?"

Her lips parted, but she shook her head as I withdrew and added a third finger to her cunt, stretching her apart as I thrust into her. She bit down on her lower lip as her thighs became drenched in her own juices. Such a little fighter.

"I'm not going to stop until you tell me," I warned her. "Tell me what you want."

Angel undulated on the table, her hips arching into my hand and her pussy squeezing against my fingers as I stretched her hole. It would feel so fucking good to fuck her. To shove my cock between these folds of hers and unload into her depths as she scratched at me and cried out when her own body shook in the throes of release.

With my thumb, I brushed against the little nub

at the top of her sex. Angel's back arched, and she cried out in shock.

"Answer me," I demanded.

"I don't know what you want from me!" she said quickly.

"You don't know?" I moved to one knee, shoving the dress farther up as I bent before her and took a good long look at my future wife's pussy. "I think you do. I think you want me to put my mouth on you." I blew gently across her sex. It was so wet it was glistening. I could feel her muscles contract around my fingers as I said that. "Tell me you want me to fuck you with my tongue, I," I said. "Tell me you want to come all over my face and then walk out there—in front of dozens of others and let me put my ring on your finger with the reminder that my tongue was in your cunt not but a few minutes before our wedding."

I looked up just in time to see her head turn back and forth as she gasped and panted, the movements making her breasts shudder beneath the dress. Soon, I'd clamp them again, attach weights that would jerk and pull each time I fucked her. Her little noises weren't good enough. I needed a verbal answer from her. I knew I would push her to her limits, possibly a little further, as I molded her. But hearing those words would make it *perfect*. To hear her want it, no, *need* it. That was what I ultimately craved. With a scowl, I shoved my fingers forward again, pushing them inside the tightest fucking pussy

I'd ever touched, and hooked them just behind her pubic bone.

"Answer. Me." I gritted the words out.

Tears sparkled in her eyes as she looked down at me. I didn't care. No, that wasn't quite right. I *did* care —I liked putting those tears there. I wanted to see more of them—on her face, on her cheeks, dripping black mascara all over those perfect features of hers.

"Say it," I growled.

"Please, Gaven," she whispered. "Please … I don't … I need…"

"What do you need?" I asked, pressing my thumb over her clit and slowly starting to rub it. I wanted to give her everything she needed. All she had to do in return was give me her life and soul.

A shiver danced down her spine. Her whole body reacted to what I was doing to her, but I wasn't nearly done. I wanted more. So much fucking more. I wanted to wreck her—my perfect, unsoiled dove.

I wasn't sure how much longer I could hold out on keeping myself from taking her right then and there. But she saved me from breaking down. When she sucked in her next breath, Angel's hands reached down, one grabbing the lapel of my suit coat as the other clutched at her skirts to keep them up. It forced me to meet her gaze.

"Yes," she panted. "I need something, *anything*. I want your mouth. I want your tongue in my pussy. *Do it…*"

That, I thought, *would have to do*. "As my bride

commands," I muttered as I jerked away from her hold and quickly pulled my fingers from her pussy. I pushed her legs up and out and settled each of her feet on the edge of the table. Leaning forward, I blew another soft breath across the wetness of her juicy, dripping cunt right before I dipped my head and tongued her opening.

I kissed the slick skin, lapping at her as a shudder rolled through her body. One delicate hand moved to my head, fingernails scraping against my scalp as I drifted up and sucked her rosy clit between my lips. She gasped and bucked against my face, her hand turning rigid as she trembled at my touch.

Licking. Sucking. Kissing. I drove her up the precipice of an orgasm only to slowly let her fall back down. It was a heady thing, having Evangeline Price under my control, under my sexual tutelage. Only when a knock sounded on the other side of the door did I finally pry my mouth from her sweet pussy.

"Sir? Miss?" a feminine voice called from the other side of the wood. "The guests are waiting…"

Angel's body stiffened, only this time, it wasn't due to pleasure. Fuck—that servant was destroying everything I'd hoped to build. If it hadn't been for Angel's open, sopping wet pussy before me, I might have removed the gun from the back of my pants and opened the door to kill whoever was on the other side.

"Gaven…" My bride's voice was accompanied by the gyration of her hips against my chin and lips.

I blinked, shocked, and diverted my gaze from the door to her. I was sure she'd ask me to stop, but instead, she bit her lip and then gently pressed my head down more.

I reached back and grabbed her hand. She would have to learn that her pleasure couldn't be sought, only given, and only by me. "Keep your eyes on me," I growled.

She nodded sharply, inhaling as I lowered my face back to her cunt and then pressed three fingers to her entrance as I took her clit between my teeth. Her pussy squeezed around me as her mouth popped open. Her skin heated and her body moved to my unspoken commands.

I didn't care who was fucking waiting. Her father. The wedding party. Hell, the entire Price Syndicate could be on the other side of that door, and I wouldn't give a single shit. What I was focused on was the way her tight cunt wrapped around my fingers and squeezed as I pumped them inside of her, feeling the way she pulsated against my skin. A groan worked up my chest. Hunger. Desire. Need. From not just her, but me as well.

I fucked her with my fingers, pulling them out and shoving them back in harder than necessary, yet she didn't seem to mind. No, instead, she responded beautifully. Quiet moans left her lips and rose to my ears. I was greedy for them, loved them, and I wanted more. Without a second thought, I dove for her pussy and locked my lips around her clit, flicking it with my tongue in a way that had her back arching off of the table and her lips parting on a muffled scream.

I sucked, licked, and nibbled at the little bundle of nerves until her thighs were quaking on either side of my head and her hands were tightening in my hair. Her breathy moans grew louder as she reached the final peak of the orgasm I'd been denying her since we started.

"Ah!"

Before she was done, I rose up and gripped her, slamming my mouth over hers. My tongue was soaked with the juice from her pussy and I didn't hesitate to push it forward, letting her taste her own desire for me. She didn't balk. Instead, she opened to me and sucked her own essence into her mouth. My cock practically *pounded* against the inside of my pants. Nevertheless, I needed to stop. I needed control—something that was in limited supply when it came to her.

It took everything I had to pull away from her. "Enough," I said, practically panting. I reached for her dress and began righting it—pulling her tiny white thong back into place and her skirts down. "It's time."

She gaped at me, a little shaken and stunned as I helped her adjust herself. *This is it. My last look at her before she officially becomes mine.* Her skin was flushed. Her eyes were glassy and unfocused in the wake of the orgasm I just forced upon her.

What a fucking glorious sight it was.

18

ANGEL

My heart pounded in my chest, my body trembling as I was ushered into one of the parlor rooms on the bottom floor of my family's estate, where my father was waiting. Electricity hummed in my veins. Every nerve ending in my body had been awakened by Gaven's sinful, dominating touch.

Why the hell had I let him do that? Why had I responded? The answer to my questions evaded me, making my head feel murky and my confusion more pronounced.

I'd fought him at first, resisted, but once it became clear that he wouldn't stop, I'd … just accepted it. His mouth was positively wicked and I had a feeling that he would easily control me and make me come again and again with that damn thing.

I strode into the small space that had been prepared before the wedding to find my father there, adjusting the cuffs of his white shirt sleeves beneath his charcoal gray suit coat. The sight made me all the more aware of how soaked my panties were and how my skin burned with the memory of Gaven's touch and tongue. I only hoped he would assume that the pink on my cheeks was blush from my makeup.

"Ah, there we are, Angel. Come, let me look at you." My father smiled and held his arms out for me. Carefully, I moved toward him. "You look absolutely stunning, sweetheart."

"Thank you," I murmured, stepping into his embrace. The hug was slightly awkward. Considering that the last time he'd seen me, he'd been angry and disappointed over my attempt at running away, it made sense. As he pulled back, I gripped his arm and stopped him from retreating. "I love you. You know that, right?" I asked.

Raffaello Price was a big man, a strong man. Before my very eyes, though, his expression softened in a way I hadn't seen since my mother had been alive. He reached up, and the entirety of his hand cupped my cheek.

"My sweet child," he said. "I know you do."

"I never wanted you to be disappointed in me," I told him. "I just … felt trapped."

"This is what's best for you." His words sounded like an assurance, and for the first time, I wondered if they really were. Perhaps the idea of leaving behind the world of criminal organizations and danger was genuinely impossible. As if he could hear my inner thoughts, my father continued. "You are my daughter," he sighed, "and that means that there are many eyes on you. Eyes that you never see. Eyes that you will likely never meet. They are there, nonetheless. Gaven is a man who will protect you from those who mean to harm you."

"I—"

He shushed me with a finger over my lips before dropping his hand away. "I know you don't understand it now, but someday you will," he said. "If I could have given you the life you wanted—the normalcy you craved, I would have. I'm sorry I couldn't. All I can do now is find safety for you."

Silence descended between us, but thankfully he didn't move away. Instead, he allowed me time to collect my thoughts as I formulated my response. "Will…" I inhaled sharply as my eyes began to burn. "Will I still see you?" I asked.

My father's face scrunched in confusion. "What do you mean?"

"I mean … well, I assume that I'll have to move out—to go live with Gaven. I just…" My eyes were watering quickly and I tilted my head up to keep the tears from falling. After a moment, I lowered my head back down to meet his gaze. "I want to know if I'll still see you often." Despite everything, I would miss my father. As much as I disagreed with what he was doing and the decisions he'd made in his life—I could hate a man's job but still love the man. I still loved him.

"Of course." My father gripped my arms and

pulled my back into his wide chest. "You're not going anywhere, Angel. My child, did you think that? Is that why you were so afraid?"

I sniffed hard. "What do you mean I'm not going anywhere?" I asked.

"Gaven is moving here." My father's response shocked me enough that I pulled away from him and scanned his face for a sign of dishonesty. I found none.

"He's moving here?"

He nodded. "Gaven is going to be the next head of the Price Family," my father replied, "with my beautiful daughter at his side." He tucked a strand of hair that had fallen loose behind one of my ears and gazed at me. "You will see me as much as you want, and as much as my schedule will allow. Perhaps, you'll even be able to do some of the things you want to."

"I have to give him an heir, though," I said.

My father nodded again. "Yes, but I'm sure that won't take long. Then there will be months between your pregnancy and the baby's birth. You can do whatever you want, love. We will give you all the opportunities—so long as you remain safe within the fold."

I bit down on my lower lip as my eyes sought the floor. *Safe within the fold*—still a part of the organization. Still a mafia wife, but … maybe he was right. Maybe it would be easier after I gave Gaven what he wanted. An heir and then … freedom. The next question would be however, would I be able to leave a child behind? I doubted it. In fact, I'd shied away from the thought, but the second Gaven did impregnate me would be the moment I'd be locked to him forever, more so than by any ring or wedding.

"My sweet Evangeline," my father said, distracting me from my thoughts as he took my free hand that wasn't squeezing my bouquet tightly. "I know this isn't the life you envisioned for yourself, but this *is* the life for you. It was the world you were born into. You were meant for this."

I stood silent, waiting for him to continue. There were no words to describe the mess of emotions that snaked through me since I'd learned my fate. Betrayal, hurt, anger, curiosity, and now ... even lust.

"I don't know what I would do if anything were to happen to you because of who I am," he continued, his words lowering to a whisper. "But now I know you'll have someone to protect you after I'm gone."

A knife sliced into my heart at the grave comment, and I squeezed his hand. "Please," I begged, "let's not think like that. You'll be around for a long time."

"Long enough, maybe, to see the next generation of Price Heirs," he teased.

My heart stuttered to a stop, but I pressed the dizziness they brought forth down. "Maybe," I squeaked out.

He grinned ruefully and, for a brief moment, I could see the handsome man my mother had fallen in love with. Despite the darkness that plagued our family, what he did and who he was, he was still the man who had held me in his arms and shielded me when I was a child. I couldn't help but love him.

"All right, my Angel, we can save all other conversations for after your wedding, but I want you to know that while you may not see it now, this is what your future needs. Do you understand?"

Not even a little, I thought, but I murmured my assent, leaning in for another hug. While still in my mind, the thoughts of only a few minutes prior had quieted, my focus shifting to the music playing in the ballroom where my wedding waited to begin. With a deep, steadying breath, I hooked my fingers in the crook of my father's arm and started forward.

Doors opened to reveal the hundreds of people who now stood as the signature bridal song started to play. Elaborate white flowers hung over the ceiling in strings. I'd chosen the lilies, my mother's favorite, but other than that, I'd had very little to do with the day's preparation. The floral scent was nearly overwhelming. I didn't know where they'd managed to get so many real flowers for the occasion so quickly, but someone had obviously worked very hard to turn the room into an interior garden.

Vines and leaves were woven over the chairs that had been set up and they even lined the walkway. Candles were lit, but overhead the chandeliers provided the most light. The room was devoid of windows, and it wasn't lost on me that it was likely because the guests in this room—Gaven and my father included—were probably enemies to very powerful people who wouldn't hesitate to see them dead, even at a wedding.

All eyes turned to my father and me as we made our way down the aisle. People I didn't even know eyed me with a myriad of expressions; awe, happiness, judgment, and hate. There were more, but I couldn't pick them all apart. All of them were focused on me. I knew, vaguely, who they all were. My father's business partners, members of our family, and I was sure even a few enemies who wanted nothing more than to see a bullet in my father's back. Perhaps one of them had even attempted to kill me on the street the day that Gaven had demanded the wedding to be moved up.

Whoever they were, they were not nearly as important or as all-consuming as the man at the end of the long path I walked down. All there was, was Gaven, standing straight and tall at the end of the aisle. A wolfish smile curled his lips with each step closer I took. I was about to seal my future with the man who scared me more than I'd cared to admit, even to myself.

The closer I drew to the end, the more nerves whipped through me. Slowing to a stop, we waited for the officiant to ask my father for his permission to have me marry Gaven.

"I do," my father agreed proudly, kissing my cheek. With a final squeeze of my hand on his arm and passing off the bouquet to Gertie as she came forward and took it from me, he stepped away. Now, it was only Gaven and me. As the officiant ran through the obligatory lines, I couldn't tear my gaze away from Gaven's intense stare, and I was *very* aware of his hands holding mine.

"Please repeat after me, Mr. Belmonte," the officiant prompted.

Gaven echoed each line with confidence, the words searing into my soul. "I, Gaven Belmonte, take you, Evangeline Price, to have and to hold from this day forward, for better or for worse, for richer or poorer, in sickness and in health, to love and to cherish; from this day forward until death do us part."

I was frozen in place by the time he finished. Everything was finally coming to fruition. This wasn't some sham or a simple business deal like my father had planned. It was *real*, and I knew that as Gaven said the vow, it was binding the two of us together. No matter for how long, no matter how far apart. I would forever belong to Gaven Belmonte.

"Now for you, Evangeline." The officiant glanced at me, a reassuring smile on his weathered face, and I nodded, echoing his words each time until I got to the end.

"... from this day forward until death do us part." The words sounded weird, steady, and smooth despite the slight tremble radiating through my body.

"Then I proudly pronounce you, Gaven and Evangeline, man and wife, Mr. and Mrs. Price. You may now kiss your bride."

Gaven didn't need any more encouragement to

do so, closing the distance between us in the blink of an eye. Cupping my head with one hand and pulling me into him with the other, he ensured I was looking him in the eye for a long moment before finally pressing his lips to mine. Possessive and intense, I felt the significance of that single kiss all the way to the tips of my toes and in the deepest recesses of my heart.

I was officially Gaven's.

Until death did we part.

19

ANGEL

Cocktail hour and photographs blew by in a flurry of activity. Posing this way and that with my new husband, greeting every single one of the hundreds of guests until finally we arrived at the reception.

"Here," Gaven instructed, holding out a flute of champagne he'd snagged from a passing waiter's silver tray. "You look a bit nervous."

"Can't imagine why," I murmured behind the lip of the glass, sipping the tart, bubbly liquid. Gaven only chuckled at my response, his grip on my hand tightening slightly. I suppose it didn't matter that I wasn't twenty-one yet. It wasn't the first time Gaven had given me a drink, and I doubted it would be the last before I was technically and legally allowed to. I'd hazard a guess that most people in this room had all done far worse than underage drinking.

"Why don't we sit for a moment? I can't imagine those heels are very comfortable," he stated, eyeing the white stilettos I'd been wearing for the last few hours. Not trusting myself to speak, I let him guide me to our designated seats at the head table.

I didn't want to admit to him or myself that despite the heavy weight I felt solidified during our ceremony, I was slowly becoming accustomed to the realization that I was now married. I was now attached to another person—a murderer for all intents and purposes—for the rest of my life. For some reason, it didn't scare me as much as it had weeks ago. In fact, I could picture the future a little more clearly now.

As Gaven pulled out my chair for me, I scanned the room, taking in all of the talking, dancing, and crowd milling about. Everyone seemed to be having fun or was at least occupied, except for two. Jackie and my father stood off to the side of the room, my father's frown hard as he glared at my sister. Jackie was dressed as pristinely as always. Her dress was formfitting, the back nonexistent with a lot of skin showing. At first, I thought that might have been the reason our father was so upset. She often pushed the limits of how he expected his daughters to dress, and I was sure he was saying something about her attire which was more appropriate for a nightclub than a wedding.

Unfortunately, there was no way to know what they were actually saying, but whatever it was, I could tell my father was not happy about it. That was nothing new, but what was new was the serene expression on her face as she spoke to him. Where he grew redder and redder in the face, hers never changed.

Whatever their problem was, it wasn't mine right now. I had enough on my plate. I brushed it off. It was my wedding day, so instead of going over to smooth their argument out, I took another sip of my champagne and looked at Gaven. After a moment of examining his features, from the droop of his eyelashes to the chiseled cut of his jaw, his lips twitched and he spoke. "Staring isn't very polite, you know," he murmured, still not looking at me.

I shrugged. "You stare at me all the time, so I thought it was only fair to do the same, *husband.*"

His gaze sliced to me at that last word, and an intensity sparked in the depths of his eyes. "That mouth of yours is going to get you into trouble." Heat laced his words, but instead of shrinking back, I merely smiled and took another sip of my champagne.

"Is that so?" I challenged in a soft whisper, earning a deep guttural growl from him as he leaned into me.

We were married now, and maybe I should have still walked on eggshells for fear of what might happen, only I couldn't stop myself. Before the wedding, I had held on to a non-existent sliver of hope that it wouldn't happen. That, by some miracle, I'd be cut free from this arrangement. Nonetheless, I wasn't; I was now tied to him and my family's life of crime, and somehow, that fear of him had lessened because of the fact that his ring now sat on my finger. This was my life now, and in spite of what Jackie had advised, I couldn't let it consist of biting my tongue.

"Oh, absolutely," he whispered, "and I'm going to enjoy every moment of punishing you for it. As will you. However, as much as I would love to fold you over my lap and paint that ass red for everyone to see, now is not the time."

Fire licked my veins, wetness pooling in my core, but before he could continue, a waiter came by with another set of champagne flutes to replace our empty ones. "Of course, it isn't," I replied, forcing my tone to stop shaking. "You wouldn't want to show Raffaello Price just what you do to his daughter behind closed doors."

"You're not just his daughter anymore, Angel," Gaven replied. "You're *mine*."

A shiver skated down my spine at that, but I didn't dignify his words with a response of my own.

"So, *Mrs*. Price," Gaven said, redirecting the conversation, "tell me … what was little Evangeline Price planning to do before being married to a hitman?"

I sighed, taking a large gulp of the fresh alcohol in my hand as I settled back into my chair. "You know what my plans were," I reminded him. " I wanted to go to college. I wanted to find a life outside of all of this. I never wanted to be married —certainly not this young." I looked down at my hand, where the heavy rock that he'd slid onto my ring finger on my left hand rested. What scared me more than his hand, more than him fucking me and locking me up to get me pregnant with his precious fucking heir, was more subtle than all of that. I was afraid that he could see right into my mind, right through me.

"What would you have gone to school for?" he asked.

I blinked, shocked that he would even be curious about such a thing. "Computers," I blurted out without thinking.

"Computers?" he repeated, his tone lilting with surprise. I could feel his attention on my face, but I didn't meet it.

I shrugged. "I'm good with numbers—but computers are more interesting. Technology is advancing quickly in the world. To understand that is to understand the progress of our society."

"You speak of progress and yet were born into a family as traditional as they come." Gaven's voice sounded amused by that fact. The contradiction wasn't lost on me, either.

"Perhaps I'm most interested in progress and technology *because* I was born into a traditional family," I suggested, grinding the words out as a newfound fire overtook me.

"How unfortunate."

I gritted my teeth at those words and finally shifted my gaze to his. "Are you pitying me right now?" I demanded.

He arched one brow as he stared down at me. "Does that upset you?"

"Yes." There was no use lying. "It pisses me off."

His lips twitched again. He liked that. Upsetting me. Pissing me off. I frowned. "Why do you antagonize me so?" I asked.

Gaven's gaze continued to hold mine. "I like seeing you emotional," he admitted. "Your face grows pinker the angrier you get." His hand lifted—slow so as not to startle me—and he gently brushed a finger down my jawline. "You have such youth and fire in you. I didn't realize how much I missed that about myself."

"I'm sure you've started more than a few fires yourself," I shot back.

He laughed, the sound startling although not at all unpleasant.

I sighed and continued to lightly sip my champagne. "I don't want to hate you," I admitted.

His laughter drifted off and silence descended. "I would prefer for us to get along as well."

"Because it'll be easier for you?" I contemplated aloud.

"Yes," he answered, "because I never imagined I'd be married. Now that I am … I find that I don't want my wife to hate me."

"After everything you've done to me?" I turned to look at him. "That's surprising."

"Act all you want, Angel, but you can't lie to me and neither can your body," he replied. "You *liked* what I did to you."

A blush burned through my face, but I pretended I didn't feel it as I met his gaze and glowered. "Whether I did or not is irrelevant," I argued.

"It's very relevant," he said.

I shook my head. "You're doing it again," I muttered, looking away from him.

"Doing what?"

"Confusing me," I snapped. I tried not to sound bitter, but it was difficult.

"Do I only confuse you because you don't like letting someone else have control?" he asked after several beats.

I inhaled sharply. "Everyone has tried to control me my entire life," I said. "I'm tired of it."

"It's different with me." It wasn't a question, but a statement.

I found myself sliding my gaze back to him. He was right. It was different with him. Aside from forcing me into this marriage, he hadn't exactly attempted to control me in any other way but sexually.

I considered my words before I spoke them. "Yes," I finally said. "It is." His control was a different beast. It was enticing as much as it was frightening.

Gaven lifted his glass and downed the champagne in one go before grimacing and setting it on the table before us. "Computer science is an interesting subject," he said, switching topics so fast it left my head reeling. I frowned at him and waited. He didn't disappoint. "I like that," he said.

"You … like it?"

He nodded before fixating me with his gaze once more. "I've never wanted a dumb bride, Angel. Intelligence turns me on, and I find you to be incredibly intelligent."

My stomach coiled. "Even though I failed at running away?" I prompted. That hadn't exactly been my finest moment.

He arched a brow but nodded. "Yes, even then. You followed your gut—even if it was wrong."

I pressed my lips together. With a rapacious grin, he continued, "Don't worry, Angel. No matter how far you ran, you would always be a Price. You wouldn't have been able to escape this life even before me, but you'll find soon enough that it's exactly where you're meant to be."

It didn't escape me that those were the exact words my father had said to me before the ceremony. What the hell did they know that I didn't? Why were they so convinced that this was the life that I belonged in?

My head throbbed at the thought of trying to dissect his words and all the hidden meanings behind them. With the weight of the jeweled metal band on my finger, all I felt as I sat there next to him was confusion and … hope.

In the end, though, even if I didn't want to admit it—they were both right about one thing. There was always a price to pay for the things we had. For me, it was remaining in this world.

Once a Price, always a Price.

20

ANGEL

The party wound down until the guests eventually filed out, one by one, leaving the mansion empty once more. The only people left were my father, Gaven, myself, and Jackie. The last of whom had gone to bed long before, and now, my father was following.

"Come," Gaven said, holding out a hand as we left the reception area. "You must be tired."

I was exhausted but, at the same time, keyed up. Tonight was a night like none before, and it was my wedding night. I was not so tired that I forgot what that meant. My virginity might be gone. The memory of his fist moving inside of me as he fucked my pussy and strummed my clit made my insides clench in anticipation for tonight. As he led me up the staircase to a bedroom, one that was not my childhood room, the fluttering of my anxiety crept back into my mind.

In one of the guest suites my father kept for

friends, Gaven quietly shut the door and turned to me. In the dark, dimly lit room, his eyes scoured my body. I was flushed, as if I'd had too many glasses of champagne—champagne that I had certainly had my fair share of. I honestly could have gone for a whole new bottle at this moment too.

I had done it—I'd married Gaven Belmonte. I was now his wife. His property. I could only hope that, given time, he and I could learn to be something other than two souls fighting for dominance.

"You looked exquisite tonight." Gaven's low voice was gruff and electrifying.

I inhaled sharply. "Thank you."

He took one step forward, and I jerked my gaze up to his. Another step and another and another until he stood right before me. With the backs of my legs pressed to the four-poster bed, I felt the heat of him against my front. Goosebumps rose along the bare skin of my shoulders and neck, and my eyelids lowered until I saw nothing and only felt the way Gaven's chest brushed against mine.

"So…" I swallowed roughly. "What does this mean now?" I asked.

He chuckled. A masculine hand lifted and drifted halfway down my arm before circling to my back. "What does it mean?" he repeated my question before shaking his head. Gaven's lips touched my neck, and I gasped, tilting my head automatically as his kiss moved to the thrumming pulse of my throat once more.

"It means you're mine, Angel."

"And you?" I prompted him, pressing for more. I was curious. "Does that mean you're mine too?" It was a daring question. *What mobster would ever allow himself to be claimed?*

His fingers latched onto the first button and began to undo it. Less than halfway down, however, I could sense his mounting frustration. I found myself smiling. Maybe he was a tormentor, but I liked to give back a little torture of my own, even if it was only in small doses. "Yes," he answered, and with a grunt, he gripped the sides of the back of my dress and ripped them clean apart. I gasped. "I'm yours, wife," he continued. "I am not a man who needs outside entertainment. I can assure you that as soon as you have my heir, you will be allowed more freedom."

"What kind…" I began breathily as cool, fresh air touched my naked back. "What kind of freedom?"

"You want to go to college?" It was the carrot dangled in front of the horse.

"You'll let me?" I asked.

"I would give my Angel anything she desires," Gaven replied as his hand moved further and further down my back, parting the fabric. He didn't stop—not until the dress was gaping open and the sleeves fell over my arms. Then it slid down my body and pooled on the floor, and I was left naked save for the silky and lacy white lingerie accompanying my wedding ensemble.

"Anything I desire..." That sounded far too good to be true coming from a man like him.

"You give me what I want," Gaven replied, his eyes locked on my form, "and I will ensure you get something you want."

A breath of air puffed over my face. I slid my gaze upward. Gaven's attention was locked on my naked breasts. On the soft skin of my stomach, and then he dragged his focus lower. To the triangle of fabric between my legs.

Why the hell was I so nervous? He'd already seen me there. He had touched me there. Licked me. Shoved his fist into my pussy. Brought me to a screaming orgasm, and it was my hope that he would do it all over again before the night was done. If I was going to get anything out of this marriage, if I was going to be forced to bear his child, then the least he could do was make the act pleasurable.

When he didn't move, though, I found my hands drifting up to the buttons lining his chest. I undid the first one and moved to the second. I was halfway down the shirt when he seemed to realize what I was doing.

"Angel..." His voice was rough, as if he was struggling to speak.

"Like you said..." I swept my hands down the front of his shirt. "We're married now, and you want something from me. We might as well get to it, don't you think? Why don't you kiss me?"

"I'm going to do so much more than kiss you, darling," he said, his eyes turning hard as he reached up and jerked the bottom of his shirt out from where it was tucked into the top of his slacks. A flush rose against my skin—heat licking across every inch of me. Gaven dragged his suit coat off and then quickly pushed my hands aside to finish unbuttoning his shirt as well. The fabric parted, revealing his broad, muscled, and scarred chest.

My hands hovered over his skin. With an amused chuckle, Gaven pulled my palms toward him. "You can touch me, love," he said. "You're allowed to touch your *husband*."

My husband. The words were foreign but no less true. This was reality. This had really happened. I was eighteen, and I was married—to a man I hardly knew. To a man eighteen years my senior. Right now, that didn't seem to matter so much. Not even when he left my hands on his skin and reached beneath my wrists to unbutton the top of his slacks.

His eyes never left mine as he unzipped and freed himself, letting his pants fall to the floor to join my dress. "There are some things you should know, Angel," he said as my eyes descended to his thick length, jutting out from between his legs. I'd seen it before, of course. I'd had my lips wrapped around that monstrous cock of his. Although right now, I felt a little faint knowing it was about to go somewhere other than beyond my lips. I shouldn't have been nervous. After all, he'd already done far worse, but this felt ... different. Almost like crossing the point of no return.

"What kind of things?" I asked.

"I like my sex a little … different," he answered, capturing my wrists once more. I knew that as much. He'd already proved to me just how vile he was. This came as no shock. Gaven pushed me back onto the bed, and I gasped as I fell back onto the mattress.

"Different, how?" I demanded still, my eyes widening as he climbed over me, spreading my legs as he shoved me up the bed.

"I'm sure you've sensed it, darling," he replied. "I like control. I'm going to do things to you, Angel, that no other man has ever done to you. That no other man ever will." His lips parted as he stared at me. My nipples tightened under the heat of his gaze. "You're my wife, Angel, and as such, you'll be subject to my interests."

"What if I don't like it?" Gaven's gaze darted back to my face, and he gently pressed my hands up as he leaned over me, caging me against the bed. "You'll like it, love," he said, his words a promise. "Your body was made to enjoy what I plan to do to you. I'm going to dominate you. I'm going to spread your legs and feast on your pretty pussy as I did earlier. I'm going to devour you, suck you down, force you to bend to my will, and when I've had my fill of you at home, I'm going to take you to some clubs."

A haze descended over me. "Clubs?"

Gaven chuckled, and with how close he was, the sound reverberated through my body. My thighs tightened, my pussy pulsing at the low noise. I bit down on my lower lip to keep myself from moaning and arching up. I wanted—no, needed—his touch. I craved it. All that had happened. I'd done this—I'd given in and married him. Didn't I at least deserve some of that pleasure he'd shown me before?

When I finally looked up and met his eyes, I realized all of my new husband's attention had fallen to my mouth. "Later," he grunted. "Much … later."

His head fell, his mouth meeting mine. And just like he'd promised, Gaven Belmonte devoured me.

I could feel his hot, hard length pressed against my stomach as he arched over me, grinding down as his hands held mine in captivity. Gaven's tongue dove past my lips, slipping against mine, rubbing insistently. I shuddered under him, relishing the headiness of his kiss. I felt as though I were falling backward, just before my body would hit the ground, and I was … limitless—floating on the bed under him.

"Angel…" His mouth dragged away from mine, and I couldn't help but lean into him, needing more as his hands moved south. He stripped my thong away, leaving on the heels I'd worn to the ceremony as well as the stockings. "You're so fucking beautiful, Angel."

I gasped when he nipped the skin of my belly and spread my thighs farther apart before dipping down and licking a path through my wet pussy. A groan rumbled out of him, and my head bowed against the pillows and comforter against my spine as he sank back and lifted my legs, each one over his shoulders, pressing his lips against me in the most intimate of ways—just like he'd done earlier.

Stars danced in front of my eyes as I gasped and moaned, but just as the crest of pleasure almost overcame me, he pulled away.

"No," I groaned in disappointment, receiving an amused chuckle from him in return.

"Don't worry, dear wife," he said. "You'll get yours soon enough, but first, we need to consummate our marriage—don't you think?"

The mention of our *consummation* made me stiffen. It shouldn't have, yet it did. *This is really happening.* The thought took my already gasping breath away, but I nodded, unable to speak through my lust-filled haze.

Gaven's hand dipped down. My back arched as he delved between my folds and his fingers came away soaked. He looked from where he held up the digits, glistening in the low light coming from the window, to me. "So wet for me, love," he said, sounding smug.

I sucked in a ragged gasp of air, and before I could think of something that would have me denying the wanton desire I held for him, I nodded. "It's just a physical reaction," I muttered, embarrassed.

Folding over me, he braced himself on the bed on either side of my head. "Keep telling yourself that, Angel, and maybe someday you'll believe it."

Dizziness assailed me. I bit down on my lower

lip as his thighs and hips pushed my legs outward a little more. Goosebumps pebbled over my skin in anticipation. A moan left me as his cock slid against my slick skin, parting my folds with each pass—rubbing over my clit and back down to my entrance as he fisted himself and directed the hot, hard length of him to where I knew I wanted him to take me.

My body was tight, so tight that I thought I would shatter under him before he even pushed in, but I forced my eyes open. Gaven pressed forward, pumping his hips as he inched into me a little bit at a time. I squirmed, feeling heated. It wasn't enough. His hands gripped my hips and held me still, and then, with his eyes centered on mine, he shoved his cock in, right to the hilt.

My lips parted with a gasp as he stretched me open. I ached, but it wasn't in a bad way. No. Instead, it felt like every nerve ending within me had been lit on fire. I panted as my back smoothed out against the mattress. Everything Gaven had promised—the pain, the pleasure, the desire—was there. Inside of me. It raged out of control, and I felt nothing but a blinding need.

Why wasn't he moving? "Please," I whimpered when he still hadn't moved.

"Please what, Angel?" Gaven tilted his head to the side and gazed down at me, a smirk playing on his lips. *Oh, but he's a wicked man.* I could feel the tension in his body, his muscles rippling as he held steady. He wanted to let go, but despite the things Jackie had said he would do, he didn't take me. He didn't hurt me. He simply held completely still above me, but that, I found, was worse.

"Fuck me, please," I begged, rolling my hips as I reached up and grabbed ahold of his forearms. "Move," I said. "*Do* something."

With a deep, masculine chuckle that reverberated through his chest and against mine, he did. Gaven pulled back until he was almost entirely out of me, and then, in a fast movement, he thrust back inside. Fireworks danced behind my eyes as I squeezed them shut. My breath shuddered in and out of my chest as he began to pump in harder movements.

"Open," he growled. My eyelids shot up once more. "There you are," he said. "Keep looking at me."

I did. I found myself captured by not just his hands, but by his gaze as well. He thrust his cock into my pussy relentlessly, ruthlessly. My back arched, and I moaned as I pressed my breasts up into his chest. My hardened nipples skated against the skin of his pecs. I ground my teeth as his hands began to move downward once more.

Gaven's fingers slipped through my folds again, and my eyes widened. I could feel him—his cock driving in and out of me, brushing against the pads of his own fingers as he reached for my clit. *What the hell is he doing?* I wondered, but I didn't need to wonder for long. Before I knew it, he was latching on to that little bundle of nerves between my legs, and on the next inward thrust, he pushed in all the way to the hilt and pinched down.

I *screamed* as he groaned and released inside of me. The heat of his cum filling me up sent me over the edge. It was more terrifying than anything I'd ever experienced before. I was consumed. My body shook. My back bowed. My limbs trembled. Yet, still, when my lips parted and something coherent came out—it was his name that I screamed.

Only his name.

21

GAVEN

E vangeline Price was everything I wanted. The openness in her gaze was addictive, but even more enticing was the fact that she was finally willing to let me have my way. It'd been a fight, and one that I'd relished in. She hadn't caved under the pressure but fought back with grit. I didn't exactly enjoy the lengths that she'd gone to get away, but I'd made sure that wouldn't be a problem again. And now, I was the only choice left for her.

My ring was on her finger. My cum filled her belly. Soon, very soon, I would ensure that she would be carrying my right to rule. My heir. She was mine. The sensation of overpowering and taking such a woman was heady, addictive. She was a new type of drug, one that I would enjoy all too well in the coming months as I fucked her across every surface of this manor and then brought her into my cold, dark depraved world and led her down even more fucked up paths.

Of all the things in this world, very few had ever actually belonged to me. My sins were the only exception. This was something entirely different. She was better than everything, and I found myself filled with an almost primal emotion.

"Gaven?" Angel gazed up at me. She blinked as confusion spread over her expression. "Are you okay?"

"Better than okay," I admitted. "I'm hungry again, *wife*." Dear God, how I loved calling her that. My wife. My bride. The future mother of my children. All the power I'd been seeking was within my grasp and she was the key.

Angel's eyes filled with a heat that matched my own. As much as she'd attempted to resist me, her body had already fallen to the desires I could stoke within her. She was fiery inside, a willing participant in my debauchery. Her body was soft in all of the right places. She turned her head away, looking over her shoulder at the clock on the nightstand. Even that, I couldn't stand.

I desired to take from her all of her attention. "Don't," I commanded. "Look at me."

Soft lashes fluttered as she followed the order, turning her head my way so that her eyes were open once more on me. She was a fucking natural at taking my commands, though I had no doubt she'd balk if I said as much. She thought herself indifferent, perhaps even independent. I knew that wasn't the case. She wanted my orders. The flare of her nostrils each time I gave one and the subtle way her body leaned towards me was proof enough. It was my deepest desire to mold her to my every will and desire, to turn her into the perfect submissive.

"I want to do something new," I told her. "Are you ready for that?"

"I don't know," she replied. "It depends on what it is."

I grinned and moved back over her. Pressing her into the mattress, I hovered over her for a moment before letting my weight come down until the air in her lungs was pushed out.

"Say yes," I said. "I won't hurt you … not unless you let me."

"I don't want to be hurt." The words were such sweet little lies on her tongue.

I grinned. "Yes, you do." I inhaled her scent. "You want me to break you apart and shove my fingers into your tight little cunt. You want me to rip you open and find all of the dirty, filthy fantasies you keep inside and let those wicked things out to play."

She shook her head back and forth, a silent denial.

"Yes," I pressed. "You act innocent, but I know the truth. You can't hide it from me, *wife*." God, I loved saying that. I'd never realized how heady it was to own a woman in this way—to completely possess her, but possess her I would. "You liked it when I forced you to do those wicked things. You can stop trying to be so virtuous. With me, you can be whatever you want to be. Vile. Mischievous. Naughty. As long as you understand that the only one who will own you is me. I'm your fucking Master, Angel. Your husband. Say it."

Her lips parted and her eyes flickered as she gazed back at me. "You're my husband." Her voice trembled slightly, but the acknowledgment made my cock throb. God, I wanted to fuck her throat again. Shove my dick between her plump lips and choke her on my shaft as tears poured down her cheeks and I came straight down into her, filling her with my essence.

"Have you ever heard of safe words?" I asked, lifting my head slightly to look down at her from some distance.

A little v formed between her brows as her lips puckered. "I've heard of them, but I've never..." She trailed off, but I understood what she was saying. Of course, she'd never used them. I chuckled. "You've heard of it before, but you didn't know people actually did it?" I guessed.

She nodded. Inside, my emotions roiled and rioted. Who? Who the fuck had taught her about them? As her husband, it should have been my responsibility, and I found myself overcome by unfamiliar irritation. Jealousy, I realized. I was insanely jealous.

"How did you learn?" My voice was even. Surely she wouldn't know how angry the thought of someone touching what was mine made me feel.

She turned her gaze away. "Does it really matter?" she muttered.

That biting jealousy swarmed my insides, and

my grip on her tightened. "It matters," I growled.

She shook her head. "Just forget it."

Gripping her chin, I directed her gaze back to my face. "I will not forget it," I warned her. "I intend to soil your mind so completely that you'll be the most deviant little creature to ever live, Angel," I said honestly. " Tell me."

My captured little bird. My pretty prey. Angel's gaze wavered over my face. Her pink tongue came out to swipe across her lower lip. *Nervous?* I wondered.

"Books," she mumbled.

"Again, darling," I said, pinching her chin harder. "I didn't hear you."

Her eyes flashed with irritation and I couldn't stop the grin that spread my lips even if I wanted to. "I read books about things like that," she huffed. "There. Happy?"

"Not quite." I released her chin and tipped down. My hands trailed over her soft skin. So pliant and unblemished, I wanted to see what she'd look like with the red markings of my palm on her backside. Of raised welts across her back or with the scratches of my beard on her inner thighs. Would she tremble in despair, or would she moan in the delicious agony of release if I were to tie her down and force her to come over and over? I had a feeling I already knew. She'd love every bit of it. Which is why she was perfect for me.

"Spread your legs," I growled. "Open that pussy for me and show me what belongs to me."

A beat passed and then, with shaky hands, she reached down. I leaned back on my knees as her legs spread beneath me and she hooked her hands under her knees. Her chest was just as flushed as her face; nipples hardened into tiny little rosy points. They were practically begging for my attention.

I trailed one finger down her body—starting at her collarbone and drifting between her breasts until I stopped at her belly button and then continued towards her mound.

"I'm pleased you didn't learn of such things from another man," I admitted. There was no use in hiding that. If she was to be my wife, then she'd learn what that meant. It meant she would belong to me and no one else. "I don't mind those naughty books of yours at all. In fact, perhaps I'll buy you an entire bookstore as a wedding present."

"Gaven…" My name was both a curse and a plea on her tongue.

"Shush." Her thighs trembled as I touched the tip of my finger against her clit as it poked free of its hood. "I'll give you whatever I desire, and you'll thank me like a good girl."

When she moaned, it made me smile.

"We'll get to safe words later, Angel," I said, circling her clit as her back arched. "For now, all you need to do is tell me to stop if you feel uncomfortable, but I hope"—I paused my movements and looked up at her, meeting her eyes. They were practically pleading—"That you'll trust me enough to let me show you the other ways I'll get you to come."

Angel's breasts rose and fell with her rapid breaths.

"Do you say yes?" I asked.

Her throat worked as she swallowed. After a beat, she finally gave me my answer. "Yes, Gaven."

I closed my eyes as I relished in that singular word. *Yes*.

"Sometimes," I warned her as I reopened my eyes and continued the movements of my finger. I circled her clit slowly, and it grew redder with each pass. "I will simply order you to strip and lay back on the bed so that I may admire you. You'll part your legs for me and let me see all of you."

My finger trailed further down and I pushed into the openness of her cunt. Despite our earlier sex, her insides gripped me tight. The muscles were practically clinging to me as I thrust into her and withdrew, only to thrust back in. Her hips rolled with need. My other hand snapped up and I slapped her thigh, earning a shocked yelp from her lips.

"Don't move," I ordered. "When I wish to admire my wife, you're to let me. Don't disrupt me."

"But——" As her lips parted and that single word escaped her lips, I pulled my finger from her clit and raised my hand, bringing it down against her open pussy. The slap rang through the room and just because I could, I grabbed her thigh to keep her legs from closing automatically and brought my hand down against the sensitive flesh of her cunt once more.

A cry erupted from her and she trembled as

tears broke the surface. Her eyes turned to me in heated confusion and … yes, arousal. Just to make sure, once I delivered my punishment, I shoved two fingers into her core and relished in the soaking wet insides of her cunt.

Devious little girl. She liked me slapping her pussy. I'd already found with how she'd reacted to my fist in her cunt that she could handle at least some level of pain. She was going to be so fun to train. To fuck. To devour. Perhaps, I'd turn her into the perfect little pain slut. Just for me, she would bend and let me hurt her. Let me wreck her completely.

"You liked that," I said with a cruel smile as I fucked her with my fingers.

Her head turned back and forth in denial, blonde hair flying around her face. "No," the denial flew out of her mouth. "I didn't. It hurt."

"Pain can be just as enticing as pleasure, Angel," I said. "Shall I show you?"

Wide, teary eyes met my gaze. "What do you mean? How?"

Pulling my fingers from her cunt, I lifted them to my lips and sucked them into my mouth. Her eyes widened as her lips parted and formed a soft little 'o' of surprise. She tasted of nirvana, deliciously wicked on my tongue as I drank her juices and licked my hand clean. Once I was done, I released her thigh and moved back.

"Turn over," I ordered, "on your hands and knees."

A beat passed and then another. Finally by the third one, she was moving. *Curious little thing,* I thought with barely repressed excitement. Despite the pain and despite her automatic denial, she was interested.

Once Angel was turned over and her hands and knees planted on the bed, I got off. The mattress shifted with the loss of my weight, and when she lifted her head and turned back, I spoke. "Don't move. Keep facing the headboard. Stick your ass out more. Yes, just like that."

I found what I was looking for on the floor, but kept it from her gaze as I set it down on the end of the bed. My hands gripped the front of her thighs, reaching around the sides and using my hold, I yanked her back until she was practically at the very bottom. Too far from the headboard to grasp for it.

A gasp left her, but I ignored it in favor of running my hand up her spine, feeling the way her muscles moved—contracting and releasing—in response. My fingers met the soft blonde locks of her hair, and I gathered them in my fist, wrapping them around my hand as I pulled sharply.

Angel's back arched upward. "Don't tell me to stop," I commanded. "Not unless you really think you can't take it. I don't want to be disappointed, Angel. I want to see how strong you can be."

"What are you going to do?" she stuttered, breathlessly.

I grinned. "You'll see." I released her again and

the front of her fell back to the bed. "Now, arch your back. I want that ass all the way out."

Hesitantly, she did as commanded. I grabbed my leather belt from the end of the bed where I placed it and took a step back. For a moment, I simply stood there, admiring the trembling of her body—the uncertainty as she waited, not knowing what I was going to do to her.

Finally, after enough time had passed that her trembling had subsided slightly, I looped the leather and held the end with the buckle. The sound of metal clinking against itself reached her ears and I saw the way her head rose. Before she could turn back, however, I lifted my fist and brought the belt down hard across her asscheeks.

"Ah!" Her scream was music to my ears. Red blossomed over the pale skin of her ass. It was a fucking beautiful sight. Her hand reached back and I slapped it out of the way.

"Don't let go of the covers," I commanded.

"What—Ah!"

She didn't get a chance to finish as I brought down the next strike—hitting a little bit beneath the first. Another streak of pure perfection. Red blossomed against her pale, milky white flesh. The mark of my ownership, of the pain I gave her.

Perhaps I would've stopped, maybe I would have asked her how she was feeling, but it was all too obvious. Her pussy was fucking dripping. Wet juices glittered against her folds as they oozed from her, streaking down her inner thighs.

"Dirty little girl," I murmured appreciatively. "Your pussy is hungry, isn't it?"

Her pants were my only response.

"That's alright," I said, cupping my palm over her ass and rubbing the red welts I'd created soothingly. "I'll give you more."

When she next whimpered, I didn't shush her. No, in fact, I enjoyed the sound so much that I rewarded her with five more strikes.

Slap.

Slap.

Slap.

Slap.

Slap.

Her ass bloomed for me. More pussy juices gushed out of her wanting cunt. They slipped down the insides of her thighs as she cried with each hit. By the fifth and final one, her head was pressed into the mattress and her ass was raised up into the air— further than it had been for the first one. She swayed back and forth as she sobbed into the covers, clenching them in her fists.

I dropped the belt and cupped her ass in both hands, relishing in the heat my hits had given her flesh. "Yes," I said admirably. "What a filthy little girl you are, aren't you?" I didn't expect an answer, so I kept talking. "You loved my present, didn't you?" I stroked the soft welts as they darkened her skin to a pretty rosy color, darker than her usual blush. "You'll remember your wedding night, won't you, Angel? Yes, you will. You'll remember how you bent over and let your husband spank you. How you shoved your ass out and begged him with your body to make it hurt."

I squeezed her cheeks, earning me a moan. My cock stood at attention, practically pounding with the need to take her again, to fuck her good and long and hard, to fill her once more with my cum. Thank God, this bed was the perfect height. Testing her cunt with two fingers speared into her insides, I withdrew them quickly and wiped the remains of her arousal on my cock before I fit myself against her opening.

My head touched her entrance and I felt her jump—her body jolting as she rose back up. It was too late, though. She hadn't asked me to stop. She'd been such a good girl for me, and that meant she deserved her reward. Gripping her waist, I yanked her back hard, and in one single stroke, I seated her entirely on my cock.

"Gaven!" Her shriek reached my ears, and I delighted in the sound for the briefest of moments.

Her insides squeezed me, rippling along my cock. I could tell she was struggling not to come. Of course, she was. She'd just taken several spankings that had made her sensitive and having the suddenness of my cock inside of her was likely driving her to the brink of insanity.

"Rock back," I whispered. "Fuck yourself on my cock."

It took a moment, but after several panting seconds, she finally followed my orders just like I knew she would. "That's right … yes, just like that." I groaned when her ass pulled away and then pressed backward once more as she took me right to the hilt. "So wet for me. You're perfect, Angel. That's a good girl—keep fucking your husband. Take my cock, take it, baby girl. Squeeze my cum out and take it into your cunt."

Angel's body moved for me, and we fell into a synchronized pattern. She would pull away and just as she pushed back again, I would thrust forward. Each smack of my hips against her ass was hard and fast, the sound of our slapping skin echoing throughout the room. Back and forth, I could hear the gasps and moans of pleasure escape her.

Soft, delirious words fell from her lips. "Please … please … I want to come. Please, let me come." Yes, this was what I wanted. A strong, fiery woman pleading for me to give her what only I could. She was begging for me to give her release—not taking it for herself. Yes, she would become everything I desired.

Submissive. Hungry for more. I would teach her everything she needed to know about giving me pleasure and gaining her own. Only from me though. I was all that she would ever know, the only man who would ever bring her to these heights.

I'd dress her up in the finest clothes and give her the most expensive jewelry. She would walk alongside me through the world of crime and violence, untouched by it all. Then, at the end of each day, I would come home to her on her knees—ready and willing to serve me as I planned to serve her.

She would suck my cock and drink my cum. She would bend over and spread her cheeks open for me to take everything from her cunt to her ass. I'd fill her so full of my cum, she would feel empty without it. I'd have everything she could give and, in return, I would make her the most powerful woman in the Price Empire. She would sleep next to me each night, knowing that no one in this world could care for her the way I could. I would ensure that no one ever disrespected her. No one would ever dare again try to kill her like they had on the street.

"You want to come?" I demanded as I fucked into her, thrusting so deeply I swore I could see stars behind my eyes.

"Yes!" she screamed. "Yes! Oh God, Gaven! Please!"

"Not God, Angel," I said. "Your husband." No God could ever fuck her the way I will—the way I was.

The rippling of her orgasm began, coursing over my cock and forcing me to still. I slapped the underside of her ass as I gritted my teeth. "Fuck, yes. Come on my cock, Angel." Wetness gushed around the base of my dick. "Come all over your husband."

And she did. Angel, as perfect and serene and pure and innocent as she'd once been, came all over my cock like the filthy slut I planned to turn her into.

My personal slave. My submissive. My fucking wife.

22

ANGEL

After the high of one of the best orgasms I'd ever had in my life finally subsided, I lay back in the bed with my skin pressed to Gaven's. My husband. For the first time since this whole ordeal began, I felt some hope that all would be well. I glanced up as he breathed deeply, his chest rising with the movement. It was actually kind of surprising that he would fall asleep next to me. Maybe he felt safer here in the mansion. We had so many guards and security systems … this had always been my home, and now it would be his too.

He might just make me take every guard in our employ with me, but he had admitted that I would be allowed my freedom. I laughed silently at that. Somehow, I didn't mind as much. I'd always been alone in this world. Jackie hadn't been a comfort, and my father hadn't understood my desire to run away. Now, though … I had him.

I closed my eyes and curled into his warmth,

trying to find a lull in my mind as I hoped sleep would consume me as it had him. All the stress had drained away, but sleep eluded me no matter how long I kept my eyelids shut.

After what felt like forever, I peeked open one eye, glancing at the windows on the far side of the room. It was still dark, and a look at the clock on the wall told me it was hardly even two a.m. The wedding reception had only ended a few hours before.

I tried again to sleep, and again, my mind was a riot of things. Despite the content glow the night had left me with, the longer I lay awake while he slept, the more my doubts crept in.

Will Gaven give up his current life? I wondered. *Or will I be left each night to wonder where he is and who he's killing? Will this mean I'll be subject to more information on the dark parts of my father's business, or will I still be kept in the dark? Did I have a choice in that?*

Gaven had said he wanted me to be his Queen, but what did that mean?

A horribly cold feeling rose within me; no matter how I tried to shove it down, it wouldn't go away. Soon, it became too much, and I found myself slipping out from beneath Gaven's arm. He turned towards me in his slumber, and I hesitated for the briefest of moments. His breathing didn't change, but I got the sense that he wasn't quite asleep.

"Gaven?" His eyes opened and I found that I was right. He looked back at me, calmly waiting. I swallowed roughly. "I'll be right back," I said. "Do you want anything from the kitchen?"

He began to move. "What do you——" I knew what he would ask, but I couldn't have it. I pushed my fingers over his mouth, stopping him from speaking and also making him freeze—halfway to sitting up. Under the sheets his stomach muscles shifted, tightening as he held the position.

"Don't," I urged, half pleading. "I just need a moment. I'm just going to grab something to drink."

His cool blue eyes examined me, and slowly, as if he were a sleepy lion giving into its mate's request, he lowered himself back onto the mattress and closed his eyes. "Don't be long," he said.

I nodded before realizing he couldn't see me with his eyes closed. "Of course," I said. "Just go to sleep. I'll be right back." I repeated the words as I finished getting out of bed and moved across the room. I picked up a robe that had been left on the back of one of the chairs and put it on, tying it at the waist as I slipped out of the suite and headed down the hallway.

A drink and maybe a snack would help me sleep. It calmed my thoughts and gave me a purpose until I could stop thinking long enough to sleep.

Halfway to the staircase, a quiet crash and thud drew my attention. I paused and straightened and then turned back, frowning when, at the very end, I saw the doors to my father's office cracked open and shadows moving on the other side.

For several long seconds, I hesitated—wondering

if I should go back to the room and wake Gaven first—but a low familiar voice sounded on the other side of the wooden doors. Jackie's voice.

Ugh, are they fighting again? I wondered silently as I released a sigh and moved toward the doors.

My feet were silent on the hallway carpet. My hand went to the cracked door and pushed against it. I opened my mouth to call out but stopped dead as something wet touched my naked toes. I looked down and my eyes widened. My insides dropped out from beneath me and horror enveloped my whole body.

All of the glow from earlier dispersed, and I turned cold. *No.*

That was all I could think. *Please, God … no.*

Blood slipped beneath my toes, coating the bottoms of my feet in red. My eyes followed its path, and as much as my mind was screaming—warning me to stop, to look away—I couldn't. My father's lifeless gaze stared upward. His eyes locked open even though there was obviously no soul remaining within them. He was still in the same suit he'd worn for my wedding; only his jacket had been removed, which made the shocking pool of red on his chest that much more startling. His body was sprawled out on the floor with his head turned slightly towards the doorway—towards me—as if that was how he'd died, searching for a way out, searching for me.

His body. My mind said it, but my heart couldn't register the truth of it. Everything in me screamed to do something, *anything*, but I was frozen in place.

It wasn't until I saw a deep red pool growing around his body that it finally hit me. He was dead. Someone killed him. My worldly, powerful father was laying there, on the floor of his office, in a massive puddle of his own blood that continued to pour from the hole in the center of his chest. My heart jerked in my chest as if being electrocuted and it kickstarted me towards him.

"Dad!" I cried, falling to my knees beside him. Warm, sticky blood coated my skin as I pressed my hands to his chest, trying to stop the bleeding. It was too late. My brain knew that, but my hands still covered the hole as the blood seeped from between my fingers. "Please ... *please!*"

"Ah, if it isn't little miss perfect, rushing in to save the day." The words were cold, though the voice was familiar. Slowly, I lifted my gaze up to my sister as her shadow came over me. Whatever expression I had on my face made her sneer. In my shock, I'd forgotten she was in the room. When I looked at her, instead of finding her freaking out about our father bleeding out on the floor, she stood there nonchalantly—leaning against one of the chairs, eyeing her fingernails with disdain. In her other hand was a serrated knife. Its steel blade was coated in blood, the red liquid dripping off the tip onto the carpet. Each inaudible splash landed in slow motion in my sluggish mind.

Despite the rapid rhythm of my heart thudding in my ears, my movements felt slow, as if I was wading through molasses as I tried to piece together everything. I felt completely numb as I glanced around. My sister didn't bother to look at me, her focus completely on her perfectly manicured nails.

No emotion. No remorse. *Nothing.*

"What—"

"Don't play stupid," she cut me off with a harsh tone, finally showing some emotion. The same hatred I'd seen briefly before the wedding filled her expression, and she angled the weapon toward me. "You know very well you were always Father dearest's favorite."

"No, I'm not." *Was that why she'd done this? Out of jealousy?* "He loved us both."

Her perfectly sculpted brow arched. "No, darling sister." Her tone was mocking. "You *were* his favorite. *I* was an obligation. Not the daughter he loved, but the one he had to raise simply because I was his blood." She emphasized the past tense portion of her statement. The reminder made the blood coating my hands, and now my legs where I knelt next to my father, feel ice cold and heavy. Swallowing the lump in my throat, I looked down at his prone figure.

"No," I whispered, shaking my head slightly. "This … you couldn't…" I couldn't wrap my head around it, almost like my brain refused to believe she was capable of this. She'd always been mean-spirited to me, our relationship never being close or even good, but *she* was the perfect daughter—not me. Jackie was exactly like our father. Her entire focus was on the family and ensuring its business thrived. Just like my father wanted. "Why?" was all I could say, my single word thick with emotion. I didn't understand—I couldn't—I would never have done something like this. It made no sense that she seemed to have no regret even with our father laying here in his own blood, like some discarded card in her deck.

Instead of answering right away, though, all she did was start to laugh, the sound manic and terrifying, and I knew it would haunt me long after this horrific night was over. "Why?" she sneered, swinging the knife around with almost detached precision as she started to pace. "Because you're just the sheltered little girl, the one with absolutely *no* fucking idea what the hell this family even needs, and yet, he hands the family off to you and your *husband*. Neither of whom has done anything to deserve it."

Her voice grew angrier, harder. "I've given my entire *life* to this family. I've done horrible things for the Price name," she growled at me. "And what have *you* done? Bitched and moaned about wanting to run away to some fairytale happy ending like the spoiled princess you are. Then, when you finally had the chance—you botched it."

Each word was accompanied by a jab of the weapon as she stepped forward. With the crazed look in her eyes, I wasn't sure if she planned on using it against me. I didn't move or speak so as not to anger her further. Her pacing finally slowed and her eyes flickered down to our father with disdain before focusing on me.

"Though I have to admit, this really is just too perfect. *Way* better than I even planned." Her angry ranting melted into a sickly-sweet tone. Jackie's signature smirk appeared, and my adrenaline began pumping harder at the sight of the cunning glint in her deep brown gaze.

Fight or flight. The reflex poured through me, a warning. Did I run, or did I stay? I had no idea how to fight, which looking back, was clearly a mistake. The realization only lent credence to her hate-filled words.

"Better how?" I bit out through clenched teeth. The cold numbness and the fear that had taken hold, transformed into sickening anger. Tears pricked my eyes, but I didn't swipe at the wet tracks as they started to fall, not wanting to smear my father's blood all over my cheek. The thought made the red-hot poker in my chest twist and turn, intensifying the pain.

Jackie strode forward, and in response, I shuffled back. There was nowhere to go, though, not with where I was crouched on the office floor. Kneeling, she chuckled slightly and before I could move, she grabbed hold of my hand and lifted it forcefully. Her nails dug into my skin, holding it open as she shoved the handle of the knife into my waiting palm. No matter how hard I tried to yank my hand back, her grip never loosened, her now free hand forcing my fingers closed over the still-warm handle.

"Father's precious angel, covered in his blood," she murmured. "And now holding the murder weapon." I attempted to shove her back, but she only moved a mere centimeter. "What are you going to do, *Angel?* Stab me? Just like you did our poor father?" she taunted. "You don't have the guts to kill. Hell, I don't think you even have it in you to maim. Pathetic, really."

Enraged, I swiped the blade towards her, slicing it through the air as soon as she let go of my hand, except she was faster. Jumping up swiftly, she missed getting cut by the serrated edge but only just.

"Hmmm, maybe little Evangeline does have it in her," she mocked. "Too little, too late however."

"What the hell does that even mean?" I seethed, shoving off the floor so I could face her fully. The weight of the knife in my hand felt odd but slightly comforting in that moment.

"The family business? It belongs to *me*, not some hitman, and certainly not my insipid, weak little sister," she spat.

"Gaven will make sure—"

"Will make sure what?" she cut me off, scoffing. "I didn't do anything. You're the one who held the weapon, dear sister. All I did was find my father's poor body, not to mention I stopped you from trying to hurt me too."

Anger and betrayal swirled in my stomach, twisting my chest and heart into knots. I stood, trembling in both my rage and fear. She was going to pin this on me, force me out of her way by getting rid of our father and me all in one night. I knew Jackie never liked me, but I'd never noticed the pure vitriol in her eyes the way I did now.

"Gaven won't believe you," I hissed. My nails dug into my palms as I curled my fingers into tight fists, the urge to punch my sister in the face growing with each passing second. To make her pay for what she did to my father. To me.

She snorted. "Do you have any idea of the connections that I have? Forget the evidence. One whisper from me and it'll be spread far and wide through the criminal underground what *you* did to our father. I guess now you'll finally get what you always wanted—a way out. Now that you'll be taking the fall for murdering the head of the Price Family, you can *never* come back."

Yes, I'd wanted an out, but not like this. Not *this way*. Not with blood coating my palms and my father's body at my feet.

"Besides," she started again when I remained silent, "if you don't take the fall, then I'll ensure that Gaven does. I mean, that knife *is* actually Gaven's." She smiled as she let that little tidbit of information sink in. "He's gotten so comfortable here at the manor, but now that the big wedding is over, I'm sure he'll notice it's missing soon. Although I must admit, I had a hell of a time snatching it from him, but thankfully he was quite distracted by you." Her narrowed gaze roved over me, making her meaning clear. He'd been distracted by me.

Her words sank into my mind. She'd been smart

when she planned this. Of course, with Gaven now married into the Price Family, if our father was gone, he would be the head that much faster—with or without an heir. People would believe her. They would fall for this whole charade. She'd set it up well and she knew it. That was why she'd been so calm earlier when arguing with our father. She knew it'd all be over soon. The thought made my stomach churn.

Gaven was a hitman; killing was what he was good at. It was what he was known for. No doubt, people had tried to persuade my father to choose someone else. It was likely why they'd attempted to stop the wedding in the first place. It didn't matter that my father had planned to step aside; the moment Gaven Belmonte had become Gaven Price, the only thing standing between him and the entire Price Family Empire was my father. All the pieces fell into place, every well-played move from my sister. Even if I hadn't meant to be here, I'd fallen right into her trap.

"You saved me the work of sneaking into your room and placing your fingerprints all over the blade," Jackie said, drawing me out of my thoughts. "I do have to thank you for that." She tapped her finger to her lips in an exaggerated movement. "Do you think Father's loyal men would torture Gaven or you first? You are his wife, after all." A sparkle of triumph filled her gaze, and my face crumbled at the thought.

"Aww, don't be sad," she scoffed. "Now we both

get what we want. I get the family business, and you get to be free of it. And your newfound husband and all the horrid things I'm sure he would have done over the years are no longer your problem."

"Because you're going to kill me," I snapped, "just like you killed Dad!"

Yes, Gaven could be cruel, but at the very least he was honest about it. Jackie was a fucking snake and I hadn't seen her until it was too late.

"Don't worry," she said. Her pleasant, satisfied tone only fueled my rage. Her features were a mask of pleasure. Her eyes glittered with amusement as she looked back at me. Smug—she was so fucking smug because she'd finally found a way to get what she wanted. "I'll give you a head start to get away. We are *sisters*, after all." She flicked her fingers towards the door and began counting. "Ten … nine … eight…"

Biting down the urge to throw up, I turned and ran. I didn't stop, didn't detour, sprinting out the door to make my final move as a Price Heir. *To run.*

I knew the moment she reached the end of her countdown because a shrill, blood-curdling scream echoed throughout the house. She was a good actress, I had to give her that. Anyone who heard it would no doubt go running towards who they assumed was a victim. I bit down harder, blood filling my mouth as I sprinted.

Weak, my mind hissed. My sister could have the family business. I didn't give a shit about that. But Gaven … he was mine. He told me as much. If I ran now, then they would all assume I was the culprit. He would be safe. I couldn't even think of coming back, of proving my innocence. All I could do was flee. It was all I was good at, apparently.

I heard doors opening on the upper floors, but I slowed to a stop next to the front door as I spotted something on the hallway table. It was one of the notepads that had been included in the wedding gifts. A pen lay next to it. It was like kismet. Before I could stop myself, I paused, realizing the knife was in my hand. I dropped it onto the table next to the pad and with shaking fingers, I wrote four words.

Four words I hoped would make things better.

Tears raced down my face. I was an idiot for considering I could find happiness in this life. Those last moments of hope with him had been nothing more than a fairytale. Happily ever after was never meant to be for me.

Despite everything—my feelings, hopes, dreams, and desires—I was nothing more than a mafia princess who'd sold her soul to the devil. A devil I was now prepared to do anything to protect. What a fool I'd been.

23
GAVEN

I was used to death. I'd dealt it out enough times in my lifetime that it had ceased to affect me the same way it might an average man. This was something entirely different. I'd known the victim. I'd been his *friend*. His demise meant that the future was changing. All of my plans needed to be adjusted.

His death meant I'd missed something, and I was not a man who *missed* things.

Raffaello's blood was everywhere. It was soaked into the carpet beneath my feet in a gruesome puddle that had dried overnight. "Sir?" One of the Price guards approached me carefully.

"Have you found her yet?" I demanded as I stared down, unseeing, at the brown dried blood.

"No, sir … there was, um, a note left." My head jerked up and I spun toward the man. "It was by the front door, along with…" He didn't have to say what it was left next to. He held up a plastic bag with a bloodied knife inside. *Fuck.*

The man looked decidedly uncomfortable, but I didn't give a shit. I reached for the piece of paper in his hand and snatched it away. I prayed it was an explanation. An excuse for her disappearance wouldn't mean she wouldn't be punished, but it might, at the very least, provide some insight into the events that had taken place while I'd been asleep.

It was a short note. Nothing spectacular and nothing with a goddamn explanation. It was four simple words.

I'M SORRY, GAVEN. — ANGEL

SHE WAS SORRY? FUCKING SORRY? WHERE THE FUCK did her 'sorry' come into this clusterfuck of a morning? I threw the paper down, cursing as I turned back toward the soiled office.

"Gaven?"

I stiffened at the sound of Jackie's voice. "Not now," I snapped.

The sound of a feminine inhale reached my ears. *Fuck.* I'd nearly forgotten. Raffaello hadn't just left Angel behind when the poor bastard had been murdered sometime in the night, he'd left his other daughter as well, and now, I had no fucking clue what to do. I was an assassin, not a family man. Angel and Raffaello were both supposed to ease me into the role. Angel, with her body, to carry my seed and bear my heir. Raffaello, to guide my hand in their businesses. Now, here I was, thrown with no remorse from the fucking universe, right into the flames.

"I'm sorry to bother you," Jackie said, her voice quiet but firm, "but I've just been informed that forensics on the weapon came back."

My body jolted and I turned to face her. She looked pointedly at the bag the guard was holding. They'd already taken it to forensics and brought it back? That seemed highly suspicious. I narrowed my eyes on her.

"They came to you?" I demanded. I'd told those bastards that I was the head of the Price Family now. They were meant to come to *me*, not her.

She nodded. Despite the ordeal of the morning, the death of her father, and the grief I figured she must be feeling, Jacquelina Price remained impassive. Or professional might have been the better term. Dressed in a pair of Louboutin heels, a black pencil skirt, and a charcoal blouse—she looked ready to attend an important business meeting *and* a funeral. I eyed her and her attire curiously. Was it just because she'd been raised in the Price household, or was there another reason for her composure?

Jackie held out a file for me and without a second thought, I took it, flipped it open, and scanned the documents. My jaw clenched as I read the words. "Tell them to do it again," I snapped, shutting the file. "There's been a mistake."

Jackie's face blanched. It was a practiced move, though, as if she was forcing the show of emotion but didn't want to interrupt the beauty of her looks. "There's been no mistake, Gaven. The blood on the blade is my father's ... and my sister's."

"She's not dead," I growled before gesturing to papers I'd thrown to the floor. "She left a note." And there was no body.

For a moment, surprise skittered across Jackie's face. Then it slowly morphed into careful consideration as she bent down and retrieved the short letter my fucking wife had left me the morning after I'd put a ring on her finger and taken her as mine. I knew, in that moment, there would be no other like her. Just as there would be no other man for her. She had, however, chosen the worst of times to get cold feet and run away.

It was too late. We were married, and I'd meant what I'd said—there was no place she could run that I would not find her. She belonged to me. She was my property. No amount of distance could change that fact.

"Gaven..." Jackie's voice was careful as she held up the note and looked from it back to me. "I'm not saying that she could be dead."

I frowned. "Then I *suggest* you tell me what it is that you *are* saying," I bit out. "I am not a patient man." Especially when I had a wife to track down.

Jackie inhaled and lowered the letter to her side. She stepped up and flicked a finger along the top of the file in my grasp. "There was blood on the knife

—hers and his," she said. "She left you a note—Gaven, you're a fine man. Handsome. Skilled. *Powerful.*" As she emphasized that last word, I narrowed my eyes on her. "My sister never wanted to marry you." I'd known that. I hadn't cared. "She wanted a *normal* life … is it really difficult to understand what happened?"

"Why don't you spell it out for me?" I offered in a cold voice.

Jackie's hand lifted from the file and moved to my chest. I willed myself not to fling her away. "She must have been quite distraught by the events of last night," Jackie surmised. "I assume she came in here and found our father. She might have thought he could do something about … well, she might have regretted..."

"Spit. It. Out." I gritted my own words out.

Jackie tilted her head to the side. "The knife found was yours, Gaven," she said. "Who else had access to your things?"

I scowled. No one. "If you're implying that Angel had access to my weapons, you're mistaken."

Jackie sighed, her chest rising and falling with the exaggerated movement. "Angel was trapped," she said. "Trapped women do awful things when they feel pinned down. Even if she loved our father, maybe she loved the idea of being free more."

It suddenly hit me what she was saying. I glanced back at the carpet in the office as two men began to cut the edges of the room and roll up the space where Raffaello had bled out and died, removing the stain of his life as if it had never been there.

"You think your sister did this?" I asked, stunned. She couldn't be serious. It just wasn't possible. "You think she killed Raff?"

Jackie's lips turned down. "I don't want to. Whatever you may think of me, Gaven, I don't like thinking of my sister as a killer, but … people do insane things when they feel like they've been backed into a corner. Did she tell you she wanted to go to college?"

"She couldn't very well go if she's on the run for murder," I snapped, stepping away from her. "Angel would never have harmed your father. She wasn't capable of it. I know her."

Jackie lifted her chin and met my gaze—something few men could even do, especially when I was this close to rage. "You met and married my sister in less than a month, Gaven," she stated plainly. "You didn't know her at all. She was a tool for you to use in order to join our family."

"She was *not* a killer," I repeated. *No, not a killer, but she* was *a liar,* I thought. She'd lied to me. Perhaps she hadn't meant to, but that pathetic excuse for an apology written on the note she'd left behind was just another one of her lies. She ran for a reason, but I doubted very much that it had anything to do with fear or cold feet.

"My sister was a woman trapped," Jackie continued. The sound of her voice was quickly becoming one of the most unpleasant things I'd ever encountered. And as a man who'd been held in a Beijing prison for a few months, there were quite a number of unpleasant things I'd been introduced to in my life. "Trapped women will do what they must if it means their freedom."

Freedom? I thought. *No. Evangeline Price had no more freedom. Evangeline Price was my fucking wife. I owned her. Body and soul.*

But to remind her of that, I would need to track her down.

Carefully, to not confuse Jackie, I lifted the file she'd handed me, and then, meeting her gaze, I ripped it down the middle. "I will get to the bottom of this," I told her. "When I find Angel—and make no mistake, Jackie, I will find my *wife*—I'll know if she murdered Raffaello and why."

A smirk appeared on the corner of Jackie's lips. Finally, an actual emotion from this woman who called herself a Price. "I think you'll find, Mr. Belmonte, that my sister—though seemingly sweet —can be just as conniving as any woman. I don't believe it will be easy to track her down. I've already got men on it."

"*My* men," I reminded her. "I'm the new head of this empire."

Jackie's smirk turned into a full grin. "No," she said. "*Mine*. My father meant to induct you into the family officially today. Alas," she paused and waved her hand towards the office, "now that he's dead, he can no longer sign over the Price properties. With

Angel missing, I'm the last Price Heir. The Price Empire is mine."

My jaw loosened. There were very few instances in my life I'd been taken by surprise. Now was one of them. She was right. Raffaello and I had meant to sign the papers today, before Angel and I left for our honeymoon. Few people had known that, but she was one of them. Suspicion burned through me. I'd met many conniving women in my life, but I must have been an idiot not to have noticed the one before me until now.

"Now," Jackie continued, "I'm going to ask my men to escort you off the premises, *Mr. Belmonte.*" Belmonte, not Price. "If I find out any information regarding my sister, I'll inform you." Her eyes met mine as two men appeared and moved toward me. "I hope you'll do the same."

Angel, I realized as the two guards Jackie had apparently called stopped on either side of me, wasn't the only liar in this family. I found myself leaning back on my heels as I tilted my head to the side and examined this new foe before me.

Tall. Elegant. Manipulative. Jacquelina Price was a careful person. Feminine but dangerous. Like a beautiful serpent. I felt the mask that had fallen away in the last few weeks with Angel settle back into place. It was one that I knew well. The mask of a killer, of a criminal, and whether she knew it or not, Jacquelina Price was now on my list. Whether she was a client or a target had yet to be determined.

"Of course," I replied, my tone even. It was a practiced sound. One that gently put clients at ease and achieved the opposite of my targets. "Please let me know if you hear anything. I want her found as much as you do."

"Oh, I highly doubt that, Mr. Belmonte," Jackie said. "I have something at stake here. My father was brutally murdered, and now the whole of his life, his empire, falls upon me. I want to know where my sister is more than anyone. I want her to pay for what she's done."

There was no doubt in my mind that Jacquelina knew more than she was letting on, and the first thing I would have to do if I was going to find out what had happened between them was to find my wife. That was where we agreed but also where our alignment on the situation ended.

Jackie lived up to her conniving and ruthless reputation, which was no different, but I needed to know the *truth* of what happened, and I didn't trust her story for a second. When I found out why Raff had been murdered and by whom, then I would deal with her. For now, I had only one focus.

My wife.

Angel would pay.

She would pay for lying to me, for betraying me, and most of all, for thinking she could run from me instead of trusting me.

"I wish you all the best, Mr. Belmonte." Jackie's words echoed as they followed me down the hall as I headed for the exit.

The best, I thought absently. That's what I was, and yet I'd been so wholly and utterly deceived by nothing more than a small, fragile-looking woman with a beautiful face.

Oh, yes, Evangeline had much to pay for.

EPILOGUE
ANGEL

5 years later ...

Dreams were like the wind. You could feel them brush against your skin, touch your presence, but you could never catch them. Never hold onto them. Attempting to do so was like trying to capture a human soul not that I believed those existed anymore, and if they did, my sister certainly had a rotten one. She was rancid and corrupt to her very core. Only now that I'd experienced the depths of her betrayal and delivered my own betrayal in return did I understand what the life of a criminal indeed did to someone.

It sucked out hope, burned it to a crisp, and then let the ashes rain back down over every fucking thing.

As I sat in the Rosemary Café on Main Street of Queens, New York City, waiting for my client to make an appearance, I absently reached up and touched the ring hanging from a slender chain beneath my silk shirt. Every morning, no matter where I was—Boston, Paris, Vancouver—I woke up and touched it. Made sure it was still there. Reassured myself that what I was doing—the person I'd become—had not been for nothing.

It was all for *him*. The only man I'd ever felt I belonged to. The only man I'd ever been so close to loving. And the only man I could never ever touch again.

Some days, the beautiful metal ring felt like it would burn a patch in my skin; other days, it felt like the only thing keeping me tethered to the ground. Today, it was a mixture of both because today was our wedding anniversary.

The bell to the café door chimed and I lifted my gaze as a tall, slender man dressed in an impeccable suit bypassed the short line of patrons waiting to be served at the counter and made his way toward me. My client's tall, gangly-thin frame outlined his body and shadowed his features as he rushed through the café. It wasn't until he sat before me that I looked up and saw the red splotches over his too-pale skin. Too thin, too pale—the poor man rarely left his lab, even less so in the past few months. He was rather sweaty, not that I could blame him. As one of the youngest scientific protégés in America, if any of Ronald Wiser's competitors even caught a whiff of what he was doing, he'd find himself on the wrong side of an assassin's scope.

"Thank God you're here," he said as he took a seat across from me. "I think I'm being followed."

My back straightened. This was not good news. My eyes shot past him and out into the busy street. "Was it a car or a person?" I clarified, scanning our surroundings.

"Car. Dark blue sedan," he answered. "I think I lost it a few blocks back, but I can't be sure."

I scowled as I watched a dark blue sedan drive past the front windows of the café. *Damn*. No, he had *not* lost it.

Ronald was neither a spy nor a criminal on the run, but he did need my protection. I sucked in a breath and slowly let it out. It wouldn't help to panic now. If I'd learned nothing over the past five years, it was that panicking merely slowed down my thinking process. If Ronald was being followed, then someone must have tipped off his competitors. If his competitors knew about the synthetic organ growth project he'd been working on for the last several months, then he was in deep shit. Anyone in the medical industry would spend billions to keep his future from happening. There was too much money on the line for them. My eyes moved from the street and back to him.

Ron was red-faced, his eyes jumping around the room as if any of them would stand up and shoot him at any moment. I leaned over and touched his hand, offering him a small smile as if we were two friends out for a friendly chat. "Calm down," I warned him quietly under my breath. "Don't make a scene."

"They're going to kill me, Eve," he hissed the fake name I'd given him when we'd first met. "I know they are. I've done everything you said. I copied all of the files, all of the information. I've sent the flash drives, but what if it's insufficient? They will want to destroy this information—or worse, take it and use it for themselves. They'll create my organs and then jack up the prices until no one but the rich can afford them. This could save lives, and they're going to use this for their own profit." By the end of his monologue, his voice had turned slightly shrill. More sweat beaded on his brow. I wrinkled my nose as the distinct smell of sweat reached my nostrils.

Discreetly, I reached into my purse, removed several tissues, and handed them to him. He took them and began blotting the sweat on his forehead.

"We don't need to worry about the research," I told him. "Right now, all we need to worry about is how to get you out of here and to a safe place before whoever is trailing you finds a way to get you alone." And *dead*, but I don't say that last part aloud.

"Do you have a safe house set up?" he asked almost pleadingly.

My smile turned pained. If only I had those kinds of connections. Had things not gone terribly awry five years ago, I might have been able to give him a better answer. I'd once thought that being the wife of a mob boss was the worst thing that could ever happen to me, but now as time had passed and the longer I'd been on the run, I knew that having contacts in the world of crime was what kept people alive—as well as fear and power. Ron had fear in spades, but his power was waning in the face of the profit-mongers.

"Come on," I said, lifting my purse over my shoulder and getting up as the same dark blue sedan crossed the street once again, this time on the other side of the traffic. "We're going out the back."

Ron's chair scraped back against the café floor as he hurried to follow me. I walked slowly though, and soon, he had to slow the speed of his gait to match mine. It was clear he didn't want to, but if I was going to get him out of here safely, then we had to be smart about it.

I lifted my head and turned past the bathrooms straight for the café's tiny kitchen. I'd been here many times—it was why I'd felt so comfortable to meet him in this location. I never went anywhere without several escape routes in mind. A few of the younger employees paused and frowned as we passed, but it wasn't my presence that made them question us back here. It was Ron's. He was sweating like crazy, and it seemed that his body odor only grew more and more intense with each second.

Look like you belong, I reminded myself, *and they'll believe it.* I'd run into an ex-thief a year or two ago that had taught me that motto. People believed confidence, no matter what it sold them. So confident, I became.

Even with Ron's sweating and shaking and his darting gaze, we made it all the way through the kitchen to the back door. I popped it open and glanced out into the alley. One side was completely open, while the other was blocked off by a set of dumpsters and a large brick wall. My heels clicked against the pavement as I led him outside. I dug my hand into my purse and pulled out a burner phone, a small wad of cash, a non-traceable credit card, and a set of keys. I was afraid this would happen, but I'd planned for it—or rather, I was still in the process of arranging things. This was my option B. Five years of learning this life. Sink or swim. Life or death. Both were good motivators that quickly made me realize I was a Price Heir, after all. But the most critical thing the trial and error had taught me was to always be prepared.

"Here," I said, reaching over and shoving the card, cash, phone, and keys into Ron's hands.

He gaped at the money and phone and then at me as we came to a stop at the mouth of the alley. "What the hell am I supposed to do with this?"

I watched the blue sedan cross the street, and before the driver could spot us, I grabbed Ron and ducked behind a low-hanging sign on the side of the building. "Listen to me very carefully," I said, keeping my eyes trained on the sedan. There had to be more, possibly an assassin already after him, but I didn't want to alert him and send Ron into a spiral of panic. He was the type who would absolutely make things worse when he panicked. I shifted my gaze back to his face.

"I want you to take that money and card and grab a taxi out of the city. Use the phone I gave you. Here—give me yours—I don't want you using it for the foreseeable future." When all he did was blink at me, I huffed and dug through his pockets until I found the phone I was searching for. I shoved it into my purse. "Now, as I was saying…" Ron still hadn't moved or said anything more. Instead, his eyes were centered on something over my shoulder. I glanced back but saw nothing. With another irritated huff, I snapped my fingers in front of his face and brought his attention back. "Focus," I said. "Take a taxi. Use the phone I gave you to contact me when you get to a safe place."

"Safe place?" he repeated, his face growing more flushed than it already was. "Where is that? Do you have a—"

"No," I interrupted him. "I don't have a specific place. You'll need to find a motel or something to hide up in. Grab some food with the money I gave you and stay put until I can come for you. There's enough money there in cash and on the card to last you for several weeks as long as you don't stay somewhere too expensive. Motels—Ron. Stay where they don't have any CCTVs."

He looked like he was going to be sick. I had to move this along. My eyes darted back to the street. That fucking sedan had turned back around. This time, it was slowing at a nearby light. The backdoor opened. "It won't be forever," I said quickly. "The phone I gave you is secure. Call me if there's an emergency, otherwise, I want you to wait for me to call."

"W-what are you going to do?"

Hope like hell that one of my contacts would come through in time for me to get him. I stepped out from behind the sign and waved my hand for a taxi. A yellow cabby caught my eye and pulled up to the curb. I stepped back to where Ron stood. Two men in black were coming down the street.

"Switch cabs often," I pushed the words out in a rush as I latched onto his arm and practically dragged him towards the taxi. "Use the cash," I snapped.

"But—what!" Ron didn't get to finish his sentence as I slammed the door closed on him.

"JFK airport, please," I told the man in front before glancing back to Ron as he cursed and rolled the window down. The men were getting closer. *Why the hell did I choose to wear heels today?* I wondered absently. "Use the chaos at the airport to switch cabs," I said, lowering my voice and leaning halfway into the cab as I tried to keep an eye on the men coming. I turned to the cabby. "There's a hundred-dollar tip in it for you if you can get him there as fast as possible, sir. He's late for a flight."

The cabby's eyes widened. "Yes, ma'am!" He nodded excitedly and then—just as every other cabby in New York when there was a hefty tip involved—threw caution to the wind and sped out into traffic. My lips twitched as I heard Ronald shriek just before the taxi was out of range.

Now, time to figure a way out of—I turned the opposite way the men were approaching and ran head-first into a massive chest. I stumbled, nearly going down on my ass, before the man's hands gripped my elbows and steadied me.

Startled, I adjusted myself. Having been to New York several times on and off, it was a rare occasion when someone was kind enough to catch a person when they fell or ran into them. Chivalry wasn't dead, after all.

My eyes lifted. My lips parted. A thank you and apology were on the tip of my tongue and as soon as I met the man's eyes, every word in my vocabulary dried up and burst into dust. Every word except one.

I gaped up at the man and let that word spill from my lips as shock overtook me.

"Gaven…"

Gaven's face was hard. Lethal. His eyes were like twin ice chips as he glared down at me. "Hello again, Angel," he said. "Or should I call you *wife*?"

THANK YOU FOR READING!

Thank you so much for reading Wicked Angel. We hope you enjoyed diving into the dark, dirty world of the Mafia Elite.

Please don't forget to leave a review for book one > here

And if you can't wait for the next installment, please make sure to pre order book two > here

ABOUT LUCY SMOKE

Lucy Smoke, also known as Lucinda Dark for her fantasy works, has a master's degree in English and is a self-proclaimed creative chihuahua. She enjoys feeding her wanderlust, cover addiction, as well as her face, and truly hopes people will stop giving her bath bombs as gifts. Bath's get cold too fast and it's just not as wonderful as the commercials make it out to be when the tub isn't a jacuzzi.

When she's not on a never-ending quest to find the perfect milkshake, she lives and works in the southern United States with her beloved fur-baby, Hiro, and her family and friends.

Want to be kept up to date? Think about joining the author's group or signing up for their newsletter below.

Newsletter

ALSO BY LUCY SMOKE

Contemporary Series:

Gods of Hazelwood: Icarus Duet (completed)

Burn With Me

Fall With Me

Sick Boys Series (completed)

Forbidden Deviant Games (prequel)

Pretty Little Savage

Stone Cold Queen

Natural Born Killers

Wicked Dark Heathens

Bloody Cruel Psycho

Bloody Cruel Monster

Vengeful Rotten Casualties

Iris Boys Series (completed)

Now or Never

Power & Choice

Leap of Faith

Cross my Heart

Forever & Always

Iris Boys Series Boxset

The *Break* Series (completed)

Break Volume 1

Break Volume 2

Break Series Collection

Contemporary Standalones:

Poisoned Paradise

Expressionate

Wildest Dreams

Criminal Underground Series (Shared Universe Standalones)

Sweet Possession

Scarlett Thief

Fantasy Series:

Twisted Fae Series (completed)

Court of Crimson

Court of Frost

Court of Midnight

Twisted Fae: Completed Series Boxset

Barbie: The Vampire Hunter Series (completed)

Rest in Pieces

Dead Girl Walking

Ashes to Ashes

Blood & Vengeance (Boxset)

Dark Maji Series (completed)

Fortune Favors the Cruel

Blessed Be the Wicked

Twisted is the Crown

For King and Corruption

Long Live the Soulless

Nerys Newblood Series (completed)

Daimon

Necrosis

Resurrection

Sky Cities Series (Dystopian)

Heart of Tartarus

Shadow of Deception

Sword of Damage

Dogs of War (coming soon)

ABOUT AJ MACEY

A.J. Macey has a B.S. in Criminology and Criminal Justice, and coursework in Forensic Science, Behavioral Psychology, and Cybersecurity. Before becoming an author, A.J. worked as a Correctional Officer in a jail and is now married with a daughter and two cats named Thor and Loki.

A.J. has two pen names in the works:

A.J. Macey - romance stories
Aria Rose - epic/high fantasy

Stay Connected

Join the Reader's Group for exclusive content, teasers and sneaks, giveaways, and more:
A.J. Macey's Minions
Join the newsletter for weekly sneaks, sales, and the ongoing NL story:
Sign-Up Here

ALSO BY AJ MACEY

BEST WISHES SERIES (A.J. MACEY):

Book 1: Smoke and Wishes

Book 2: Smoke and Survival

Book 3: Smoke and Mistletoe

Book 4: Smoke and Betrayal

Book 5: Smoke and Death (coming summer 2021)

FSID AGENTS SERIES (A.J. MACEY):

Book 1: Whisper of Spirits

Book 2: Whisper of Pasts

Book 3: Whisper of Blood (coming summer 2021)

HIGH SCHOOL CLOWNS & COFFEE GROUNDS (A.J. MACEY):

Book 1: Lads & Lattes

Book 2: Misters & Mochas

Book 3: Chaps & Cappuccinos

Book 4: Fellas & Frappés (coming spring 2021)

Post-Series Novella: Getting Lei'd & Iced Lemonade

(coming summer 2021)

THE ACES SERIES (A.J. MACEY):

Book 1: Rival

Book 2: Adversary

Book 3: Enemy

THE CAT'S CREW SERIES (A.J. MACEY):

Book 1: Rumors (coming late 2021)

CUT THROAT LOVE SERIES:

Book 1: Feral Sins (coming late 2021)

VEGA CITY VIGILANTES SERIES (A.J. MACEY):

Book 1: Masked by Vengeance

Book 2: Cloaked in Conspiracy (coming Halloween 2021)

Book 3: Revealed through Redemption (coming Halloween 2021)

NOT YOUR BASIC WITCH CO-WRITE SERIES WITH JARICA JAMES (A.J. MACEY):

Book 1: Witch, Please

Book 2: Resting Witch Face

Book 3: Witches Be Crazy

Epilogue Novella: Born to be Witchy

CRIMINAL UNDERGROUND CO-WRITE BOOK COLLECTION WITH LUCY SMOKE (A.J. MACEY/MACEY ROSE):

Sweet Possession

Scarlett Thief

Sinister Engagement (coming spring 2021)

Sinister Obsession (coming summer 2021)

THE SENTINEL TRIUNE (ARIA ROSE):

Book 1: Heart of Gold (coming 2021)